PRAISE FOR JACI BURTON AND HER NOVELS

"Jaci Burton's stories are full of heat and heart."
—#1 *New York Times* bestselling author Maya Banks

"A wild ride." —#1 *New York Times* bestselling author Lora Leigh

"Jaci Burton delivers."
—*New York Times* bestselling author Cherry Adair

"One to pick up and savor." —*Publishers Weekly*

"Jaci Burton's books are always sexy, romantic and charming! A hot hero, a lovable heroine and an adorable dog—prepare to fall in love with Jaci Burton's amazing new small-town romance series." —*New York Times* bestselling author Jill Shalvis

"A heartwarming second-chance-at-love contemporary romance enhanced by engaging characters and Jaci Burton's signature dry wit." —*USA Today*

"Captures everything I love about a small-town romance."
—Fresh Fiction

"Delivered on everything I was hoping for and more."
—Under the Covers Book Blog

"A sweet, hot small-town romance." —Dear Author

"Fun and sexy." —Fiction Vixen

"The perfect combination of heat and romance."
—Heroes and Heartbreakers

"Plenty of romance; sexy men; hot, steamy loving; and humor."
—Smexy Books

"An extraordinary novel—a definite home run!"
—Joyfully Reviewed

"Lively and funny . . . intense and loving."
—The Road to Romance

"An invitation to every woman's wildest fantasies."
—Romance Junkies

"Burton is a master at sexual tension!"   —RT Book Reviews

Titles by Jaci Burton

Brotherhood by Fire Series

HOT TO THE TOUCH

IGNITE ON CONTACT

Boots and Bouquets Series

THE MATCHMAKER'S MISTLETOE MISSION
(an eNovella)

Hope Series

HOPE SMOLDERS
(an eNovella)

HOPE FLAMES

HOPE IGNITES

HOPE BURNS

LOVE AFTER ALL

MAKE ME STAY

DON'T LET GO

LOVE ME AGAIN

ONE PERFECT KISS

Play-by-Play Series

THE PERFECT PLAY

CHANGING THE GAME

TAKING A SHOT

PLAYING TO WIN

THROWN BY A CURVE

ONE SWEET RIDE

HOLIDAY GAMES
(an eNovella)

MELTING THE ICE

STRADDLING THE LINE

HOLIDAY ON ICE
(an eNovella)

QUARTERBACK DRAW

ALL WOUND UP

HOT HOLIDAY NIGHTS
(an eNovella)

UNEXPECTED RUSH

RULES OF CONTACT

THE FINAL SCORE

SHOT ON GOLD

Wild Riders Series

RIDING WILD

RIDING TEMPTATION

RIDING ON INSTINCT

RIDING THE NIGHT

Stand-Alone Novels

WILD, WICKED, & WANTON

BOUND, BRANDED, & BRAZEN

Anthologies

UNLACED
(with Jasmine Haynes, Joey W. Hill, and Denise Rossetti)

EXCLUSIVE
(with Eden Bradley and Lisa Renee Jones)

LACED WITH DESIRE
(with Jasmine Haynes, Joey W. Hill, and Denise Rossetti)

NAUTI AND WILD
(with Lora Leigh)

NAUTIER AND WILDER
(with Lora Leigh)

HOT SUMMER NIGHTS
(with Carly Phillips, Erin McCarthy, and Jessica Clare)

MISTLETOE GAMES
(*Holiday Games*, *Holiday on Ice*, and *Hot Holiday Nights* in one volume)

eNovellas

THE TIES THAT BIND

NO STRINGS ATTACHED

WILD NIGHTS

IGNITE ON
CONTACT

JACI BURTON

JOVE
New York

A JOVE BOOK
Published by Berkley
An imprint of Penguin Random House LLC
penguinrandomhouse.com

Library of Congress Cataloging-in-Publication Data

Names: Burton, Jaci, author.
Title: Ignite on contact / Jaci Burton.
Description: First edition. | New York : Jove, 2020. | Series: Brotherhood by fire
Identifiers: LCCN 2019031817 (print) | LCCN 2019031818 (ebook) |
ISBN 9780440001379 (paperback) | ISBN 9780440001386 (ebook)
Subjects: GSAFD: Love stories. | Erotic fiction.
Classification: LCC PS3602.U776 I38 2020 (print) |
LCC PS3602.U776 (ebook) | DDC 813/.6—dc23
LC record available at https://lccn.loc.gov/2019031817
LC ebook record available at https://lccn.loc.gov/2019031818

First Edition: February 2020

Printed in the United States of America
1   3   5   7   9   10   8   6   4   2

Cover photo by Claudio Dogar-Marinesco
Cover design by Sarah Oberrender
Book design by George Towne

This book is dedicated to family—
whether blood or found.
Thank you to mine for being
all that I've ever needed.

ACKNOWLEDGMENTS

Gracias por todo, Carmen.

CHAPTER 1

FLAMES LICKED ALL AROUND RAFE DONOVAN, THE HEAT from the house fire causing sweat to drip down his face and inside of his SCBA mask. Since he couldn't wipe his face, he blinked instead, clearing the perspiration from his eyes.

Rafe firmly gripped the lead hose to douse the blaze threatening to drop a fiery ceiling on their heads. Tommy Rodriguez had his back, feeding him more line. They soaked the flames in the living room, pushing through the dining room and into the kitchen, driving the beast back.

"It's wearing down," Rafe said, watching as the inferno tried to roar, then inched back into the walls as he blasted it with water. "You don't win today, you bastard."

"You tell that fucker, Rafe," Rodriguez said.

Fire was his nemesis, the thing that had almost killed him back when he was a kid. It had also saved his life, turned it around and given him a new beginning. But it still had to die. Every day he faced it, it had to die.

When the blaze was finally extinguished, he exhaled. The Engine 6 team did a walk around, pulling down walls to make sure fire didn't lurk in the Sheetrock, waiting to reignite. He made his way outside and pulled off his mask, sucking in a deep breath of Ft. Lauderdale's hot summer air.

It might be humid as hell, and he might be drenched under his turnout gear, but he'd survived. No one was inside the house when the fire broke out, so he'd call this one a success.

He looked at the one-story ranch, charred but still standing. It looked a little beaten down, but the old house would come back.

"Nice job in there." Jackson Donovan, his brother and his lieutenant, patted him on the back.

"Thanks."

He grinned and headed back to the truck, elation blasting through him as it always did when they were successful.

He loved his job. If he could do it every day, he would.

They began to wrap up. They were folding the hoses and packing up equipment when smoke started pouring from the roof.

"Dammit," Rafe said. How had they missed that? He heard Jackson's voice ordering them to get back into the house. Rafe loaded a fresh tank of oxygen on his back and put his mask on, then waited for his backup.

Rodriguez was right behind him as they returned inside.

"Be careful in there, all of you," Jackson said. "I don't like the looks of that smoke."

"Yeah, got it," Rafe said. He didn't like the skittering feeling crawling down his back. He had a sixth sense about fire, and which scenes posed a danger. This one didn't feel right to him. Something was off.

Inside looked clear, which meant the smoke was hiding in the walls somewhere. Hendricks and Richards were inside, too, helping them inspect. They'd broken off, going in the opposite direction.

"There's no heat, no smoke," Rafe said as they made their way around the house, testing more walls for fire. "So where's the smoke coming from?"

"Attic, maybe," Rodriguez said.

"Already up in the attic and cleared it," Hendricks said into his radio. "So whatever we saw, it isn't up here."

Damn. It wasn't unusual for a fire to snake along the walls, lurking, moving from one location to another. Which meant they'd have to check behind the drywall in every room until they found it and extinguished it. Rafe used his drywall hook to cut open a section of wall, checking for smoke in one of the smaller back bedrooms.

"Anything?" Jackson radioed.

"Still looking," Rafe radioed back. "Not finding anything."

"I don't like this," Jackson said. "Keep a sharp eye."

Rafe was already doing that. The whole team was in here now, cutting through and dragging down sections of walls to search for smoke, looking for hot spots.

When Rafe got to the closet in the hallway, he felt the door. It was hot, and the paint on the outside of the door was bubbling.

"There you are," he whispered, then turned to Rodriguez. "We need to vent this through the roof."

He was about to notify Jackson that they were exiting when he was knocked back off his feet by an explosion.

And then everything went dark.

BUSY SHIFTS IN THE EMERGENCY ROOM AT FT. LAUDER-dale Medical Center were Carmen Lewis's jam. It was a big-city emergency room, serving a large population that made for demanding days. Carmen's shifts went fast because she rarely stopped moving. She relished the fast pace, but even more, she loved helping the sick and injured.

She was charting in the station when her friend and fellow nurse Tess Blackstone stopped by. "The patient in room seven is ready for discharge according to Dr. Lange. Scrip for pain meds and a follow-up with his personal physician in a week. Room six is still waiting for someone to take her up for a CT scan. I just administered another bolus of morphine to room eight with Dr. Chan's approval."

Carmen nodded and updated the patient charts, signing off on the discharge for room seven. "Call CT—again—and tell them we've been waiting an hour and a half for that scan. What's the status on the patient in room three?"

"Waiting to be taken up for an angiogram."

"Okay, thanks."

"I'll see what's up with CT—again," Tess said, picking up the phone and rolling her eyes at Carmen.

Carmen grinned, confident Tess would do her job well. All her nurses did. She had the best staff in the hospital, in her opinion. As triage nurse and supervisor of the department, Carmen had her hands in everything in the ER, which meant she was always managing chaos. Just the way she liked it.

EMTs rolled in with a firefighter strapped to a stretcher, bringing Carmen to instant alert. She recognized Rafe right away since he and his brothers lived in the house next door to hers. As a nurse running an ER, she never panicked, but she hated seeing someone she knew on that stretcher.

His face was covered with ash and grit, but she was happy to see he was awake and seemingly alert as she directed the paramedics to take him into room five.

The attending physician came into the room at the same time to do an assessment.

"Explosion at a house fire," EMT Miguel Acosta said. "He took a pretty good blast that knocked him unconscious."

Acosta and his fellow EMT Adrienne Smith unstrapped Rafe and moved him from the stretcher onto the ER bed.

"But as you can see," Rafe said, "I'm not unconscious now."

"Patient was down for approximately three minutes but roused quickly," Miguel said.

"And then he was a royal pain in the ass in the ambulance all the way here," Smith said, glaring at Rafe. "So he's alert and oriented times three."

"Any vomiting?" Dr. Lange asked.

"None," Smith said.

"Thanks, Adrienne," Carmen said. "We'll take it from here."

Miguel smiled at Rafe. "Behave yourself."

Rafe tried to sit up, but Carmen laid a firm hand on his shoulder. "Nope. Stay put until we assess you."

Dr. Lange did a physical and neurological exam.

"No burns, but he does have a bump on the head. No external injuries. Get him set up on an IV and EKG and do his vitals and blood work," Dr. Lange said. "Let's order a CT scan."

She nodded and Dr. Lange stepped out. Carmen went to the cabinet to get the leads and everything else she'd need, then alerted one of the other nurses to bring her IV fluids.

"I shouldn't even be here," Rafe said.

"You know the protocol, Rafe," Carmen said, giving him her standard nurse stare. No one ever argued with her stare. It was pretty fierce.

Rafe, apparently, wasn't fazed by her glare.

"Whatever, Carmen. I'm fine."

"Sure you are. Let's get you out of that turnout gear."

He grinned. "Getting me naked. Now we're talkin'."

She laughed and shook her head. "Can you sit up?"

"Yeah, sure."

She held out her hand. He grasped it and sat up, much too fast for her liking.

She noticed he winced, and then he wobbled on the table a little.

"Head hurt?"

He reached for his forehead, cradling it in his hand. "A little. Damn backdraft caught me unaware, and the door knocked me backward. And out cold, I guess."

She'd known Rafe and his brothers since they moved next door to her four years ago. Rafe helped her all the time with her grandfather. Over the years, they'd grown close, and the thought of him being hurt made *her* hurt.

She helped him unlatch his jacket and slide it off. "You're lucky it wasn't worse."

He shrugged out of his coat, and Carmen couldn't help but admire his broad shoulders encased in his tight T-shirt, something she shouldn't be noticing right now.

"Can you stand so we can get the rest of your turnout gear off?"

"Yeah."

"Hold my hand."

His lips curved, revealing his amazing smile. "Carmen, I never knew you were interested."

She rolled her eyes at him. "Up. Hold my hand."

He took her fingers and dropped his suspenders, letting the pants fall while he stepped out of his boots.

The hottest man she knew was undressing in front of her. At least partially undressing. Even in his T-shirt and standard uniform pants, standing this close to him made Carmen feel things she hadn't felt since—

Longer than she'd like to admit. Which she wasn't going to think about, because right now Rafe was a patient. And that's all he was to her.

"Come on, climb back into bed. Shirt off."

"See, you flirting with me like this makes my head feel a lot better."

She shot him a look. "At least your sense of humor is still intact."

He gave her a lopsided grin. "Always."

He pulled his shirt off, and she refused to notice his wide shoulders and muscled chest, or the very interesting tattoo on the back of his right shoulder.

Okay, she did notice the tattoo, the Maltese cross with the three fists and the words "Brotherhood by Fire" surrounded by flames. She wanted to ask. She didn't. He was hurt and she was his nurse and it was none of her business. She got him into a gown and hooked up to the machines so they could chart his vitals, all of which were ridiculously normal. She checked his eyes, which were dilating normally as well—a very good sign.

Amy, one of the nurses, brought her the fluid bag, so she started the IV. Rafe didn't even flinch when she inserted the needle, which wasn't a surprise. The guy was tough. She wet a washcloth with warm water and brought it over to clean the soot and grime off his face.

"I didn't know a bath was included," he said, his warm brown eyes studying her the entire time.

Heat sang through her body. Normally, cleaning a patient was an emotionless task. She did it because it was part of her job. But with Rafe it felt . . . different. Intimate. Unnerving.

"I thought we might want to clean off some of this residue from the fire."

"A nice hot shower would feel really good right about now."

She swept his thick dark hair away from his forehead and finished cleaning his face. Such a gorgeous face, too, with angular lines and a very strong jaw. "Can't do that for you, but does this feel better?"

He reached up and wrapped his fingers around hers. "You touching me feels good."

That heat she felt earlier was replaced by an incredible tingling sensation that settled somewhere in the vicinity of her sex.

Whoa, girl, back up.

Which she did. "Okay, I can actually see your face now."

He smiled, as if he knew exactly the effect he had on her.

She needed to remind herself that Rafe Donovan was a patient, and her neighbor, and that nothing was ever going to happen between the two of them.

Ever.

No matter how many times she'd fantasized about him.

CHAPTER 2

RAFE'S HEAD FUCKING HURT.

But the rest of him felt damn fine because Carmen Lewis was the most beautiful woman he'd ever laid eyes on. Black hair wound into a bun at her neck, full lips, beautiful smoky hazel eyes, curvy in all the right places, and the woman was smart. She was the perfect package. Living next door to her was hard enough. But having her leaning over him, washing his face, breathing in her scent—what was that? Hand sanitizer? How could hand sanitizer be so hot? And having her hands on him? Now that was torture. Even gloved up, her hands made him feel better. All he wanted to do was draw her closer and kiss her. He saw the way her incredible eyes went dark with desire when she got near him, the way her breathing stilted and her lips parted when he put his hand over hers.

He knew when a woman was interested, and Carmen was definitely interested. And then she backed away like he was a hot stove and she'd just burned her hand on him.

So she was wary. The question was . . . why? They were in the wrong damn situation for him to ask that question.

"How's your head?" she asked.

"Huh?" He'd been watching her gorgeous ass as she had her back turned to him and honestly wasn't paying attention to what she'd been saying.

"Your head, Rafe. How's your head?"

"Oh. It hurts."

"Any queasiness?"

He grimaced, trying to quell the nausea that kept rising up like a rocky sea. "No, I'm good."

She cocked a brow, as if she knew damn well how he felt. "This isn't tell-a-lie time to get out of here fast, Rafe. I really need to know how you feel. If you hide things from me or from the doctor, it could affect your diagnosis."

He blew out a breath. "Fine. Kind of queasy."

"Okay. I want you to lie still, and no getting up without buzzing for help. Understood?"

"Yes, ma'am."

"I appreciate the cooperation. No going to sleep, either."

"I'm too wired to sleep." Though he wasn't sure if the adrenaline rush was from the fire or from having Carmen so close to him. Both, maybe?

Before she could leave the room, Rafe's brothers, Jackson and Kal, appeared in the doorway. He was glad to see them, though he wasn't going to tell them that.

"Hey, Carmen," Jackson said. "Okay if we come in?"

"Sure. I'd like someone to keep him company anyway while we wait for the CT scan."

Kal smiled. "We can do that." He pulled up a chair next to Rafe, grabbed the remote to the television and turned it on, scrolling through until he found a football game.

Jackson stepped out to talk to Carmen for a few minutes. Rafe watched the two of them in conversation. Carmen's hands moved as she talked. Then she tucked a loose hair behind her ear, nodded and grasped Jackson's arm as if to soothe his worry before walking away.

Jackson stepped inside.

"Well?" Rafe asked.

"Well, what?" Jackson slid into the other chair.

"Am I dying?"

"How the hell should I know? Do I look like a doctor?"

Rafe rolled his eyes, which only made his head hurt more. "What did Carmen say?"

"She said she thinks you're a dick."

"Very funny."

"She said she thinks it's a concussion, but they'll know more after the CT scan. And if you have to get up to go down the hall to take a piss, one of us has to come with you so you don't faint."

Rafe frowned. "Fuck that."

"No, seriously."

"Don't worry, bro, I'll hold your hand," Kal said, giving him his signature smart-ass smirk.

Rafe stared at the TV. "This whole situation sucks."

"If you didn't bang your head against doors, you wouldn't be in this situation."

He glared at Jackson. "How's the house, by the way?"

"Fire's contained. Finally. You did good in there."

"Yeah, right up until the backdraft knocked me on my ass."

"Hey, we've all been there."

"Not me," Kal said, his face glued to the game.

Rafe glared at his brother. "You'll get your turn, asshole."

Kal let out a laugh. "I'm not as dumb as you."

"Ignore him," Jackson said. "His time will come."

Honestly, Rafe hoped his little brother would never have the same experience Rafe had had today.

Because this pretty much sucked.

• • •

"WHO'S THE EXTREMELY HOT FIREFIGHTER IN FIVE?" TESS
asked when Carmen returned to the desk.

Carmen kept her focus on charting. "My next-door neighbor."

"Shut the front door." Tess's jaw dropped. "He is not."

"He is."

"What's his status?"

"Possible concussion. We won't know more until after his CT
scan."

"Carmen Lewis, you've been holding out on me."

"About his diagnosis?"

Tess tilted her head to the side. "No. About you and the hot
firefighter."

Carmen finished charting Rafe's vitals, supplies they'd used on
him and details about his status, then looked up at her friend.
Tess Blackstone was a beautiful redhead with a killer smile who'd
been Carmen's best friend since nursing school. Carmen had been
terrified her first day of nursing school, didn't know anyone, felt
inept and unprepared for what was ahead. It must have shown on
her face, because Tess had sat next to her, leveled her signature
bright smile on Carmen and told her they were going to be best
friends forever.

And they had been ever since, including falling in love with
emergency medicine together and ending up getting a job at the
same emergency room. Carmen had been matron of honor at
Tess's wedding to her husband, George, and Tess had been there
to offer a shoulder to cry on when Carmen's marriage had ended
so badly.

They'd been through it all together, and there was nothing
that Carmen wouldn't tell her.

"I hold nothing back from you, Tess, and you know it."

"Apparently, you do, because you've been living next door to an extremely sexy firefighter for—how long?"

She shrugged. "A few years."

"What? And I'm just now hearing about it?"

"Those are his two brothers in there with him. They live with him."

Tess looked at the room, which just so happened to be across from the nurses station. She gaped, then turned to face Carmen. "Dear God in heaven, Carmen. I don't think we can be friends anymore."

Carmen laughed. "You're so dramatic. There's nothing to tell. We're neighbors. That's it."

"And yet you never once thought to mention to me that three—count them, three—extremely good-looking firefighters were living right next to you."

She signed out of her terminal, grabbed her netbook to do some inventory and left the station. "Nope."

Tess followed. "Hmm."

Carmen stopped. "What does that mean?"

"That means you're interested. In which one?"

She shook her head. "None of them. You know I don't date."

"Which is weird enough on its own. Your vagina didn't put up a *Closed for business* sign after your marriage ended, you know."

Carmen looked around to make sure no one had heard that. "Tess."

"What? Just stating the facts. You're beautiful and vibrant and healthy and you should be having all kinds of sex."

"Hmph." She started walking again.

"No hmph. Hump. You should be humping. Everything with a penis."

She reached the drug room and used a key card and password to enter. Tess followed.

"And you have sex on the brain."

Tess laughed. "The key to a happy marriage, honey."

Carmen shook her head and ordered some refills on a few of the drugs they needed.

"So the hurt one. He's amazingly beautiful, Carmen."

"Rafe? Yes, he is. He comes over and helps me with Grandpa."

"Oh, he does? That's so sweet. And after you get your grandpa to bed, does he help you out with anything else?"

She glanced over at Tess. "Like what?"

"I don't know. Orgasms?"

Carmen laughed. "No."

"Then you're using him in all the wrong ways. Does he have a girlfriend?"

"Rafe? I . . . don't think so. I've never asked."

"For the love of . . . Girl, we need to get you laid."

"No, we don't." She shut the drug cabinet, withdrew her key and walked out of the room, Tess on her heels.

Tess's pager went off. "I gotta run. This conversation isn't over."

Carmen raised her hand to object, but Tess had already disappeared down the hall. She needed to go check on Rafe anyway, as well as general department status.

When she stopped by Rafe's room, he was gone, but Kal and Jackson were hanging out there watching television.

"The CT people came to get him about five minutes ago," Jackson said.

She nodded. "Good. It won't take long, and we should have results soon."

"You don't think it's anything serious, do you?" Kal asked.

"I couldn't say, since I'm not a doctor."

"Come on, Carmen," Jackson said. "You see this kind of stuff all the time. We're not asking for a diagnosis. We're asking what you think."

She liked that they cared so much about their brother. She also didn't want to give them false hope. There were a lot of things that could show up on a CT scan. Sometimes bad things.

"He seems fine. A little dizzy and nauseated. If I were to guess, I'd say it's a concussion. But you know as well as I do that we have to wait for the CT scan results to know for sure."

Jackson nodded. "Thanks."

She went back out to the desk, looking over at Rafe's room every few minutes.

She expected—or at least hoped—that his CT scan would be negative, which meant he'd be cleared to go home with concussion protocol. She told herself Rafe would be fine.

He had to be fine.

Then she could get back to doing her job without having Rafe so close. Without needing to worry about him.

Which meant she could stop thinking about him, and stop remembering how he smelled, and what it felt like to touch him.

Because none of that was good for her sense of well-being. She didn't need or want a man in her life, despite what Tess thought. She'd already had a man in her life once, and that had ended in disaster.

She wasn't about to go through that again.

CHAPTER 3

STAYING AT HOME SUCKED. RAFE WAS ON A NO-ACTIVITY restriction, which was total bullshit. After a half-assed sleep last night because his brothers had taken turns waking him up every damn hour, he thought maybe he could nap this morning. But his body didn't work that way. The sun was up, and that meant coffee and awake time.

Jackson and Kal had gone to their mom and dad's. Becks, Jackson's live-in girlfriend, had left for her job at her tattoo shop early today, because she needed to stop and buy some ink.

He'd thought about going along with his brothers just to hang out, but his mom would come home at some point, and when she saw him not working on the house she'd ask questions. He'd asked his dad not to say anything to her. He was going to be fine, and his mom had enough on her mind with her job and getting the house ready to sell.

He leaned back in the kitchen chair and finished off the mango juice he'd poured for himself, then stood, wincing as he did.

He lifted his shoulders and turned his head from side to side, feeling the strain in his neck. Then he held on to the chair and bent forward to stretch out his back, taking it slow in case he got dizzy. His muscles felt tight, but when he straightened, he felt okay. That was a good thing, because he'd definitely felt woozy last night in the ER.

At least things were moving in the right direction there. He wished he could go to the gym and do a solid workout, but he'd been banned from doing anything strenuous—including his damn job—for the next five days until he followed up with his doctor and got cleared to return to work.

He looked around, wondering how to occupy himself in a useful way that wasn't considered strenuous. He'd already made breakfast and done the dishes, which wasn't much. He'd wiped up the stove and counter along with the table, which also hadn't been much, since everyone who lived here always cleaned up after themselves.

Becks was even cleaner than him and his brothers. She routinely did a thorough scrubbing of the house, and yesterday was her day off, which meant she'd done a top-to-bottom scouring of the entire place. In fact, Jackson and Becks had gotten into an argument about it, because Jackson was worried she was doing more than her fair share. He'd said they could all pitch in and clean the house, but Becks claimed cleaning was one of the great joys in her life.

That had been a fun argument to watch. Jackson had lost, of course, because Becks was amazing, and who was going to deny her something she enjoyed? Rafe didn't understand how mopping floors or scrubbing bathrooms could be a life-fulfilling task, but to each their own.

Rafe ventured into the game room and played a few video games, but the flashing lights on the TV gave him a headache, so he quit, disgusted.

Running out of ideas, he slid on his sunglasses and went outside to sit by the pool. Since it was summer and hot as fuck, he slid onto the bottom step of the pool to cool his body down.

He closed his eyes and let the water lap around his chest, content to relax here. It was better than staring up at the ceiling. He'd rather be swimming laps, but he knew that would be considered strenuous activity.

It was going to be a long five days.

He jerked his eyes open when he heard the gate to the backyard swing open, then smiled when he saw Carmen come in. She was holding a baking dish in her hand. She spotted him and waved.

"Hey, Rafe. I rang the bell, but no one answered," she said. "I'm going to put this in the fridge."

"Sure."

He climbed out of the pool and dried off, then put his T-shirt back on and went into the house.

Carmen was just coming to the door. "Oh. You didn't have to get out of the pool. I'm headed out again. I just stopped by to leave you some food. You shouldn't have to worry about cooking in the next couple of days."

She looked amazing in her shorts and skimpy tank top, her hair piled on top of her head. Her skin was glowing like wet sand, and all he wanted to do was lick the drops of perspiration beading between her breasts.

Okay, dude. Take a step back.

Which he did. "You don't have to leave. How about a glass of iced tea? It's hot out there."

"Sure is," she said, following him back inside. "And I made it even hotter by baking in my kitchen this morning."

She'd done that for him. He appreciated it. He moved around her and went into the kitchen, pulling two glasses from the cabinet. He poured tea, handing one to Carmen, who'd taken a seat at the island.

"You baked? For me?"

"Enchiladas verdes."

He walked around and pulled up a chair next to her. "That's my favorite."

She took a sip of tea and laid the glass on the counter. "I know."

"Thank you, Carmen. You didn't have to do that."

"I wanted to. I know you're stuck at home for several days, so I wanted to make sure you had something to eat."

Even though he'd just finished breakfast a little while ago, his stomach was already rumbling at the thought of Carmen's enchiladas. "It's probably time for lunch."

She laughed. "It is not. And there's plenty there for everyone."

"Yeah, as long as Jackson and Kal don't see it. I'll have to bury it somewhere."

"Seriously. There's more than enough to share."

He shook his head. "Not a chance. I'm marking it *Rafe's Recovery Food*."

She rolled her eyes. "Whatever. I can make more, you know."

He picked up her hand. "Can you? You'd do that for me?"

"Sure. As long as you don't milk this injury for weeks. I do have a full-time job, a grandfather to take care of, grocery shopping and housecleaning, bills to pay. You know, an actual life."

He let her hand drop. "Okay, now I feel guilty."

She laid her hand on his arm. "Not my intention. I was joking with you. We all have things to do."

"Not me. Not for the next five days, anyway. I'm not allowed to do a thing. I can't go to the gym, I can't swim laps, I can't go to work. I can't do anything . . . strenuous."

She made a sad face. "Aww, you poor baby. Relaxation must be killing you."

"You have no idea."

She slid off the barstool. "Come on."

"Where?"

"For a walk. You can't do anything strenuous, but you can go for a walk. With me."

"I thought you were busy."

"Not too busy to take a walk with you."

He wouldn't turn down the opportunity to spend some time with Carmen. And getting out of this house sounded like the best idea ever. "Sure. Let me grab my shoes."

He went upstairs, put on his sneakers and started back down, pausing to gape at the glorious sight of Carmen leaning over. She was holding on to the barstool and bending from the waist, no doubt stretching her hamstrings.

Damn, she had a very fine ass and some spectacular thighs. She wasn't overly thin, which suited him just fine, because he liked a woman who looked like she had some flesh on her. But every part of her looked firm. Of course she was on her feet at work all the time, so she got plenty of exercise.

He made his way downstairs. "Ready."

She straightened and smiled at him. "Me, too. You should stretch."

"I'm not running. I'll stretch as I walk."

She shrugged and said, "You know best."

He liked that she didn't lecture him. He'd dated plenty of women who thought they knew best and didn't hesitate to nag him about what he should and shouldn't do. Those women didn't last long in his orbit. He already had a mother. He didn't want to date one.

The humidity blasted him full in the face as they stepped outside. "You sure you want to do this?" he asked.

"Do what?"

"Walk. Outside. In July."

She laughed. "It's fine. I've lived here my entire life. I'm used to this heat."

Another bonus point. She didn't complain. He'd once tried to get a woman he'd met at the gym to run a 5K with him. It was even during the winter, but she complained about how messed up her hair would get in the humidity.

Sometimes finding a woman who was down with his interests

was as impossible as trying to win a game of *Alien: Isolation* on his Xbox.

"How did last night go?" Carmen asked.

"Miserable."

She looked concerned. "Really? Any vomiting?"

"Nah. I was tired. I wanted to sleep. My asshole brothers woke me constantly."

She slanted a smile at him. "I'm sure that was very annoying. But necessary."

"Yeah, I know. At least I'll sleep good tonight."

"Yes, that's the payoff."

They turned right at the end of the road. They lived in an established neighborhood, all the homes having been built in the late seventies, which meant a lot of mature trees on both sides of the road. School hadn't started back yet, so kids played in the yards and rode their bikes up and down the street. Rafe often thought about what it might have been like to grow up in an environment like this, with great parents and friends who lived next door.

But that hadn't been the hand he'd been dealt.

"You're quiet," Carmen said. "Are you all right?"

He turned his head to look at her. "Yeah. Whenever I walk the neighborhood, I always think about what it might have been like to grow up here. You know, to be born into something like this. Good parents. Friends. Riding my bike up and down the street without a care in the world. Never being hungry or thinking about where my next meal would come from."

Carmen reached out and laid her hand on his upper arm. "You ended up with great parents, Rafe, growing up with amazing brothers."

"Yeah, I got lucky with Jackson and Kal and our parents. I just didn't start out there."

"I don't know the whole story other than what you all have told me."

"Nothing much to tell. Jackson, Kal and I were all homeless and we bonded. We stuck together. One night we got caught in a fire in an abandoned house, and Josh Donovan saved our lives. He was one of the firemen who rescued us. Then he and his wife, Laurel, adopted us and became our parents, and we became Donovans."

She nodded. "I've heard that part. What about before that?"

He sidestepped a pothole in the street. "You mean when we were homeless?"

"No. Before you became homeless. Your family life before you hit the streets."

He hadn't thought about that part of his life for a long time. "Not really much of what I would call a family life. It wasn't a great time, so I try not to think about it."

"Then I'm sorry I brought it up."

"Don't be. I just don't focus on it. I'm a Donovan now, and have been for most of my life. It's all that matters."

She smiled at him. "Sure."

He hated his childhood memories, before he met Jackson and Kal. His birth parents never parented him, not in the traditional sense. To them he had just been some kid who got in the way of their drug business.

He had never been happier than when he'd run away from them. If he'd stayed, he'd probably be dead.

He took a deep breath, inhaling the humid air, clearing his head.

"Tell me about your tattoo."

He frowned. "My—" His lips lifted. "You ogled me while I was half-naked in the ER yesterday, didn't you?"

She rolled her eyes. "I was not ogling. I was doing my job. But your tattoo is amazing."

She'd totally ogled. Which was fine with him. Better than fine, actually. "Thanks. Jackson and Kal got the same one. Becks did them. It represents all of us and our bond as brothers and as fire-fighters."

"Really? That's very cool. Something else the three of you have in common now."

"True."

Then it went quiet again. The funny thing was, it wasn't an uncomfortable silence. Carmen seemed content to just walk alongside him, and he was pretty happy to have her company.

"Great day for a walk, isn't it?"

She shot him a look. "It's hot, Rafe."

"Yeah, but we're alive and healthy and life is good, isn't it?"

She arched a brow. "You always carry this annoyingly positive outlook?"

"Always. Why? Does it bother you?"

"Depends on my mood."

"Yeah? And how's your mood today?"

"I'm fine."

That wasn't a happy *I'm fine*, so clearly, something was on her mind. "Want to talk about it?"

"There's nothing to talk about. I'm off work today. I made an extra batch of enchiladas, so dinner's handled. And I've already done two loads of laundry."

All domestic bullshit. "And what about you, Carmen? What are you doing for fun on your day off?"

She held her hands out. "I'm taking a walk, with you."

"And I appreciate it. But that's the nurse in you, making sure I'm okay. I'm talking about fun. What do you do to get out there and have a good time?"

She didn't answer.

"Got a boyfriend?"

She looked flustered, as if the question made her unsettled. "Oh . . . no. Not me."

"Girlfriend?"

She laughed. "Not one of those, either."

"So you don't date?"

"No. Not lately, anyway."

"Why not?"

"Too busy. And I don't want to."

"Again . . . why not?"

They turned the corner, and she focused her attention on the park, watching kids play on the swings. "I . . . just don't."

Now he was really curious. Carmen was beautiful and had a lot to offer. She worked and cared for her grandfather, but surely, she took time out for herself. "Maybe you should consider it."

They'd made it back to their street. She tilted her head up and gave him a curious look. "Why? Do you have someone in mind?"

He didn't know why or how the words fell out of his mouth, but they did. "Yeah. Me."

"Oh, God, no."

The look of horror on her face would have made him laugh if he hadn't been so insulted.

"Hey, I'm not that bad."

"Oh, I didn't mean it that way. I mean . . . look at you." She gave him a head to toe once-over. "You're . . . amazing. Hot. Incredible looking. Any woman would be lucky to . . . What I'm saying is . . ."

Her eyes widened, and then she glanced over at her house. "Well, we're back. Thanks for the walk. And for the invitation for the date, but I'm just not . . . Anyway, thanks, Rafe. Hope you enjoy the casserole. See you later, okay?"

She gave him a quick wave over her shoulder as she disappeared into her house.

Rafe stood there for a minute or so, trying to digest their conversation and coming to no conclusion other than he was totally confused.

What the hell just happened?

CHAPTER 4

CARMEN TRIED TO BUSY HERSELF WITH CLEANING HER grandfather's bathroom, but even the sweet lemony smell couldn't scrub away the utter mortification from her earlier conversation with Rafe.

What. A. Moron. It was like she'd opened her mouth and idiocy had fallen out.

First she'd insulted him by acting as if going out with him would be the worst thing that could happen to her, and then she'd stumbled all over herself trying to correct that mistake by practically drooling all over him with compliments.

Ugh. He probably thought she was the dumbest woman he'd ever known.

"Nothing good ever comes from me interacting with a man," she muttered.

Her grandfather walked slowly into the bedroom, then leaned on his cane. "Who are you talkin' to?"

She lifted her head. "No one. Myself."

"You losing your mind?"

"Maybe." Probably. Definitely. She went back to cleaning the sink.

"Or maybe something's on your mind and you need to talk it out."

"Nothing's on my mind, Grandpa."

"Yes, it is. When you start scrubbing like you want to take the top surface off my bathroom counter, it means you've got a problem. Start talking."

The very last thing she wanted to do was tell her grandpa about how she acted with Rafe. So she tossed the sponge into the cleaning bucket, straightened and smiled. "I was just working out some aggressions from my job on your counter, which is now shiny and clean. Are you ready for some lunch?"

"I guess."

He gave her the side-eye, and she knew he didn't believe her. But since he turned and left the room, that meant he wasn't going to push the subject further—at least for now.

She made turkey sandwiches and salad, which would keep the house cool. They sat at the kitchen table and ate.

"You look stronger today," she said. "I notice you're using the cane and not the walker."

"The cane makes me feel a little wobbly, but my physical therapist said not to rely so much on the walker, and to give the cane a try for a few hours a day."

"Good." He was so much stronger now than he'd been a month ago. The new therapy he'd been doing was working wonders for him.

"Did you take that food over to Rafe's house?" he asked.

"I did."

"How's he feeling?"

"He seems to be doing fine."

Her grandfather chewed thoughtfully for a few minutes, then

took a swallow of milk and set his glass down. "You were gone awhile."

"Oh, we went for a walk. Since Rafe is on activity restriction for the next few days, I thought it would be good for him to get out and do some minimal exercise."

"That's nice of you."

"Just returning the favor since he often helps out here."

"True enough."

More chewing, more staring off into space. Grandpa did that when something was on his mind, so she waited, figuring he'd get around to saying whatever it was he needed to say.

"That Rafe is a fine young man, Carmen."

And there it was. "Yes, he is, Grandpa."

"You know, you've been divorced for four years. I don't recall you bringing anyone over for me to meet. Or, for that matter, dressing up and going out anywhere. With anyone."

Now it was time for her to focus on her sandwich. She took a bite, waiting for the subject to drop. Instead, her grandpa stared at her. Waiting.

Damn.

"I've gone out. I'm just busy." Which was partly true. And it wasn't like she hadn't dated at all in the past four years. She'd had dates. Not in the first year after her divorce. But after she'd gotten over the sting of ending her marriage, she'd ventured out here and there. Though nothing serious, and certainly no man had interested her enough to bring him home to meet her grandfather.

"Life didn't end for you just because your marriage did. You should get out, have some fun. Date a nice boy. Like Rafe."

Ouch. "I'm not going to get serious with anyone right now, Grandpa. I have my hands full with work and with—"

His brows shot up. "With me? I don't need a damn babysitter, girl."

"That's not what I was about to say. I just . . . I'm not ready yet."

He laid his hand over hers. "Not every man is going to be like Tod."

She gave a quick nod, her throat closing up as a lump gathered there. She finally swallowed and said, "I know."

"It's time to move on. Find someone who'll treat you nice. Who'll appreciate the fine woman you are."

She laid a smile on him. "Thank you. I'll think about it."

"You do that."

For the remainder of the afternoon, thinking was all she did. Unfortunately, all she thought about was Rafe. His amazing body, the way he smiled at her and how she'd unceremoniously said no to his offer of a date. She felt badly, and she shouldn't.

So what if she'd said no to him? She had every right to turn a man down. Yes, he'd helped her out with her grandfather on occasion, but that was just him being a good neighbor. She owed him nothing. Nothing.

Oh, come on, Carmen. The real issue here is you wanted to say yes. But you're afraid.

She shook her head and carried the load of folded towels into the bathroom.

CHAPTER 5

AFTER TWO DAYS OF UTTER DULLNESS, RAFE GOT UP early to watch his brothers get ready for their shift at the fire station. He even made breakfast for everyone, since he had nothing else to do with his time.

"You? Making breakfast again, Rafe? This is getting to be a habit." Becks, the first one up, surveyed the smorgasbord of food he'd laid out on the kitchen island.

"What can I say? I'm bored."

He'd prepared biscuits and gravy, plus eggs. He'd sliced a couple of melons and placed those in a bowl and then had squeezed fresh orange juice. At least he'd felt he'd used his muscles—in the most minor way possible.

Jackson came downstairs, slinging his arm around Becks to brush his lips across hers before looking at the spread Rafe had laid out. He arched a brow. "Maybe we should keep you at home more often."

"Funny. Shut up and eat."

Kal was the last one downstairs. "Hot damn. Becks made breakfast?"

She laughed as she took her plate to the table. "Not me. Rafe."

"What? Is it the apocalypse?"

Rafe rolled his eyes. "Come on. It's not like I can't cook."

"No," Kal said, "but you usually don't. And besides, I'm the best cook out of all of you. Other than Becks, of course."

Becks blew him a kiss.

"Hey, this is good," Jackson yelled from the table. "You're on cooking duty for your entire house arrest."

"Screw you, Jackson."

Rafe filled his plate and joined the others at the table.

At least they'd been home with him last night, so he'd had some company. Today they'd start a twenty-four-hour shift at the station, and Becks would be at her tattoo shop until after eight, so he'd be completely alone. Not that he couldn't handle being alone; it would just up the boredom factor.

"I don't know, man," Kal said. "If I had five days off to just lie around, I'd catch up on some sleep, float around in the pool, watch some TV and play video games."

"The TV and video games make my head hurt."

Kal grimaced. "Sucks for you."

Becks gave him a sympathetic look. "I'm sorry this is so hard for you. Hopefully, you'll start feeling better soon."

"You don't have much downtime left," Kal said. "You'll be on next shift."

Rafe was so ready for that.

Jackson took a swallow of orange juice. "How did you sleep last night?"

"Fine. Though it was hard to fall asleep."

His brother shot him a look of concern. "Headaches?"

Rafe shook his head. "No, I think it's more the inactivity. I'm used to working out or running or being on shift. Even on my days off I'm active. So my body was restless. But no headache."

Jackson nodded. "That's good. Not that you couldn't sleep, but that it was attributed more to restlessness."

"Yeah. I'll get through it. I feel less sore this morning, so I'm healing."

"Good," Jackson said. "Try to walk if you can. Just getting the blood going a little will help with healing."

"I plan on it."

After breakfast, everyone else headed upstairs and Rafe did the dishes. At least he felt like he was doing something. Jackson and Kal came down and headed out to work. Becks wasn't due in to the shop until ten, so she hung out with him on the sofa in the game room.

"Maybe you could call one of the women you date and go do something with them," Becks said.

"Not really seeing anyone right now."

She smiled at him. "It doesn't seem to be a hardship for you to find someone to go out with, Rafe."

He wasn't sure if that was a compliment or an insult. "Are you calling me a manwhore?"

She laughed. "No. I'm saying women like you. You're charming."

"Thanks. I asked Carmen out the other day."

"You did? I didn't know you were interested in her."

"I am. I know you two didn't exactly have the best first meeting."

"Hey." She laid her hand on his forearm. "It was just a miscommunication, and we settled it. She seems nice, and you obviously like her."

"Doesn't matter. She turned me down."

"Oh. Well, maybe she's seeing someone."

"She's not. I asked. And, anyway, her reply when I asked her was . . ."

She drew her knees up to her chest. "Was what?"

"I don't know. She seemed . . . horrified. And then she apologized and stumbled all over herself complimenting me."

"Huh." She frowned.

"What does that mean?"

"I don't know. You should ask her to clarify."

He laughed. "I'm definitely not asking her again."

"Why not? Maybe you caught her off guard and she wasn't prepared for the question. Maybe she was flustered and didn't know how to answer."

"And maybe she's just not interested."

"Maybe she's not. But if *you're* interested, you should ask her again."

"I don't know."

She nudged him with her shoulder. "I realize being turned down is new territory for you, Rafe, but if you like her, ask her again. Or at least ask her to explain her answer."

There was no way in hell Rafe was going to push things with Carmen. They lived next door to each other. If things went bad, they'd have to see each other all the time. It would be awkward—forever.

Nope. Not gonna happen.

"And you know, Becks, I get turned down all the time."

She laughed. "Sure you do." She slid off the couch. "I have to go get ready for work. But if you want to talk about this some more, I'm always here for you."

He watched her walk away.

He trusted Becks. She'd been part of their group when they were homeless kids. They'd been close. She was like a sister to him. When she and Jackson had fallen in love, it had made Rafe so damn happy he could hardly hold it all in. Becks was family.

But on this? She was way off base.

Though after Becks left for work, he thought about it some more. Had he misinterpreted Carmen's response? Rafe knew no meant no, in all things regarding women. His mom had taught him that early on when he'd first started dating, and that was the way he'd always operated. So the thought of pushing Carmen on this seemed like a bad idea.

He decided the best way to handle it was not to handle it at all. He put on his tennis shoes and decided to go for a walk to stretch his muscles and clear his head.

He did three miles and wished like hell he could have run those three miles, but until he got the all clear from the doctor, he knew he had to obey the edict. At least he was moving. As he walked past Carmen's house, he noticed Jimmy, Carmen's grandfather, sitting in his wheelchair outside. Jimmy waved to him, so he walked up to the porch.

"Morning, Jimmy."

"Rafe. Out for a walk?"

"Yes, sir. How are you doing today?"

"Just fine. Catching a little hot summer air. You doin' the same?"

Rafe smiled. "Seems that way."

"I was about to grab some iced tea. Can I interest you in a glass?"

"That sounds great. Thank you."

Rafe held the door while Jimmy wheeled himself inside. His electric wheelchair offered him decent mobility, which was good. In the kitchen, he noticed that Carmen put everything in the lower cabinets within Jimmy's reach, but then he saw Jimmy park the wheelchair and stand.

"Hey, look at you," Rafe said.

Jimmy nodded. "I'm workin' on it. My physical therapist is a bastard. Making me stand and move around with the walker and the cane."

"You probably hate it, and then you also love that you're more mobile."

Jimmy smiled. "Yeah, something like that."

There was nothing more important to a man than being independent, so Rafe stayed out of his way while Jimmy grabbed two glasses, filled them with ice and took a pitcher out of the refrigerator. He didn't offer to help, because you didn't take away a man's dignity by doing things for him when he already had physical restrictions.

Jimmy handed the glass to him.

"Thanks." Rafe took a couple large swallows. "This is good."

"Carmen makes the best iced tea in Florida."

Rafe laughed. "I don't disagree with you."

"Come on over and let's sit by the window."

They had a similar floor plan to Rafe's house, except that Rafe and his brothers had renovated their house before they'd moved in.

They sat at the table, and Rafe noticed Jimmy had a deck of cards sitting there.

"Are you playing some solitaire?"

"I'm looking to play a little poker. You up for it?"

"You know it. Let's get started."

Jimmy dealt and then promptly kicked Rafe's ass. The man was lethal at poker. But since they weren't playing for real money, it wasn't like Rafe was losing anything. Except maybe his dignity.

Rafe studied his cards on the current hand. "I'll take two."

Jimmy handed him the cards, then took two for himself.

He looked around. "I take it Carmen is at work today?"

Jimmy didn't look up from his cards. "Mm-hmm."

Rafe placed his bet. "I call."

"Four kings," Jimmy said.

"Dammit, Jimmy." Rafe laid down his three jacks. "You got a loaded deck or something?"

He laughed. "No. I'm just better at this than you are."

They played several more rounds, and Rafe managed to actually win a couple of hands, so he didn't feel like a total loser. Rafe refilled both their glasses with iced tea while Jimmy went to the bathroom. After that, they ate some sandwiches for lunch.

Rafe munched on his chips and looked around. "Carmen keeps herself busy, doesn't she?"

"She does."

"Work and keeping this place up. Does she . . . date anyone?"

Jimmy's lips curved. "Asked her out, didn't you?"

Obviously, he couldn't slip anything past the sharp old man. "Yeah."

"And she turned you down, didn't she?"

Rafe sighed. "Yeah."

Jimmy nodded. "She's a tough woman, my *bebita*. Her exterior—like a hard shell. But she's soft on the inside, Rafe. She's had some very hard times. It's made her wary about men."

Hearing Jimmy talk about Carmen like this shed an entirely new light on her and made him want to know more about her. "I didn't know. She hasn't told me anything."

Jimmy gave him a look that meant serious business. "It's not my place to tell her story. Just . . . if you're interested, don't give up on her. She's worth it."

"Okay. I won't." He sat up straighter after that lecture, leaning into this conversation. Jimmy had given him a lot to think about.

Despite getting his ass handed to him in poker, Rafe found the day enlightening.

And he changed his mind about asking Carmen out again.

CHAPTER 6

"I WANT YOU TO MONITOR THE PATIENT IN SEVEN. HIS breathing is uneven, his white cell count is elevated and his BP is through the roof. No history of asthma or COPD. We're waiting on blood test results, and I need to make sure that now that he's had a treatment, his breathing improves. I asked for a report every thirty minutes. If you don't mind actually doing your job, make sure you give me those reports."

Carmen counted slowly to three in her head before answering the doctor. "I'll make sure that's taken care of, Dr. Ventura."

The doctor turned and walked away while Carmen took her internal count all the way to ten to avoid throwing her extremely expensive portable netbook at Dr. Ventura's head.

Brody Anderson was thirty-three years old, had never smoked, held a job as a grocery store manager and had a wife and three little boys. He seemed very nice. He was also very sick right now. She checked his vitals, which seemed stable, and his blood pressure appeared to be coming down, which was a good sign. His wife, Karen, sat at his bedside, looking almost as pale as Brody.

"The fact that he's resting right now is good," Carmen told her.

"I just don't know what happened. He never gets sick. Then he woke up this morning short of breath and looking deathly pale. It came out of nowhere."

"Don't worry. We'll get it figured out. You should try to rest, too."

Karen shook her head. "I can't. All I want to do is . . . watch him breathe."

Karen's eyes filled with tears.

Carmen had seen a lot of crying in the ER over the years and steeled herself against the emotional aspect of her job. If she didn't, she'd fall apart every day. But that didn't mean she'd lost all sense of empathy.

"We're doing everything we can to find out what's wrong, Mrs. Anderson. And you should try to rest. If you tax yourself too much with worry, you won't be able to help your husband."

She nodded. "You're right. Thank you. Everyone here is so nice."

Carmen smiled at her, then left the room.

Almost everyone here was nice.

She sent her report in, though she doubted Ventura would pay attention. The man had a typical God complex. She'd seen it countless times over the years. Some doctors would come in, do their jobs and get along well with everyone. But every now and then there'd be one like Forrest Ventura who thought he was owed something. He had a connected family, came from money, and because his father was a big name in the city, he thought everyone should bow down to him.

To Carmen, the only way you earned respect in the ER was to do your damn job, just like everyone else. If you cared about the patients, if you worked as hard as everyone else, you were appreciated. If you didn't, you needed to get the hell out of everyone else's way.

Her responsibility was to monitor what her nurses were doing, which included all the patients on her wing. Because she hired exceptional nurses, she rarely had anything to worry about. Today, everything was running smoothly, which meant she had more time to concentrate on the one patient who needed extra care—Mr. Anderson.

"Front desk said someone's asking for you," Bonita, the unit clerk, said.

She frowned. "For me?"

"Yes. Some good-looking guy in a firefighter's uniform."

He wouldn't . . . Well, maybe he would. "Okay, send him on back."

She would have gone out to the front, but she wanted to stay close to her patient in case anything changed.

Rafe walked through the double doors a few minutes later. He looked amazing in his dark blue firefighter pants and T-shirt.

"Back to work?"

"Just left the doctor and got a clean bill of health, so I'm released to full duties. And since I was next door at the medical offices, I thought I'd stop off here and say hello."

She pushed back the giddy sensation in her stomach. "I'm kind of busy."

"I know you are. But I wanted to take a few seconds to ask you out to dinner tomorrow night."

"Rafe, I already said—"

"Just as a friendly thank-you for being there for me the night I got hurt. It gave me peace of mind to have you taking care of me. You made me relax."

"I just did my job."

"But I knew you. If you hadn't been there, I'd have fought the whole thing."

"Still, I—"

"Just let me take you to dinner to thank you. Kind of like you make me casseroles when I help take care of your grandpa? Only I'm not cooking."

She couldn't argue with that. Well, she could, but what harm would a thank-you dinner do? "Okay, sure. Dinner tomorrow night."

"Great. Are you on shift tomorrow?"

"Yes. I get off at six."

"You just let me know what time I can pick you up."

"Seven thirty?"

He gave her a grin that made her tingle all over. "Sure. Seven thirty sounds great. I'll see you then."

"I didn't get a report thirty minutes ago, Ms. Lewis."

Just the sound of Dr. Ventura's voice sent electric rage surging through her nerve endings. But she turned and smiled at him. "I've sent you two reports in the past thirty minutes, Dr. Ventura. Mr. Anderson's vitals are stable, and the blood reports are in."

He looked at her with a tight-lipped expression. "Fine. But you can entertain your boyfriends on your own time."

He walked away.

Rafe frowned. "Who's the dickhead?"

"Chief resident and resident pain in my ass."

"Want me to go kick the shit out of him?"

"No, thanks. I can handle him."

Rafe gave her a knowing smile. "I'll just bet you can. I gotta run. I'll see you tomorrow."

"Okay. See you, Rafe."

She leaned against the nurses station desk and watched him walk away.

That man had a very fine ass.

"Did I hear right?" Tess asked, coming up to stand next to her as Rafe disappeared through the double doors. "You have a date with hottie McFireman?"

Carmen shook her head. "Not a date. Just dinner."

"He asked you out to dinner, right?"

"Yes, but just to thank me for taking care of him when he was here in the ER."

"Uh-huh."

"What does that mean?"

"Nothing. Very nice of him. I hope he takes you to a good place for dinner."

She knew Tess. And the one thing she knew was that Tess always spoke her mind. She definitely had something to say, and whatever it was, she wasn't saying it.

"Okay, spill."

Tess looked around. They were currently alone at the desk. "Fine. He likes you, Carmen. It's obvious. So why not enjoy him? Go out to dinner, and then see what happens."

"Nothing's going to happen."

"Why not? You don't have to make him your forever and ever. No commitment required. But aren't you tired of sleeping alone at night?"

She had to admit the answer to that was a resounding yes. But the thought of dating again made her shudder. Tod had made such a mess of their marriage, leaving a sour taste in her mouth for all things love.

"I don't know, Tess. I don't associate dating with anything pleasant."

"Which is your ex's fault. You can't blame the entire male population for his mistakes. Give men another chance."

Since she was tired of this conversation, and mainly because she knew Tess was right, she nodded. "Fine. I'll have dinner with Rafe. But just dinner. Nothing else."

Tess's lips curved. "Of course. Just dinner. But I'm coming over after work tomorrow to help you choose an outfit."

"You don't trust me to dress appropriately?"

"I think you'd toss on a pair of capris and a random shirt and call it good. I'm going to make sure you're dressed to kill."

Ridiculous. "I'm not Cinderella, Rafe isn't the prince and we're not going to a ball. It's just dinner, Tess."

"Maybe it's just dinner, and maybe there'll be dessert. I aim to make sure you're dressed for dessert."

Carmen rolled her eyes at Tess's insinuation that there would be any fooling around. She could barely bring herself to have dinner with a guy, let alone have sex with him. "I'm not having dessert."

"Depending on how dinner goes, you might be interested in whatever decadent dessert Rafe is offering."

"Whatever. You can come help me pick out clothes, okay?"

Tess grinned. "Outstanding. Now I need to go check on Mrs. Fillipo."

"You do that."

Carmen was going to go do her job and not think about dinner with Rafe tomorrow night.

Where there would absolutely be no dessert.

CHAPTER 7

AFTER NEARLY A WEEK OF NO ACTIVITY, WALKING INTO the fire station felt exhilarating. And the welcome from Rafe's firefighter brothers and sisters made his heart swell. It felt like coming home again. These people were part of his family. He'd missed them.

Rafe never took his job for granted. He knew what it took to be a firefighter. He also knew the risks. His dad had taught him that from an early age, when he came to live with the Donovans. After he came off shift, Dad would tell him stories about what had gone down. His father had never shied away from honesty, and when they asked questions about the fires, he'd always been honest with them.

After all, Rafe and his brothers had lived through one. He figured that's probably why they had all joined the squad. Not only surviving a fire but being rescued by an amazing man.

Being lucky enough to be adopted into that world was something Rafe was incredibly grateful for, especially considering where he'd come from.

He walked down the hall and stopped as he saw Captain Kendall Mathias. The captain shook his hand.

"Welcome back," Captain Mathias said.

"Thank you, sir."

"Got your release?"

"Yes, sir." He handed the paperwork to the captain.

"You took a hell of a hit from that backdraft. Glad your injury wasn't more serious."

"Me, too."

"Don't let it happen again. Good firefighters like you are hard to come by."

It was a warm compliment, shrouded in an admonishment. But Rafe took it for what it was—his gruff captain's welcome back.

"I'll be more careful in the future, sir."

Captain Mathias nodded and disappeared down the hall. His captain was a man of few words, but Rafe respected him. He got the job done and wasn't afraid to put himself on the front lines with his team.

He found the rest of the squad in the kitchen. With the welcome he got, he felt like he'd been gone for months, instead of just a couple of shifts. They had even held breakfast so they could all eat together.

"Glad you didn't die," Tommy Rodriguez said, winking at him.

"He's just glad you took the blast instead of him since you were in front of him," Zep Richards said.

Rafe laughed and scooped the egg-and-ham casserole onto his plate. "Hey, that's what a firefighter brother does for another."

"And maybe next time you can get out of the way before the door blows up in your face." Ginger Davidson grinned.

"That would mean he'd have to use his brain," Kal said. "We already know he doesn't have one."

"And what little brains he did have leaked out when he got conked on the head," Mitchell Hendricks said.

"Very funny. Shouldn't you be shoveling food in your mouths so you can all shut up?"

Fortunately, the food was more important than talking shit about him, though it was natural to give an injured firefighter a hard time. Rafe knew it meant they cared about him. And as he looked around the table, he realized how much he cared about them, too. These people all had his back, no matter what.

That meant a lot.

"So, what did you do with all that time off, Rafe?" Callie Vassar asked. "Lie in the sun and work on your tan?"

"He probably took a lot of naps," Rodriguez said. "You know how Rafe is. We always catch him napping around here."

The reprieve didn't last long. "Not much, since I was on activity restriction. I'm looking forward to a hard workout today."

"You'll get it," Jackson said. "Truck needs washing, and there's a knocking sound in Ladder 6's engine. See if you can figure out what the problem is."

Everyone knew Rafe was the mechanic of the fire station. If any of the rigs had a problem, they'd call on him first rather than sending it out for service.

"I'll get right on it. As soon as I eat a second helping of this breakfast casserole."

"He's back to normal," Ginger said, grinning.

"Yeah, normal, all right," Kal said. "Eating all the food."

Rafe ignored them and finished breakfast, then moved the Ladder 6 truck into the mechanic's bay where all the diagnostic and repair equipment was located. It didn't take him long to figure out the problem in the timing system. He adjusted it and then drove the truck outside to wash it.

It felt good to be doing something again. He liked staying active, and five days of doing nothing had been frustrating. Being able to use his muscles again felt like he'd received a second chance at life.

He knew that the backdraft at the house could have gone much worse. He'd been lucky to end up with only a concussion.

He got up on a ladder to scrub the top of Engine 6.

"You could have yelled for someone to come in and help you."

He turned around to see his brother Kal staring up at him.

"I'm okay."

Kal grabbed a long-handled brush and a ladder, then appeared on the other side of the truck. "I know you're okay. But I'll still help you."

Rafe cocked his head to the side. "You've gotta wash Ladder 6, don't you?"

Kal grinned. "Yeah."

"So now you'll want me to help you do that."

"Well, yeah. Brothers help brothers, don't they?"

Rafe rolled his eyes, but he didn't mind. He planned on washing the ladder truck anyway. Not that he was going to tell his brother that.

With the two of them working, they had both trucks washed and dried in no time. They cleaned the windows, then rolled the trucks back into their bays.

Rafe and Kal picked up all the towels and tossed them on top of the washing machine. They hosed out the shop and started sweeping out the water to dry it.

"So, I asked Carmen Lewis out to dinner."

Kal stopped and stared at Rafe. "Did she say yes?"

"She did. She's reluctant, though. I had to tell her it was a thank-you for bringing that casserole over the other day."

"Maybe she doesn't like you."

Rafe shook his head. "Not possible. All women like me."

Kal laughed. "*In your mind*, all women like you."

"Whatever. Carmen likes me."

Kal leaned on the broom handle. "And you like her."

"Yeah, I do. She's feisty and smart and beautiful. What's not to like?"

"She's also our next-door neighbor. If you start dating her and things go south, she's still going to be our next-door neighbor. Have you given that any thought?"

He had thought about it. Too much. And he didn't want to think about it again. "I'm not going to get into a relationship with her. We're just going to dinner."

"Uh-huh."

"And anyway, I don't hurt the women I date. I'm always honest with them, letting them know that we're just going to have a good time, and I'm not looking for more. I'm pretty sure Carmen isn't looking for anything more, either. I think we'll be fine."

Kal shrugged. "As long as you don't screw things up with her and make her mad."

"Have I ever done that with a woman?"

"Not that I know of. But then again, you've never dated a woman long enough to have what I would consider a relationship."

He was about to respond to that with a denial, but he paused.

Was Kal right? He'd gone out with Kaylee for a month. And then there'd been Gina, but that had been only a few weeks. Maria had lasted six weeks, and she'd probably been his longest relationship. And she was a flight attendant, so she'd been gone for half of that time.

"Huh."

Kal slanted a smug smile at him. "See? You've never had a long-term girlfriend."

"I guess not. I don't know why not. I like women."

Kal swept the broom down to the end of the shop and out the door before turning to face Rafe. "Yeah, for short durations. Then you get bored. Or maybe they get bored with you."

He frowned as he swept. "I am not boring."

"Are the women you date boring?"

"No."

Kal shrugged. "Then you must be the problem."

"Fuck you."

His brother laughed and grabbed Rafe's broom, sliding both of their tools back in their spots on the wall in the workshop. "Maybe it's time for some self-reflection."

"Oh, this coming from a guy who also doesn't do relationships?"

"We aren't talking about me. Plus, I had a long-term girlfriend in high school. So at least I know I *can* have one. Can you say the same thing?"

He couldn't, so he let the subject drop and went back into the fire station. They got a call right after that, so Rafe had to clear his head and concentrate on his job.

It felt great to be back in his rig again, to have his gear on, to hear the sirens roar, to know that he was healthy and capable of doing his job. The ride to the scene took about five minutes, and it was the best damn five minutes he'd ever had. The rush of adrenaline made him feel alive.

They pulled up in front of an older one-story. A middle-aged man came running toward them from the side of the house.

"It's my wife. She was cleaning out the storage shed, and a shelf fell on her."

Their EMTs had also been called to the scene, but Engine 6 was going into the shed first.

"What's your wife's name?" Jackson asked.

"Shelly." The man was shaking. "I told her I was gonna get to cleaning it out, but she got mad and she went in to do it. I told her not to."

Jackson grasped the man's arm. "It's okay. We'll get her out."

Jackson turned to them. "Rafe, you and Mitchell take lead.

Ginger, see if you can get up on a ladder and shine some light into that shed."

"Yes, sir." Rafe never gave a second thought to taking orders from his older brother. At least, not on the job. Jackson had earned his lieutenant's bars, and on scene, he was in charge.

The oversize shed was filled to bursting with junk piled so high it wasn't a surprise that it had tumbled down on Shelly. Rafe had no idea how an actual person was in there. But then he saw a path off to the left, so he made his way in.

"Right behind you," Mitchell said.

Rafe took careful steps. There were plastic boxes, cardboard, file cabinets and all kinds of things in his way. And the piles weren't steady, so the last thing he wanted was stuff coming down on top of Mitchell and him. Then there'd be two more people to rescue.

"You hear anything?" Mitchell asked.

"No."

But then Rafe thought he heard a moan. He raised his hand to halt Mitchell, hoping the quiet would let him hear it again.

He did. It was a soft moan, coming from the back of the shed.

"This way," he said to Mitchell.

As they rounded the corner, Rafe bumped a tower with his shoulder and a couple of boxes came tumbling down on top of them. He braced himself for the impact, wincing at the weight. Fortunately, they were only cardboard boxes, so he was able to lift them up and stacked them to his left.

"You okay?" Mitchell asked, helping him readjust the pile.

"Yeah. How about you?"

"Fine."

Rafe nodded. "Let's keep moving."

The moans were getting louder, and then they were blasted by a bright burst of light.

"Does this help?" Ginger asked, holding a flashlight.

"Better, thanks," Mitchell said.

"More to the left, Ginger," Rafe said.

The light moved to the left, which guided them to a woman on the floor. A sizable amount of debris had fallen on top of her. She had a cut on the side of her head, and she was in and out of consciousness.

"We found her," Rafe radioed to his team. "She's semiconscious. We're going to free her from the debris."

"Roger that," Jackson said.

"Shelly," Rafe said, "can you hear me?"

She blinked, then frowned. "Yes. My head hurts."

Okay, at least she was coming around now. "We're going to fix that, Shelly. You just stay still."

They had to maneuver in a tight space and pull the debris off of her, including a damn heavy file cabinet. Fortunately, Rafe and Mitchell were able to lift it upright, freeing Shelly.

They checked her for broken bones but didn't find any. They put a c-collar around her neck to stabilize her spine and strapped her on the portable stretcher, winding out the way they came in.

Since they now had Shelly between them, it was even more slow going. It was hot as fuck in the shed, too, with sweat pouring off them, so the sooner they got out of this hot box, the better.

This time, Rafe followed Mitchell. At least they had light and communication with their team outside.

And when they made it outside, Miguel and Adrienne took over, loading Shelly onto the stretcher and doing their assessment before putting her into the ambulance and taking her to the hospital.

Rafe finally exhaled, then headed to the truck, where cold water was waiting for him. He needed hydration in the worst way, so he guzzled it down.

"A little tight in there?" Jackson asked.

Rafe's lips curved. "Good thing I'm not claustrophobic."

Jackson slapped him on the back. "Good job. Go put up your gear and let's head back."

It had been crazy tight in there, but it had also felt good to be at work again.

But as he sat in the truck on the way back, he thought about his earlier conversation with Kal. He wondered what it was about him that made him pull back from women just as things were heating up.

Kal might be right. Maybe it was time for some self-reflection. Because he liked Carmen. And the last thing he wanted to do was screw anything up with her.

Even if it was just dinner.

CHAPTER 8

CARMEN HAD SCOURED HER CLOSET AND DECIDED SHE had nothing to wear.

Of course, she hadn't been on a date in . . . She was pretty sure the last actual date she'd been on had been her first date with her ex-husband. She'd had coffee with a couple of guys that hadn't amounted to anything, and she couldn't call those dates.

She grimaced and closed the closet door with a resounding slam.

At least her grandfather wasn't home tonight. Mario and Javier, a couple of his old friends from his club, had picked him up for a night of cards at Theo's house. It was good for her grandfather to get out and socialize, and she trusted his close friends to take good care of him, so she wasn't worried.

Much.

But Grace, Theo's wife, promised she'd call Carmen if there was any problem.

She trusted Grace even more than Grandpa's buddies.

Her doorbell rang, so she went to answer it. Tess stood there with several dresses slung over her arm.

"I have nothing to wear," Carmen said, turning and walking away.

Tess followed. "I knew you'd say that, so I brought a few items."

"That's because your amazing husband takes you out all the time."

"You bet your sweet ass he does."

She'd known Tess's husband, George, for as long as Tess had known him. He was kind and sweet and funny and treated Tess like a treasure. Tess was a lucky woman.

Carmen led Tess into her bedroom, where Tess laid four dresses on the bed.

She looked down at the selection Tess had put on display. "You didn't have to bring me dresses."

"I know. But I also know you haven't been on a date in ages and you probably haven't bought a new dress since you last went out with Tod."

"This is true."

"So, you can borrow one of mine until you get your feet wet and decide to go splurge on something new for yourself. Or maybe a few new pretty things."

She shrugged. "I don't need a few new pretty things."

"Actually, you do. Do you know how amazing it is to dress up, to feel good about yourself? No one deserves that more than you. Even if it's new lingerie."

Carmen just looked at her, and Tess's eyes widened.

"You did buy new lingerie, didn't you?"

"Of course I didn't. When would I have had time to do that?"

"I don't know. On your lunch? There's a mall two miles from the hospital."

Carmen shrugged. "It never occurred to me. Besides, it's not like he's going to see my underwear anyway."

"You sure about that?" Tess raised a brow. "Do you really want to get yourself all tricked out in some hot dress with your makeup on and your hair looking amazing, and then underneath you'll have ten-year-old underwear?"

"They're not that old." They were seven years old, but she wasn't going to admit that to Tess. "Besides, it's too late to do anything about it, anyway. And if by some chance I get undressed in front of Rafe—which isn't going to happen—he's just going to have to deal with my raggedy underwear."

Tess shrugged. "If you say so."

Carmen didn't plan to have sex with Rafe tonight. Just dinner.

She tried on the dresses. She and Tess were roughly the same size, though Carmen had bigger breasts, which meant that her cleavage spilled out of all of them.

"You look amazing in that red one," Tess said.

Carmen stared down at the dress. "It is super cute and fits me well, but I don't know." She smoothed her hands over her breasts. "It's cut a little low."

"I know," Tess said, waggling her brows. "It makes you look hot as hell."

She lifted her gaze to Tess. "I don't know that I want to look hot as hell."

"Really. What do you want to look like?"

"I—" She didn't have an answer off the top of her head. "I don't know, Tess. Just, normal me, I guess."

"You are normal you. Just in a dress. What do you want, Carmen? To wear scrubs to dinner?"

"No. Maybe, you know, capris or a sundress or something."

She pointed. "Then try on the sundress that I brought."

"Okay."

She grabbed the brightly colored sundress and slipped that on next. It was just as low-cut but not as fancy as the red dress. She could wear her beige sandals with the turquoise beads and a bracelet and grab a wrap and the look would be more casual. She already felt much more at ease, more herself.

"Dynamite!"

She lifted her gaze to Tess. "It's so pretty. How come you've never worn this?"

Tess shrugged. "It doesn't look as flattering on me as it does on you. It doesn't fit me the same. I think it's your rack. You fill it out better than I do."

Carmen looked at herself in her closet door mirror. Okay, so maybe it wasn't quite as low-cut as the red dress. The sundress hit just above her knees, and it had a nice silky flow to it. She could already imagine herself walking, or even dancing in it. Or strolling along the beach. Whatever they did, she'd feel good. Not self-conscious. And that was what was important.

She smiled, then turned to Tess. "Thanks for letting me borrow it."

"You can have it. I bought it at an end-of-season sale for practically nothing, and I'll likely never wear it."

"Then I'll pay you for it."

Tess sighed. "It was twelve bucks, Carmen."

"Then I'll pay you twelve bucks for it."

"Fine. As long as you're happy wearing it."

"I am happy. Thanks for letting me play dress-up."

"You're welcome. Now I need to get back home, because George tossed ribs in the smoker this morning, and they should be falling off the bone by now."

Talking about the ribs made her stomach grumble. All she'd had for lunch today was a package of cheese and crackers and a chocolate milk. "That sounds delicious."

"Doesn't it?" Tess gave her a hug. "I want all the details tomorrow."

They walked to the front door. "I don't know if there will be any details other than dinner details, but whatever they are, you'll get them."

"My guess is you might be surprised just how much dirt you'll have to spill to me tomorrow."

Tess was so off base about her dinner with Rafe.

"We'll see. Thanks again."

Tess gave her a quick wave and headed out to her car.

Carmen noticed lightning off in the distance and smelled rain in the air.

Great. She should have just opted for her capris and maybe a baseball cap. But if she did that, Tess would never forgive her. Not that her friend would ever know.

But she was committed to the sundress, so she decided to go for it.

She closed the door, then went back into the bedroom to finish getting ready. She'd already taken a quick shower after work. So after she did her hair and makeup, she got dressed, put on a pair of chandelier earrings, then headed into the kitchen, debating whether she wanted to pour herself a glass of wine to calm her nerves.

Why was she nervous, anyway? It wasn't like this was a big deal. It was just dinner with her friendly next-door neighbor.

Oh, right, Carmen. Your hot-as-hell, abtastic, sexy next-door neighbor who you've fantasized about for years.

Then again, for all she knew, Rafe really was just interested in dinner, and nothing more.

Wouldn't that be the most ironic thing of all? Here she was, obsessing over tonight, when likely all he wanted to do was thank her with a nice dinner and a handshake by the door at the end?

She laughed and went to the fridge to pour herself a glass of wine.

CHAPTER 9

RAFE COULDN'T REMEMBER OBSESSING SO MUCH OVER what to wear for a dinner date. He finally settled on dark jeans and a blue-and-white thin-striped button-down shirt. Who knew this was going to be such a big deal?

But he had to remember to make this as laid-back and casual as possible, so he wouldn't spook Carmen into bolting from the restaurant. After talking to her grandfather, he decided to take things easy. She was obviously skittish about dating and men in general since her marriage broke up. He didn't know the details, and it wasn't his business to know. All he wanted to do was show her that he was one of the good guys.

He backed his truck down the driveway and pulled into Carmen's. He could have walked over, but he figured since this was a date he'd pick up Carmen the right way rather than having her walk across the lawn to his house. Plus he'd seen the lightning, and he didn't want Carmen to get wet if it started to rain.

He rang the doorbell and waited. No one answered, so he frowned and rang the bell again.

He heard footsteps, and Carmen opened the door, knocking him back on his heels.

She had on a sundress that clung to her gorgeous curves. Her hair was down, she had makeup on, her lips were painted some dark color that drew his attention to her mouth and suddenly all he wanted to do was kiss her. And maybe run his fingertips over all her exposed skin to see if it was as soft as it looked.

Slow. The. Fuck. Down.

Good reminder. So he smiled and said, "You look amazing."

She gave him a hesitant smile. "Thanks. So do you. Also, you didn't mention where we were going, so if this outfit is too much, or not enough, I can change."

"You're perfect for where we're going."

"Oh, good."

"Is your grandpa here? Do you need to do anything for him before we go?"

"No. He's out tonight with friends, and they'll settle him in when they bring him home."

"Great. Then we can go."

"Okay. Let me grab my wrap and my purse."

He watched her as she walked down the hall toward the living room, then leaned over to fetch her purse from the sofa. He tried not to ogle the way the sundress caressed her butt, making him itch to explore her globes with his hands.

Dude. Get your head in the game.

He cleared his throat and turned his back on her, forcing himself to think of anything other than Carmen's hot body.

When she pulled the door shut and brushed by him, she offered up a smile. "I'm ready."

So was he. So, so ready.

He went out to his truck and opened the passenger door. She gave him a curious look as she stepped up.

"What?" he asked.

"Nothing."

He closed the door, then walked around to the driver's side and got in. He pulled out of the driveway and down the street, making his way toward the highway.

After he pulled into a lane on the highway, he said, "You gave me a look."

She shifted to face him. "I did?"

"Yeah. When you got into the truck."

"Oh." She let out a soft laugh. "It's been a long time, like, a very long time, since someone has opened and closed the door for me when I got into a car."

"Really?"

"Yes."

"So you don't date much."

"Honey, I don't date at all."

He slanted a quick look at her. "Then I'll do my best to make this one good for you."

She gave him that look again, the one that told him she didn't believe that what was happening to her was real.

Who the hell had she been out with before? And what kind of an asshole was her ex?

Don't worry, Cinderella. I'll make you feel special.

He had thought to go low-key tonight, to approach this as a friendly dinner. But now he saw that Carmen needed to be treated like a princess, that it had been far too long since someone had put her needs first.

He was just the guy to do that.

They made small talk about their workday during the twenty-minute car ride, which reminded him how well they got along, how easy it was to be with her. Usually, first dates were full of tension, not knowing the person, trying to grasp at what to talk about. With Carmen, conversation flowed naturally. They always seemed to have a lot to talk about.

He pulled into the parking lot at Serafina.

"I hope you like Italian," he said after he turned off the engine.

"I love Italian. I've never eaten here. I've heard this place is fancy and expensive."

His lips curved. "The food is great. Come on, let's go."

He got out and came around to her side, holding out his hand to help her out of the truck. She hesitated, then took his hand and stepped down.

"Thanks."

They started toward the door, but she stopped, so he did, too.

"You know, I'd have been fine with some taco place near the water," she said.

"Good to know. I like tacos, too. We'll do that some other time." He held out his arm, and she looked at him, then sighed and linked her arm with his.

She might not be fully on board with this yet, but before the night was over, he intended to make sure Carmen had zero hesitations about the fact that the two of them were on a date.

CARMEN WASN'T SURE WHAT TO MAKE OF THIS WHOLE thing with Rafe, but she was hungry. Plus he was gorgeous and he smelled good, so she was going to follow through.

The restaurant was beautiful with its blue light undertones, lending it a warmth that was romantically atmospheric. Rafe gave his name at the front desk, and they were seated right away at a table outside next to the water.

Their server presented them with menus and a wine list.

Rafe looked over the wine list, then handed it to her. "Let me know what looks good to you."

"You don't like wine?"

"I like wine. I just thought you might want to choose a bottle for us."

That was a first. Tod always ordered wine and food for her, as if she didn't have a mind of her own. One of the many things she'd wholeheartedly disliked.

She perused the list, then looked up at him. "I like both reds and whites. Do you have a preference?"

He shook his head. "I'm good with whatever you decide."

She couldn't help but sigh with happiness.

When their server returned, she ordered the Bortoluzzi Merlot.

"Very good," their server said.

Rafe smiled.

"Is that okay?" she asked.

"Yeah. I like merlot."

She leaned back in her chair and opened her menu, then studied Rafe. "I didn't take you for a wine drinker."

"Why's that?"

She shrugged. "I don't know."

"Because of my looks? Because of my job? My background? You do realize those things have nothing to do with liking wine."

She realized she had preconceived notions about Rafe, and that was her mistake. "I'm sorry. You're right."

"I took a wine trip with a friend a few years back. Decided I liked the taste. Not as much as beer, mind you. But a good wine is worth drinking."

She laughed. Now that sounded more like Rafe. "Of course."

She studied the menu as their server returned with the wine, opened the bottle and poured a sample into each of their glasses. Rafe deferred to her—again—so she tasted the wine.

It was smooth, and excellent, so she nodded to the server, who filled both glasses.

"Nice choice," Rafe said, swirling the liquid around in his glass.

She was mesmerized by his hand on the glass, the expert way he held his fingers on the stem. And, okay, maybe she just liked his hands, and had thought about what it would feel like to have his fingertips exploring her neck, her collarbone, and lower.

She shivered.

"Cold?" he asked.

It was about eighty-five degrees out, and her shivering had been all about her fantasies and had nothing to do with the weather. She shook her head. "No, I'm fine, thanks. So, where was your wine trip?"

"Napa Valley."

"With a woman, I'm guessing?"

"Yeah. She was in sales and won the trip for hitting her goals. So she asked me to go with her."

"Nice perk."

"Sure was. A weekend in Napa, wine tours, great hotel, amazing food. We had fun."

She swirled her finger over the rim of her wineglass. "And then what happened?"

"We dated for a couple of weeks after that, but she got a job transfer to Boston, so we ended things."

"Just like that? No sad goodbyes?"

His lips curved. "No sad goodbyes. She had already put in for the promotion, so she knew she might be moving soon and was up front about that from the time we started dating. I let her know I wasn't interested in anything serious, so we knew from the get-go that we were just in it for a good time."

"Easy for both of you, then, I guess."

"It was."

"I suppose that's how you like it."

"Like what?"

"Your dating life. Easy, with no emotional investment."

He took a sip of wine and set the glass down on the table. "Makes it uncomplicated that way. No one gets hurt."

"But you don't get to fall in love that way."

They were interrupted by their server, who came over to take their order. Carmen ordered the Fra Diavolo, and Rafe ordered Osso Buco D'Angello, along with salads.

After their server left, Rafe slanted a smile at her.

"Is that what you're looking for?" he asked.

"What?"

"To fall in love?"

"Oh, God no. Never again."

He laughed. "That sounded definite."

She hadn't meant to put it out there that forcefully, but now that it was, she supposed she should explain why. "I was married for two years. Granted, we were both very young and we shouldn't have done it. It was a stupid mistake, and one I don't intend to make again."

"I don't know, Carmen. If you were young, you probably learned something from it. You don't mean to tell me you're planning to spend the rest of your life alone, are you?"

She finished off her glass of wine and reached for the bottle. Rafe grabbed it and poured for her.

"Thanks. And my life is full right now. I have my job and my grandpa, and there's no room in it for me to make another stupid mistake."

"So you don't trust your own judgement when it comes to men? Is that what you're saying?"

"Not at all. I'm a lot smarter now than I was when I was twenty-one."

"Which means you know exactly what you want—and what you don't."

"True."

"And who the good guys are versus the bad guys."

"Of course."

"Well, you're out to dinner with me. That makes me one of the good guys, right?"

She smiled at him, admiring his confidence, but she needed to set him straight. "We're not on a date."

"Let's say we were."

"But we're not."

"What if I wanted to make this a date? Officially."

She tilted her head to the side. "Rafe."

"Carmen."

The way he looked at her, his lips tilted just short of a full smile, his eyes dancing in a way that told her he was amused, should irritate her. But for some reason it didn't. Maybe it was because he was so incredibly fine looking, and maybe because he wasn't a stranger to her. She knew Rafe. He was fun and playful, with an incredible sense of humor. He wasn't making fun of her, he was trying to engage her. The man oozed charm, and she found that a bit irresistible.

Fortunately, she could resist just fine.

"You don't want to date me."

"Why?" he asked.

"Because I'm not the dating type. I'm cranky and I have baggage."

He arched a brow. "We all carry baggage around, babe. And you're not cranky. Not with me, anyway."

"Have you ever had your heart broken?"

"Yes."

His answer was quick. "I didn't know you'd ever been in a relationship."

"I'm not talking about a relationship."

"Oh." Now he was delving into deeper waters, and she wasn't sure either of them was ready to talk about that. "Okay. So you know what that feels like."

"Yeah. And how hard it is to trust that anyone you care about won't do the same thing to you."

He was hitting all her buttons right now, and she didn't know what to do about that. But saying all the right things didn't mean she was going to fall into his arms, because she'd already been with someone who'd done that. And when it had come down to *doing* all the right things, he had failed.

So she sipped her wine and thought about the things he had said. And all through dinner they talked, getting to know each other in ways they hadn't when they'd just been neighbors.

"I moved in with my grandpa after the divorce. He'd had a home care worker who was coming in twice a day to cook and help care for him, but it was becoming obvious he needed more."

"It seems to have worked out well for both of you. Jimmy has you there, and you have a place to hide out from the world."

She frowned. "Hey. It's not like that at all."

"Isn't it? I mean, yeah, in the beginning it was great. You needed to heal, and staying there was perfect. Family is everything when you're hurting, and Jimmy needed you."

"He still does."

"Jimmy likes feeling independent."

She stabbed shrimp onto her fork, then lifted it and pointed it at him. "Oh, he told you this himself?"

Rafe shrugged. "He didn't have to. He's a man who's still in good enough shape to mostly take care of himself, with a small amount of assistance. But you baby him and treat him like an invalid."

She'd never been more insulted in her life. "I'm a nurse, in case you forgot that, and I'm more than capable of assessing my grandfather's medical needs."

Rafe pushed his plate to the side, seemingly unaffected by her rising anger. "I didn't mean to insult you, Carmen. I'm just saying that it seems to me that your grandpa gets along just fine. He goes out with his friends to play cards, he gets regular therapy for the side of his body weakened by the stroke he had several years ago, and other than maybe requiring some assistance now and then, he appears to be able to care for himself just fine."

She lifted her chin. "He needs me."

"Or maybe it's you that needs him. And so in your mind you've decided that he's worse off than he really is."

Fucking douchewipe. She should walk out of there, grab a Lyft and head home. She didn't need this. Unfortunately, her food was delicious, and she'd be damned if she'd bail on an excellent Fra Diavolo. No man was worth leaving a good meal.

So she pierced her fork into her noodles and swept some up. "How is it that you think you know me so well that you can make assumptions like this?"

While she was chewing, he said, "I don't. I'm just trying to liven up the conversation."

She swallowed and took a drink of her wine. "By pissing me off?"

"Oh, come on, Carmen. You don't want to talk about the weather, do you?"

"Wait. Those are the only topics? My hiding from relationships by living with my grandfather, and the weather?"

"Not the only topics. Do you want me to tell you how beautiful you are? Because I could spend about an hour on how soft your hair looks, on the way your eyes sparkle in the moonlight, how delicate your fingers are and how much I'd like to kiss your shoulders."

She blinked. Hold on. What was happening here. First he insulted her, and now he was waxing poetic about her damn shoulders?

Who the hell was this guy? Some Jekyll and Hyde personality? One minute he was an insulting dipshit, the next a romantic?

"I don't know what to make of you, Rafe. I thought you were a nice guy."

His lips curved. "Whatever gave you that idea?"

She rolled her eyes. "Oh, so now you're going to tell me you're a bad boy? Because if you are, I'm not interested."

He laughed, seemingly so relaxed she even found that irritating. "I don't even know what that means. I'm neither, Carmen. I'm just me. I like to tease, and I also like to compliment. But I'm always honest. And sometimes that means saying things that people don't like to hear."

"Oh, you mean about me living with my grandfather. Or, should I say, hiding out at my grandfather's house."

He shrugged. "Just calling it like I see it."

"Well, you're wrong about that."

"Prove it."

"How?"

"Go out with me."

This was ridiculous. "I am out with you. Right now."

"No, I mean really go out with me. You bent over backward making sure tonight was going to be labeled nothing more than a thank-you dinner."

"So it wasn't?"

"It was. I want more."

She cocked a brow. "Excuse me?"

"Not like that. I mean, yeah, like that. I like you, Carmen. I want to see you. Like, a lot. Going out. Dating. Doing fun things together. Romance. Kissing. Sex. The whole thing that you do when you're attracted to someone."

Her face flamed hot at the mention of sex, though she didn't know why, since it was often Rafe she fantasized about when she was alone in her bed, naked with her hand between her legs.

And just the thought of that made her even hotter.

"You want to go out with me."

"Hey, I'm not proposing or anything. I'm just suggesting we have some fun. Get you out of the house."

She frowned. "I wasn't suggesting marriage, either, idiot. And I'm hardly wasting away in my castle."

He laughed. "No, you're definitely not wasting away. You stay busy. I get it. It's one of the reasons I admire you."

"And yet you think I'm a lost cause."

He reached over and grasped her hand. The contact between them was electric. He must have felt it, too, because she saw the heat reflected in his warm brown eyes.

"No, I think you're dynamic, sexy, desirable, and smart as hell. I also think you're hiding because someone hurt you and you're afraid to put yourself out in the dating pool again."

He was so on the mark it was scary. "Thank you for the compliments. And maybe."

"So . . . baby steps. I'm not asking for anything other than some fun. And I promise not to break your heart."

She inhaled deeply, then released it. Rafe was right. She had been hiding ever since her divorce. What would be wrong with a no-strings fling? As long as her heart could come through it intact, then no harm, right?

"Fine. We'll . . . go out and have some fun."

He laughed. "You make *fun* sound about as pleasant as taking out the trash."

"I'm sorry. I'm just not used to this yet. It's been a while, you know? I really want to go out with you, Rafe."

He grinned. "Great. I promise to show you a good time."

She was counting on it. Because she was definitely ready for one.

CHAPTER 10

AFTER WORKING TWO DAYS OF TWELVE-HOUR SHIFTS, Carmen was looking forward to a day off. She had a house to clean, and laundry was piling up, plus she had grocery shopping to do.

But instead of diving into this morning's to-do list, she sat in the kitchen inhaling a cup of coffee and thinking about her date last night with Rafe.

After dinner, he'd driven her home and walked her to the front door. She'd expected him to invite himself in. Instead, he'd thanked her for coming to dinner with him and waited for her to let herself in. She said good night. He said good night, then turned and walked to his truck.

Just said goodbye and left.

She'd been stunned, and if she was honest with herself, a little disappointed.

He hadn't even kissed her.

For some reason, she'd built that kiss up in her mind the entire drive home from the restaurant. How he'd do it, what it would feel like. Would he lean over and just gently put his lips on hers, or would he pull her into his arms and give her the kind of kiss she'd remember forever? And what kind of kiss would she want from him?

A passionate one, of course. It had been a while, and she was long overdue for some passionate kissing. She wanted him to lay one on her, the kind of kiss that would leave her breathless and aching all over.

By the time they'd pulled into her driveway, she'd worked up some serious imaginary momentum for that kiss, only to be disappointed when absolutely nothing had happened.

She sighed and took another sip of coffee.

What had she expected, though? She'd pushed hard against the whole idea of going out with him. She'd more than made clear she wanted to take things slow. So when he had, she couldn't complain.

Except she'd really wanted him to kiss her.

You can't have it both ways, Carmen.

At least now she'd have time to go buy some new underwear. She jotted that down on her to-do list.

The doorbell rang. She frowned and looked at her phone. It was eight freaking thirty in the morning. Who the hell was at the door? She got up, went to the door and pulled it open, surprised to find Rafe standing there. She wasn't surprised at the kick in her heart rate. Seeing him always seemed to do that to her.

"Hi," she said.

"Hi, yourself. You mentioned you had the day off today."

"I do."

"Got any plans?"

"Oh, tons."

"Yeah? Like what?"

"Come on in."

He did, and she closed the door, inhaling the smell of soap as he walked by. She tried hard not to lean into him, instead leading him into the kitchen. "Would you like a cup of coffee?"

"Love one."

She poured him a cup of coffee and handed it to him. Then they went to the table and sat.

"So, what do you have going on today?" he asked.

"Very exciting things. Laundry. Housecleaning. Errands to run."

He held the cup in his hands, motioning to her notebook. "Is that your errand list?"

"Sort of."

"Let's take a look." He reached for the notebook before she had a chance to grab it.

"Groceries. Light bulbs. New kitchen faucet." He looked up at her with a gleam in his eyes. "New underwear."

"It's for my grandfather."

He slanted a knowing look at her. "Bet not."

"Okay. For me."

"Awesome. I'll go with you."

"You will not."

"But I like shopping for faucets."

She cocked her head to the side, knowing that wasn't at all what he was interested in.

"And underwear."

She laughed. "Fine. You can go with me. But I'm going in the underwear store alone."

"The hell you will. That's like the cherry on top of the errand list."

She rolled her eyes. "Seriously? Are you some kind of lingerie aficionado?"

He slanted a confident smile at her. "As a matter of fact, I can choose the lingerie that will rock your world."

"Oh, this I have to see."

"You have no faith in me. I intend to prove you wrong."

She couldn't wait. Plus, it would be fun having some company on her errand runs. And Rafe was definitely some fine-looking company.

"Have you had breakfast yet?" he asked.

"No."

"Go get dressed. We'll stop for breakfast, then shop. By the way, where's your grandpa?"

"He's at therapy until two. Then Theo is picking him up and they're going to some AFL-CIO dinner. Grandpa brought a change of clothes, and he'll change at Theo's house."

"Kind of a heavy day for him."

She appreciated that Rafe was aware of how taxing the day would be for her grandfather. "Yes. But he'll have a couple of hours to rest at Theo's house, and Theo promised me he'll make sure Grandpa puts his feet up and they'll watch TV. Grandpa always falls asleep in front of the TV."

"Good. My guess is his butt will be parked in front of the TV all day tomorrow, too."

Carmen laughed. "Yes, he'll need a recovery day for sure." She stood. "Okay, give me ten minutes and I'll go get ready."

"I'm not in any hurry."

She went upstairs to change, feeling excited about Rafe going with her today. Which was ridiculous. They were only running errands together. It wasn't like a date.

But they were going to hang out together today. And she liked him, enjoyed spending time with him. Nothing wrong with that, was there?

And maybe she'd tear through her to-do list a lot faster now that she'd have help. Then she could come home and dive into cleaning and laundry. And that would suit her just fine.

Today was shaping up to be much more interesting than she originally planned.

• • •

WHILE HE WAS WAITING FOR CARMEN, RAFE WASHED their cups and turned off the coffee maker, then wiped down the counter. After that, he took a seat at the kitchen table and made a list on his phone of all the places Carmen needed to stop today.

Of course, he was particularly interested in helping her buy underwear. He could already envision her in some sexy red lacy bra with matching panties. Then again, Carmen was practical, so she might be the cotton type and prefer beige or white or black.

She'd look hot in those, too.

Mainly his preference was to get her naked, so he could stroke his hands across her skin and taste her all over.

That train of thought was making his dick twitch, so he got up and went to the bay window, looking outside.

Her backyard looked well manicured. He wondered who did the mowing and trimming for her.

"I'm ready."

He turned and smiled. She'd put on a pair of blue shorts and a silky white-and-blue polka-dot sleeveless button-down shirt that pressed nicely against her full breasts. Her hair was pulled up, and even dressed casual like that she looked damned gorgeous.

"You look pretty."

She glanced down at her feet where she wore a pair of navy blue and brown sandals. "Really?"

"Yeah. You're always beautiful, Carmen."

She sighed. "And you always know the right thing to say. Thank you."

They stopped at a local breakfast place not too far from their house. It was small, cramped. The owner was a cranky bastard named Gustav Lopez. His father hailed from Puerto Rico, his mother from Sweden, and the guy was six feet four, mean as he could be and made the best damned pancakes Rafe had ever eaten. Fortunately, his wife, Sofia, was the polar opposite, as sweet a woman as you'd ever meet, and Gustav's bluster was all for show. The guy was a local treasure, as least as far as his cooking.

"I can't believe you know about this place," Carmen said as they were seated at a table in the corner. "It's one of my favorites."

"Mine, too. Jackson and Kal and I stumbled onto it not too long after we moved into the house. One bite of Gustav's Swedish pancakes and I was a goner."

Carmen nodded. "They're my favorites. So delicate and delicious. And the sausages he makes are perfection."

Their waitress, Roxanne, came over and brought menus and took their drink order.

"How's it going, Rafe?" Roxanne asked, offering up a bright smile.

Rafe smiled back. "Good, Rox. How are you?"

"I'm great. Got that new apartment I was telling you about."

"Did you? I'm glad to hear that."

Roxanne hesitated, then finally glanced in Carmen's direction. "So, what would you like to drink?"

They both ordered coffee, and Roxanne scurried off.

"She has a crush on you," Carmen said.

Rafe frowned. "What? No, she doesn't."

Carmen's lips curved. "Oh, she does."

He shook his head. "She's just a kid. Barely nineteen. She's been working here for a couple of years, so she knows me."

"Kid or not, she likes you. I'm surprised you didn't see the emoji hearts falling from her eyes."

He laughed. "Knock it off. I have never encouraged her."

"I'm sorry to have to tell you this, Rafe, but you're good-looking and friendly. Women probably fall all over themselves around you."

"No, they don't. I'm just nice."

She arched a brow. "Uh-huh."

Roxanne brought their coffee, set Carmen's down with barely a look in her direction, and kept her gaze firmly fixed on Rafe.

"Could I get some cream, please?" Carmen asked.

Her attention still fixed on Rafe, Roxanne nodded. "Oh, sure."

She skirted over to an empty table, grabbed the bowl with the cream containers, then brought it over to their table, smiling at Rafe as she did.

"Thanks," Carmen said, smirking at Rafe.

"So, Carmen," Rafe said, turning his attention on her. "You ready to order?"

"Absolutely."

Roxanne took her pad and pen out of her apron pocket. "What would you like, Rafe?"

"How about we let Carmen order first?" Rafe asked.

"Of course," Roxanne said, reluctantly dragging her gaze away from Rafe. "What would you like, ma'am?"

Carmen ordered, and then Rafe did as well. It was obvious to Rafe at that point that Roxanne paid way more attention to him. Like, all the attention.

"Well. Damn," Rafe said after Roxanne left to put their order in. "She is a little infatuated."

Carmen's brows rose. "A little?"

Rafe held his hands up. "Like I said, I've never encouraged her."

"I believe you. Not that I can blame her. You're kind of irresistible."

"See, I knew I was growing on you."

"Yeah. Like a fungus."

He laughed. "I'm wearing you down. Soon you'll be knocking on my door at all hours, just begging for my attention."

She took a sip of coffee, smiling over her cup. "You are a dreamer, Rafe."

"No, I'm a realist. And you and me, Carmen? We're meant to be."

"Surely you aren't telling me you believe in that whole soulmate thing."

"I don't know about soulmates, but there's chemistry between us."

He waited for her to deny it. Instead, she took another swallow of her coffee and stared out the window of the restaurant.

Yeah, that's what he thought. No way could she deny the spark between them.

He noticed Roxanne coming toward them with their tray of food. He grabbed Carmen's hand.

She gave him a curious look.

"Just go with it."

As soon as Roxanne arrived at their table, he started in. "And then I thought we'd hit the Keys next weekend when I have extra time off. We could reserve the penthouse suite at your favorite hotel—the one right on the water. Dance all night at the club, then take a cruise."

He gave her an intense look and rubbed his thumb over the top of her hand while Roxanne gaped at him.

Carmen must have noticed, because she immediately smoothed her hand over his forearm in a slow, sensual way.

"Oh, babe, that sounds fantastic. You know how much I love spending time alone with you."

"Perfect. I can't wait for us to be alone, too." Rafe lifted his gaze to Roxanne. "Oh, breakfast. Thanks, Roxanne, I'm starving."

Roxanne laid their plates down and walked away without a word.

Carmen's lips lifted. "A little harsh."

"But necessary. I think she's grabbed a clue that I'm not available."

Carmen looked down at their entwined hands and extricated hers. "Right. Good call. Now we can eat."

Rafe had to admit that it felt good to touch her, to feel her fingernails raking over his forearm. He wanted a lot more of that.

Breakfast was great. Rafe scarfed down his waffles and sausages and eggs, then snatched a piece of Carmen's bacon and a bite of her pancakes.

Carmen arched a brow.

"What?" he asked.

"You're done already."

"Yeah?"

She looked down at her plate, then at his empty one. "Did you even taste your food?"

"Sure, I did."

She laughed. "Uh-huh."

He wasn't sure what she was getting at, but he definitely liked the sound of her laugh. He wanted to hear it again. "What do you mean?"

"You eat fast."

"Oh. Yeah. When you grow up homeless, you never know where your next meal is going to come from. Or when. My mom always tried to get us to eat more slowly, but I guess I never grew out of it."

She reached across the table and laid her hand on his. "I understand. But maybe you should take a breath, slow down and enjoy every bite."

He wanted her to keep touching him. "I'll keep that in mind in the future."

"I'll try to remind you."

His lips curved. "You do that."

By the time Roxanne came to clear their plates, he noticed she was much more subdued and treated him like a regular customer instead of a potential boyfriend, so he was satisfied that there'd be no more flirting. He was going to have to bring Carmen with him again. Not that that would be a hardship.

He paid for their meal and they left the restaurant, climbed in his truck and drove to the home improvement store.

"What do you need light bulbs for?"

She pulled out a list of the types of bulbs she needed and for which rooms, so they hit that aisle first.

"You should let me put some LEDs in your kitchen. Make it much brighter in there."

"My can lights aren't wired for LEDs."

"I can rewire those in an hour or so."

She leaned against the cart. "Really? And what might that cost me?"

He shrugged. "Empanadas?"

She laughed. "Sounds like a deal to me."

"Great." Once she told him how many can lights she had on her ceiling, he grabbed everything he'd need for the retrofit project and put it in the cart.

Carmen looked down into the cart, then up at him. "You know what to do with all of that?"

He nodded. "I've got this, Carmen. Trust me."

She gave him a dubious look. "I divorced the last guy who asked me to trust him."

Rafe swooped his arm around her waist and tugged her against him, right there in the light bulb aisle. He lowered his gaze to hers, forcing her attention on the seriousness in his warm brown eyes.

"First, hopefully you didn't divorce him over electrical issues. Second, the one thing I want to make clear to you, Carmen? I'm not your ex. And I *can* be trusted."

For a few seconds, she couldn't breathe, because she was mesmerized by his eyes, and by the feel of his strong, muscular body aligned with hers.

There were so many things she wanted to do in this moment, the first being explore every inch of his body, from his broad shoulders to his amazingly sexy forearms to what she was certain were rock-hard abs, none of which she could do in the electrical aisle of the hardware store.

Dammit.

So, instead, she nodded and took a step back, taking a strong breath so she could gather some oxygen into her lungs.

"Okay, on to faucets, then?" he asked.

She nodded enthusiastically and smiled, mainly because her throat had gone bone-dry and she couldn't form words. Or maybe her brain cells had fled south, fueling all the quivering currently going on in her sex.

Her libido could just calm the hell down, because they weren't going to have sex in the bathroom fixture aisle, either.

Deciding to focus on faucets instead of sex, she wandered the department, looking around until she had narrowed her decision down to two. She was surprised Rafe didn't interject his opinion, but she was happy about it, too. Her ex would have never let her pick out her own kitchen faucets, since he was big into traditional gender roles.

"I know many people like the touchless ones, but I'm not sure having the fancy option is worth the money." She looked up at Rafe.

"We had one for a while," he said, "and then two years later the touchless feature stopped working. But that's entirely up to you if you think it's something you need. The other one you picked out is just as good; it just doesn't have the touchless feature. I don't think you can go wrong either way."

And again, he left the decision up to her. She pointed to the nice stainless steel faucet that had the pull-down faucet, but without the touchless feature. "I think this one."

"Nice choice." He picked up the box and put it into their cart.

Now that they had everything they needed, she figured they'd head to the checkout. Rafe surprised her by deviating into the plumbing aisle.

She frowned. "Where are you going?"

"Your grandpa needs a new showerhead."

"Really. And you know this how?"

"Because I gave him a shower that night he fell in the bathroom, remember? There are only like three holes working in that showerhead."

She slanted him a disbelieving look. "I don't think it's quite that bad."

"Maybe not. But it's pretty bad, and since he sits when he showers, he needs a more powerful showerhead, one that offers a wider spray area."

She couldn't argue with that. "Okay, let's get a new showerhead." She'd figure out where to sacrifice in the monthly budget to adjust for the cost of that.

But when Rafe picked out some fancy rainfall showerhead that also had a handheld shower wand to go with it, she looked at the price and her eyes widened.

"I don't think so," she said.

Rafe turned to her and frowned. "Why not? This way he can be more independent."

Dammit. "Yes, but that's a little pricey."

"But this was my suggestion, so I'm buying it, and I'll install it."

She shook her head. "Absolutely not."

He laughed. "You can't stop me from buying this. It's my treat for Jimmy."

She blew out a frustrated breath. "I don't need your charity, Rafe."

"This isn't charity, Carmen. Quit being so defensive. I like Jimmy.

He's my friend. And he needs the damn showerhead, so stop arguing with me and let me do this."

She wanted to put her foot down, but since this was for her grandpa, she kept her mouth shut. And Rafe was right. Anything that would give Grandpa more independence was a good thing.

"Okay, fine."

Rafe put the box in the cart and added a few more plumbing supplies, which made her give him a side-eye, but, true to her word, she didn't say anything. Then they headed for the front of the store.

After checking out, they walked to the truck and she slid into the passenger side. As she was buckling up her seat belt, she turned to Rafe.

"Thank you."

He smiled, and that smile could melt a million cold hearts. "You're welcome. What's next?"

She wanted to say the grocery store, since the thought of him going to the lingerie store with her made her skin tingle in a not-unpleasant way, but instead, she told him to head to the mall.

His lips curved, and all she could think about was Rafe hovering above and giving her that same hot smile while her legs were spread and he was just about to slide his incredible cock inside of her. Not that she knew if his cock was incredible or not, but she'd just bet it was.

Despite the air-conditioning blasting in the truck, she was sweating between her breasts because she was fantasizing about sex.

You are so doomed, Carmen.

CHAPTER 11

IT WAS A WEEKDAY, BUT IT WAS ALSO SUMMER, WHICH meant every teen was going to be at the mall. Not Rafe's favorite thing to do, but since Carmen wanted to shop for underwear, he'd make the ultimate sacrifice.

Oh, who was he kidding? He was dying to do this with her. She was going to allow him to be in the same lingerie store with her, and that was an intimate thing. He recognized the privilege being afforded him, and he wasn't about to do anything to jeopardize it, especially knowing how skittish Carmen was about the whole dating and relationships thing.

Not that he was big on relationships himself; he just wanted Carmen to get her feet wet with a guy who wasn't going to lead her on or hurt her. And in doing so, help her remember that dating and sex were fun. She was young and vibrant and beautiful, and she should be out there leading men around by their dicks. Guys should be lined up at her front door begging for a chance to take her out.

He aimed to wake her up and make her look at herself in the mirror and help her see all the fun she was missing out on. Then, once she had her confidence again, he'd let her go with a smile and know that he'd done a good deed. And had some fun himself in the process.

"You sure you're up for this?" she asked, standing outside the lingerie store with a dubious look on her face.

"I'm totally up for it. How about you?"

She stared at the lingerie store sign as if it was some gauntlet she had to run. "It's been a while for me."

Obviously, it had been a while for her for a lot of things. He was more irritated at her ex than ever. What the hell had this guy done to her?

He slid his arm around her waist. "Have I ever mentioned you have a fantastic ass, Carmen?"

Her eyes widened and she looked around. It was the middle of the afternoon. The mall was crowded, but no one was paying any attention to them.

"Rafe."

Her voice had gone low. Cracked a little.

"Carmen."

She inhaled, let it out. "Maybe I should do this alone."

"Up to you."

She nodded. "I think I'll do this alone."

He had to admit he was disappointed, but he understood. "Sure. I'll be on the bench here. Take your time."

She turned to face him and smiled. "Thanks for . . . understanding."

"Hey, no problem."

She walked inside . . . slowly . . . as if she were facing execution.

Rafe shook his head and went to find a seat on the bench.

ADMITTEDLY, CARMEN HAD PANICKED. THE THOUGHT OF rifling through underwear and bras with Rafe looking over her shoulder had made her break out into a sweat.

She could barely tolerate the idea of doing it by herself. With Rafe by her side? No way.

But now that she was inside the store and staring at all the options, she had no idea what to do.

Correction. Of course she knew what to do. It wasn't like she had no idea how to buy underwear. She was a grown-ass woman. But the reason she was in here buying new underwear was the expectation that someone—that someone being Rafe, of course—would be seeing said underwear.

You're way overthinking this, Carmen. That expectation is only in your head.

She wasn't required to do anything she wasn't ready for. Rafe hadn't even said anything to her today about sex.

He did mention her having a nice ass, though, which had made her blush to about a thousand degrees. But it also made her feel sexy, something she hadn't felt in a long time.

When was the last time she had thought of herself as a desirable woman?

Way too damn long ago. It was high time she womaned up and reminded herself that she was smart, beautiful and desirable. And the first place to do that was here, in the lingerie store.

With that confidence-building thought in her head, she plunged into the lacy underwear section, realizing she was doing this for her and no one else. It was time to push the past aside and start feeling good about herself.

She'd chosen the right day to shop, because the store was having a buy one, get one sale. The prices were way more reasonable than she'd thought. She ended up with six new bras and twelve new pairs of panties, in all different colors and fabrics, from satin to lace to the softest cotton. Some were more practical, and a couple downright sexy as hell.

She couldn't wait to wear them all. She also couldn't wait to throw out all her old underwear.

Fling the past aside. The new Carmen was about to be revealed. At least the new lingerie-clad Carmen.

Baby steps, right?

When she left the store, she looked over at the benches but didn't see Rafe.

Huh. Maybe he'd had to go do some shopping of his own. She decided to wait for him on the bench, so she took a seat and composed a text message to Tess.

At the mall. Bought tons of new underwear.

Tess had the day off today as well, so it didn't take her long to reply. *Awesome! Did you buy any pink ones? I know it's your fave color.*

Carmen grinned and replied. *Of course. And black, purple, red, white . . . all the colors!*

Tess sent back a text that said: *About damn time*, along with a congratulatory emoji.

Carmen laughed and sent her another text. *Spending the day with Rafe. Will fill you in at work tomorrow.*

Tess replied: *Want ALL the deets!*

She would, too.

"Finished already?"

Rafe stood in front of her holding two cups. He handed one to her.

"Yes, finished." She took the cup from him. "And thanks, shopping makes me thirsty."

"I don't know why, when it's so entertaining."

"Entertaining, how?"

He took a seat next to her. "Watching everyone go by. You know, people watching."

She leaned back against the bench. "Oh, really? This is your favorite pastime."

"I wouldn't say favorite, but it's entertaining."

She took a sip of soda, letting the cold liquid slide down her parched throat. "Do tell."

He motioned with his head to the group of teen girls walking. "They're all on their phones while they walk."

Carmen nodded. "Probably texting each other, too."

He laughed. "Probably."

"I think it's how they communicate now."

"I guess. But keep watching them. They're waiting for boys."

"How do you know?"

He shrugged. "I can tell."

She looked over at him. "Really, how?"

"Hey, it wasn't that long ago that I was a teenage boy, scoping out the girls at the mall. Just watch."

It didn't take long. Within five minutes, a group of boys around the same age walked up to the girls and started a conversation. There was a lot of hair flipping by the girls and thumbs hooked in pockets by the guys.

"It's like watching a nature show on mating rituals," Carmen said in between sips of her soda. "This is interesting stuff."

"Told ya. And then there's that couple." He motioned with his soda cup to the young twentysomething couple headed their way. "They're fighting."

Carmen's attention diverted from the teens to the couple. "How can you tell?"

"She's walking three steps ahead of him, and he's got his head down and his hands jammed into his jeans pockets as if he doesn't want to be anywhere near her. And she's got her chin held up high, her lips compressed tightly. It's like she's fighting the urge to turn around and yell at him."

Carmen studied the couple as they made their way toward them, then walked past.

"You could be right," she said. "It was like you could feel the tension in both of them as they walked by."

"Yup."

She chewed on the end of her straw as she smiled at him, then said, "You're pretty good at reading body language."

"I am, aren't I?"

She laughed. "And you're so humble as well."

"I am, aren't I?"

She rolled her eyes, then squeezed his thigh. "Come on, Mr. Humble. Let's hit the grocery store."

He wrinkled his nose. "My least favorite thing to do."

"Oh, but you've never shopped with me. I make it so fun."

As they made their way toward the exit, he dropped his arm around her shoulder. "Not even you could make grocery shopping fun, Carmen."

She tilted her head back to look up at him. "But I'll be cooking for you later. Does that help?"

"Does cooking include modeling your new underwear for me?"

She laughed. "I can't even imagine what's going through your head right now."

He gave her a half smile, one loaded with steamy promise. "Yeah, you can."

Which reminded her that her grandfather was going to be gone tonight. And that meant being alone with Rafe.

And being alone with Rafe tonight had infinite possibilities.

CHAPTER 12

CARMEN HAD TO ADMIT THAT RAFE WAS HANDY. WHILE she did some housecleaning, he'd installed the new showerhead and handheld in Grandpa's bathroom, then the new faucet in the kitchen, and was halfway through rewiring the kitchen lights.

She'd made guacamole and salsa and put those in the fridge, then made a marinade for the flank steak she'd bought, intending to put it on the grill for fajitas. She sliced onions and peppers and put those in the fridge as well, then poured two tall glasses of iced tea, handing one to Rafe, who had just climbed down from the ladder.

"Thanks."

"You're sweating. You should take a break."

He took a couple of gulps of tea, then set it on the kitchen counter. "I'm good. I want to get this finished."

She resisted the urge to lean into him, to rub herself against his sweaty T-shirt and *oh, God*, what was wrong with her? She was turned on by man sweat? Then again, Rafe smelled good. Maybe there was just something about the guy's pheromones that got to her. All she knew was she wanted to climb him like a rock wall and have her way with him right there on the kitchen floor.

She sighed.

"You okay?" he asked, tilting his head to the side in question.

"Oh. Me? Sure, I'm fine." She picked up her glass of tea and took several long swallows.

Walk it back a bit, Carmen. The man is doing your lights, not you.

Unfortunately.

Clearly, it was time to try out the new underwear.

She watched his extremely awesome ass climb back up the ladder.

"Do you need help?" she asked.

"No, thanks, I've got this."

She chewed on her bottom lip and balanced on the balls of her feet, making sure he wasn't going to check on her. He was focused. Not on her.

"Okay, then. I've got to go . . . fold laundry in my room. I'll be back shortly."

"Sure," he said, not even looking at her.

While his attention was diverted on her kitchen ceiling, she dashed into her bedroom, stripped out of her clothes and took a quick shower. She lotioned her body from top to bottom, then grabbed one of the new bras and panties from the laundry basket, happy she'd washed those first while Rafe had been busy plumbing her grandpa's bathroom. She'd chosen the hot pink one because the color looked sexy against the bronze hue of her skin.

And she was so ready to be sexy.

Not wanting to be too obvious, she threw on a pair of shorts and a tank top, keeping things casual. She slipped on her sandals, quickly blow-dried her hair and headed back downstairs.

Rafe was just coming back inside when he saw her. "Hey, where's your vacuum? I want to clean up the mess I made in here."

"I'll get it."

"No, I'll get it. Just tell me where it is."

"In the entry closet."

He nodded, grabbed the vacuum and cleaned the kitchen floor. And not just where he'd made the mess. He vacuumed the entire floor. She shook her head.

He just wasn't like any man she'd ever known. Certainly not like her ex, who wouldn't know a vacuum from a scrub brush, considering he'd never used either. Tod was an old-school traditional man who thought anything inside the house was a woman's job to do. Even after she worked a twelve-hour shift, he expected her to cook and clean and do the dishes and the laundry.

Carmen, on the other hand, was a very modern woman who said *bullshit* to all that nonsense and expected a fifty-fifty balance of sharing the workload of household chores. Especially since when they were married they lived in a condo that required zero work *outside* the house other than taking out the trash, which Tod had complained about having to do.

Basically, the guy had been worthless. Not to mention a serial cheater.

Refusing to think about Tod any longer, she concentrated instead on Rafe.

What was it about a good-looking man running a vacuum cleaner that was such a turn-on? Maybe it was the fact that he was doing it so she didn't have to that made it so damn sexy.

She expected him to finish up in the kitchen and put it away. Instead, he continued into the living room.

She took a seat at the island and grabbed her iced tea, feeling flushed while she watched him.

Rafe was every woman's dream, and—for today at least—he was hers.

He finished in the living room, wrapped up by vacuuming the entry, then emptied the canister and put the vacuum away.

She sighed in contentment.

If he was as good at sex as he was at plumbing, electrical and household chores, she might just hold him prisoner here for the rest of his life.

He went to the sink to wash his hands, giving her an opportunity to watch him from behind, which was quickly becoming one of her favorite pastimes. His sleeveless shirt fit tight across his broad shoulders, and his shorts hung low on one very fine ass. He had biceps that just begged to be caressed, and all she wanted to do right now was press a kiss to the back of his neck.

Honestly, if she got any hotter around him, she would spontaneously combust. Something was going to have to be done about this. And she knew exactly what that something was.

But first, she was going to feed him dinner, because the man had worked hard today.

He dried his hands on a paper towel and turned to face her. "Okay, let's go check out your grandpa's bathroom."

She batted her lashes at him. "I thought you'd never ask."

He laughed.

They went into the bathroom, and he turned on the shower, demonstrating the rainfall shower and the handheld.

"Grandpa's going to love that so much."

"It'll give him a little more freedom. He won't have to be monitored so much when he's in here."

"He'll love that even more. Thanks."

"No problem. Should we try the new kitchen lights?"

"Absolutely."

They went into the kitchen. Rafe hit the light switch, and her normally dull and dim kitchen was bathed in brilliant LED lights. She blinked a few times, amazed by how bright it was in the room.

"Wow. This is magnificent. I'll actually be able to see what I'm cooking now."

He grinned. "Yeah, it's a huge improvement, isn't it?"

She couldn't get over the difference changing out the lighting had made. She went over to him and wrapped her arms around him, feeling all that muscle she'd previously ogled. "Thank you."

He put his arms around her, tugging her closer. "You're welcome."

He leaned in, pressing his nose against her neck. She shivered at the contact.

"You showered."

"Mm-hmm."

"You smell good, Carmen."

Was it her imagination, or did his lips brush her neck? Every inch of her skin reacted with goose bumps. Her nipples hardened, and her sex quivered in response.

She could stay like this or push for more. But she needed to reward the guy for a hard day's work, so she pulled back. "I bet you're hungry."

The hunger she saw in his eyes had nothing to do with food, making the temptation to stay in his arms even more difficult.

But he took a step back, too. "I could eat."

"Great. I'll get the grill started."

"I'll do that."

"I think you've done enough. How about you grab yourself a beer and go put your feet up."

"What I need is a shower. But are you sure you don't want me to grill?"

She tilted her head. "I'm perfectly capable of doing it."

"Okay. I'll be right back."

"Sure."

He left the house.

That could have gone in such a different direction. She could have tilted her head back and stayed right where she was, and she knew Rafe would have kissed her.

She'd wanted him to kiss her. So why had she put a stop to it? Because she thought he needed a meal?

Bullshit, Carmen. You're the one who's hesitating. You had a hot guy in your arms, and you didn't pull the trigger. You need to go for it.

Deciding hindsight was getting her nowhere other than supremely frustrated, she took the meat out of the fridge and laid it on the counter, started rice cooking in her Instant Pot, then went outside and fired up the gas grill.

Fortunately, the steak wouldn't take long to cook, and she didn't have to linger to watch it, which was a good thing, because the humidity level was off the charts today. By the time she was ready to go outside and pull it off the grill, Rafe was back, looking amazing in black-and-white shorts and a white sleeveless shirt.

"You're just in time," she said, handing him a plate. "You can go fetch the steak while I do the veggies."

"You got it," he said, heading out back.

She grilled the onions and peppers until they were sizzling, then warmed the tortillas and quickly fluffed the rice before pouring it into a bowl. She took out the salsa and guac she'd made earlier.

"Where do you want this?" Rafe asked as he closed the slider.

"On the counter so I can slice it."

After slicing the flank steak into strips, she brought over the rice, and Rafe helped her set the table and carry the rest of the stuff over. He held her chair out for her, making her smile.

"Thanks."

"Thank you for making me dinner. You didn't have to do that."

She pointed at the kitchen. "You didn't have to brighten my kitchen or do any of the other things you did. The new faucet works great, too, by the way. Thanks for everything you did today."

"It was my pleasure. Thanks for letting me tag along."

She fixed herself a tortilla and rolled it up, then took a bite, not realizing how hungry she was. They'd both worked hard today. But her house was clean, laundry was done, and with Rafe's help, she'd accomplished a lot more than even she'd intended.

"These are great, Carmen."

She lifted her head and smiled at the compliment. "I'm glad you like them."

"Who taught you to cook?"

"My mom died when I was ten, and my dad split not too long after. Never knew what happened to him. So I went to live with my grandparents. I used to cook a lot with my mom before she died. After that, I hung out in the kitchen with my *abuela*. Unfortunately, my grandmother passed away when I was twenty."

He laid his hand over hers. "That's rough, losing both your mom and your abuela. I'm sorry."

The warmth of his touch was comforting. Even if it had been years, she still missed her mom and her abuela. "Thanks. It was. But I had my grandpa, and he was there for me when I needed him most."

"Which is why you've been there for him."

"Yes."

"He's a great guy."

She smiled. "Always has been. He was my lifesaver after my abuela died. She and I had grown so close after my mom passed. She got me through my teen years and pushed me to enter nursing school. She believed in me when I didn't believe in myself. I told her everything that was going on in my life. All my hopes and dreams and heartbreaks. So when she died, I was lost. Grandpa stepped in and picked up where she left off. He offered his ear and his heart, and I leaned on him in ways I could never repay."

"But you're doing that now, being there for him like he was for you."

"True. It's not a hardship, though."

"I'm sure it's not. That's what family is for. Still, I know it's been a rough few years for both of you."

She shrugged. "Life's hard sometimes. You know all about that. You didn't have the easiest life, either."

He scooped some rice onto his fork. "Earlier part of my life sucked, that's for sure. I had shitty parents. It was easier for me to live on the streets than live in fear of getting shot during a drug deal gone bad."

She leaned back in her chair, shocked at how matter-of-fact he'd made it sound, when she knew it had been anything but. "Good God, Rafe. I had no idea. Did you run away? Is that how you ended up homeless?"

He nodded. "It got dicey at the house. People coming and going all hours. I never slept. My mom would disappear for weeks to head down to Mexico to visit family, or so she said. My old man mostly forgot he even had a kid, so I was on the streets anyway. And there were always shootings in the neighborhood. I was scared all the time. I ran into Jackson one night, and he took care of me. Then I just didn't go home."

"And they never came looking for you?"

He laughed. "They were happy to be rid of me. One less mouth to feed, one less thing to worry about. I stopped by the house not long after, but they'd split. They were always relocating to avoid the cops. I'm sure they were happy to be rid of me."

She reached across the table and squeezed his hand. "They were horrible people, and you were the one lucky to be rid of *them*."

"Yup."

"But then being homeless on top of the hell you lived in. That couldn't have been easy."

He swallowed and took a sip of beer. "Surprisingly, the homeless part wasn't as bad as the hell I came from. And then it got a lot better. The Donovans are amazing." He smiled as he thought of his *real* mom and dad.

She cast a look of concern at him. "No one comes through something like that unscathed."

The last thing he wanted was to talk about his past, especially his birth parents. "I imagine with what happened to you, you didn't, either."

She leaned back. "I didn't. I got married to the wrong guy at twenty-one and got divorced at twenty-three."

"So what made you choose him? The wrong guy?"

"He seemed like the right guy at the time. And I guess I was tied up in grief over losing Abuela, and my heart and my mind were mixed up. Grandpa was mourning as well, doing the best he could with me, you know? But I was in my last year of nursing school, and the grind was tough. I had gone out with my girlfriends on Friday night, and I met Tod at a dance club. He and his friends actually got rid of some guys who were bothering us, so we asked them to sit with us.

"Tod and I started up a conversation. He had just graduated from UCF with his degree in Criminal Justice and was preparing to apply to the police academy in Ft. Lauderdale."

Interesting. Rafe knew a lot of Ft. Lauderdale cops. "Yeah? Is he still on the force now?"

She shook her head. "He was. I mean, he's still a cop, but he transferred to Orlando a couple of years ago. Anyway, we hit it off and talked about how tough college was, and he asked me out and I said yes. In the beginning, everything was great. We'd been dating for about six months when he asked me to marry him. And I was so into the whole romance of the thing that I didn't see the signs."

Rafe frowned. "What signs?"

"That he always put himself and his needs first. I saw that as his commitment to his career, and I put the same emphasis on finishing school, so it was one of the things I admired about him. What I didn't see at the time was that he was always going to put himself first, no matter what."

"Ouch."

"Yeah. But we got married, and the first six months were great. We got an apartment. I graduated nursing school and started my job. And that's when things started sliding downhill in a hurry. I had second shift, so I was gone nights, and he was on day shift, and I wasn't there to put dinner on the table when he got home, and sometimes the laundry and dishes piled up and the house wasn't clean, and who was going to cook him his dinner if I was at work?"

Rafe's jaw clenched as Carmen ticked off her ex-asshole's list of items he could have done himself. "He did realize those were all things he could have been doing while you were working, right?"

"Oh, he said he wasn't going to cook, and cleaning was a woman's job, and his job as a police officer was way more important than mine, and he worked way harder than I did and he was sooo tired when he got home."

Rafe could do nothing but blink.

"It gets better. Turns out he was sooo tired because he was banging one of the rookie cops while I was working. Some really cute blonde who had no idea he was married because he left his wedding ring on the bedside table before he went to work. Until I showed up at the precinct one day to bring him his wallet, which he forgot, and found the two of them making out in the parking lot. She was shocked as hell to discover he had a wife and slapped him—hard. I found that very satisfying. So the affair wasn't her fault and entirely his."

"What a prick."

Carmen smirked. "I know, right? Anyway, that was the end of our marriage. I moved out that day and filed for divorce, while he called and texted me, telling me I was being totally unreasonable and it only happened that one time, blah blah blah. Asshole."

"You are so much better without him."

"You said it. But that was a harsh lesson to learn. And a really rough year."

Now it was his turn to grab her hand and give it a squeeze. "It wasn't your fault, Carmen. That was a painful time in your life. No one makes great decisions when they're hurting."

"That much is true. Easier to never let yourself get hurt. Then you don't make bad decisions."

"I don't know about that. You've grown since then. One person can't rule over your future just because they hurt you in the past."

She stared at him. "Maybe. I don't know. I like my life the way it is. I have control over the decisions I make, and no man can ever tell me what to do or how to feel."

She definitely still stung from being hurt by her ex. Not that he could blame her. The guy had put her through hell and made her wary of trusting men again.

But Rafe intended to show her there were nice guys out there. And he was one of them.

CHAPTER 13

CARMEN WORKED SIDE BY SIDE WITH RAFE IN THE KITCHEN putting leftovers away and doing dishes. It was nice to have him in there, especially after the conversation she'd had with him about how little her ex had done to help around the house. Not that there was any comparison. Rafe had proved that earlier today. He'd busted his ass doing things she'd never even asked him to do. Which was ten times the amount of work her ex had ever done around the house.

She hadn't intended to blurt out her past to Rafe in such detail. She hadn't intended to tell him anything. But she'd been so relaxed at dinner, and then he'd told her all about his parents, and he'd commiserated about her mom and her abuela, and before she knew it, all the details of her marriage had come spilling out.

He had taken it well. He hadn't bolted or told her she was an idiot for marrying so young, or choosing the wrong guy or not waiting until she knew him better, which was what her grandpa had told her when she'd gotten engaged after only six months. But she'd been in love—or so she'd thought—and at the time, she'd been convinced Tod was the right guy.

She'd been so wrong.

But that was in the past, and she didn't linger there very often, because she couldn't change what was. She could only be sure she didn't make the same mistakes again.

Like buying new fancy underwear and thinking you're going to have sex with this guy? Those kinds of mistakes, Carmen?

She needed to shut up her inner voice, because it was really beginning to annoy her.

But yeah, maybe. Though her situation with Rafe wasn't at all like it had been with her ex. First, she was much older now. Second, she'd already known Rafe longer than she'd known Tod. And third, they weren't dating or having sex or rushing into anything, certainly nothing like love and marriage.

So her inner voice could suck it.

And now he'd grabbed a wet paper towel and cleaning spray and was wiping down her table.

Could the man be any hotter? It was time she took advantage of what was right in front of her.

She finished wiping off the kitchen counter, then washed and dried her hands. Rafe tossed the towel in the trash and came over to her.

"I think that's everything," he said, looking around the kitchen.

"Not quite everything."

He glanced down at her. "What else do you need?"

She raised up on her toes and cupped the back of his neck. "You."

She brought his head down, and he obviously caught the drift of what she was after, because he scooped his arm around her waist and pushed her against the kitchen island. His mouth met hers in a mix of expelled breaths and tangled tongues and fiery-hot passion that nearly melted her toes to the tile floor.

This kiss—this kiss was everything she'd imagined it to be.

His lips were soft, yet demanding, promising her a passion she so desperately needed.

Rafe lifted her—with one arm—onto the kitchen island. She wrapped her legs around his hips, and he stepped into her, his hot body making contact with hers. As the kiss deepened, Carmen felt an explosion of heat as his lips molded to hers.

Dulce Dios ten piedad, the man had incredibly soft lips. And he knew what to do with his mouth, making her wonder what else he could do with it—and where.

She was on fire, and as he began an expert exploration of her back with his fingers, she couldn't wait to touch him, to taste him, to—

She heard the garage door, effectively dousing the fire of passion that had flamed up between them.

Rafe must have heard it, too, because he quickly pulled her off the kitchen island.

"I'm going to need to slip into the bathroom for a few seconds," he said.

She looked down, supremely disappointed she wasn't going to be able to play with his sizable erection.

She blew out a breath then nodded. "Okay."

She was flushed, hot and sweaty and needy, so she stepped to the sink and turned on the cold water, running it over her wrists in the hopes it would cool down the heat burning her from the inside out.

"Oh, you're home." Her grandfather used his walker to slowly make his way inside, followed by his friend Theo. "And why's it so bright in here?"

"Rafe did some work around here today," Carmen said after she shut the water off. She turned and smiled at him. "And then I fixed him dinner."

"Oh, Rafe's here?" her grandfather asked.

"Yes. He's in the bathroom."

"Great."

Rafe came out of the bathroom. "Hey, Jimmy. Hi, Theo."

"Rafe," Jimmy said, offering up a smile. "Carmen said you did some work around here today. Did she put you on laundry duty, or do I have you to thank for the brightness in the kitchen?"

Rafe laughed. "No laundry. I put LEDs in here."

Jimmy nodded. "Looks great, doesn't it, Theo?"

Theo looked around. "Gonna need my shades on for poker nights."

"We also got a new kitchen faucet," Carmen said. "And wait 'til you see what Rafe did in your shower, Grandpa."

"Oh yeah?"

They followed her grandfather as he made his way into the bathroom. Carmen turned on the shower, and Jimmy stared up at the rainfall showerhead.

"Hot damn."

"You also have a handheld to use yourself."

Jimmy turned around and shook Rafe's hand. "Thanks for doing this. I don't know why you did, but I sure appreciate it."

"Your showerhead was crap. It needed changing. My treat."

"Thanks, kid. I'm gonna enjoy the hell out of my next shower."

"Hey, Rafe, you wanna come over and check out my house?" Theo asked. "I've got a few fixtures that need replacing. I'm sure my wife won't mind."

Rafe laughed and grasped Theo's shoulder as they all made their way back into the living room. "Sure, Theo. Anytime."

"No way," Jimmy said. "He's my personal handyman now."

"And your personal handyman is heading home. I've got some laundry to do before I head on shift tomorrow."

"Sure," Jimmy said. "Thanks again, Rafe."

"I'll . . . walk you out. I'll be right back, Grandpa."

Carmen stepped outside with Rafe. "I'm really sorry about my grandfather's terrible timing."

Rafe shrugged. "Don't worry about it. There'll be another time."

Even now, he was kind about their make-out session getting interrupted. She wanted to kiss him right there, but she knew if she did, she wouldn't stop.

"So, I'll see you later?" she asked.

He nodded and smiled. "Yeah. Later, Carmen."

As she watched him head across the lawn toward his house, the feeling of loneliness crept over her for the first time in a very long time.

She walked inside and shut the door.

CHAPTER 14

"NINETY-SEVEN, NINETY-EIGHT, NINETY-NINE, ONE HUN-dred."

After those hundred push-ups, Rafe jumped up and did a walk around the workout room to cool down, moving in circles around Kal, who was doing shoulder presses with kettlebells.

"One hundred push-ups."

"Yeah, whatever." Kal set the kettlebells down and rolled his shoulders. "I did a hundred yesterday on my day off."

Rafe downed a couple of gulps from his water bottle, then screwed the cap back on and shot a look at his brother. "Video or it didn't happen."

Kal laughed and went over to pick up the sandbag. "Unlike you, I don't need the attention. You'll just have to trust me."

"Not buying it."

"Okay, fine. We'll put hundred-pound sandbags on our backs and do a mile around the track."

"You're on."

By the end of the mile, sweat poured heavily down Rafe's neck and back, and his legs felt like limp noodles.

They both collapsed onto the floor.

"I sure as hell hope we don't get a call right now," Kal said. "I don't think I can walk."

"Hey, dumbass. This challenge was your idea."

Kal stared up at the ceiling. "It was a stupid idea."

Jackson stuck his head in the door.

"Kal."

"Yeah."

"I'm still waiting on your CEU certificates. You're missing two."

Without looking at Jackson, Kal said, "Yeah, I'm on it."

"You've been saying that for two weeks. I need them by the end of this week's shift, or you'll be sitting out calls until you get them done."

Kal sighed. "I'll get them done, okay?"

"Make sure you do." Jackson waited until Kal gave him his attention, then pinned him with a look that made Rafe wonder what was going on with his two brothers.

After Jackson left, Rafe rolled over to face Kal. "What's up?"

"With what?"

"With you and Jackson."

Kal frowned, then popped up to a standing position. "Nothing's up. I just have some work to do."

"Not that." Rafe got up and grabbed two towels, tossing one at Kal. He took a seat on the bench to look at his brother. "I felt the tension. You two fighting?"

"No. It's not that." Kal took a seat on the bench across from Rafe and ran the towel over his face, then stared down at his feet. "I don't know. I just feel . . . frustrated."

"About the job?"

"I guess. I'm not sure."

This was the first time Rafe had heard his brother complain. "Are you unhappy being a firefighter?"

Kal looked up. "God no. I love this job."

"Then what is it?"

Kal hesitated, and Rafe added, "You know this won't go anywhere but this room."

Kal nodded. "I just feel that since I'm the youngest Donovan, I'll never get a leg up as long as I'm at the same station with you and with Jackson. Jackson's a lieutenant, and he's making his move up the ladder toward captain. You know with your seniority you'll be the next to make lieutenant. And I'm just . . . stagnating with nowhere to go. There are three people ahead of me, rankwise. I'm not even on engine. And I'm not happy where I'm sitting. So I'm frustrated."

Rafe could see his point. "That's fair. So what do you want to do?"

"I don't know."

"I think you do. Maybe you just haven't voiced it yet."

"I love the job I do, but being under Jackson's thumb makes me feel as if I'm being double judged. First as a firefighter and second as a brother."

"You know he pushes all of us to be our best."

"Logically, I know that. But I just want to be treated like anyone else. And I don't feel like I can shine as long as I'm in this station."

"I had no idea, man. I'm sorry."

"Thanks. I just want what I do to matter."

Rafe laughed. "And you think what you're doing now doesn't?"

"That's not what I meant. I just need more than what I'm getting here."

Kal paused, but Rafe knew there was more he wanted to say, so he waited. He'd known his brother for a long time. Kal was thoughtful when there was something on his mind. And when he had something to say, he'd mull it over first.

"There's a training class for the Technical Rescue Team coming up."

Rafe arched a brow. "The TRT does some dangerous work. High-angle rescue. Confined spaces. Water emergencies. High-risk, Kal."

Kal grinned. "I know."

"They're the best of the best."

"Yeah."

This was some big-time shit. He knew Kal could do it, but . . . damn. Then again, no matter what, he'd always stand behind his brothers.

"And they're probably all current on their CEUs."

Kal rolled his eyes. "Fuck you."

Rafe laughed. "Hey, I can't help that I was in the room when Jackson popped in to tell you what a loser you are."

"Fine. I'll do those today."

"You should. And then you have to talk to Jackson. And Dad. Because if there's something you want, you should go for it."

"You're right. Hey, thanks for not telling me my idea is stupid."

"I think it's dangerous. But elite as fuck. You're a great firefighter, Kal. And you can do anything you set your mind to."

They stood and hugged.

"I appreciate your faith in me," Kal said.

"Anytime. You know you can talk to me about anything."

"Thanks."

"Now go do your CEUs."

Kal grinned. "On it."

"Let me know what Jackson says."

"I will."

Kal left the room, and Rafe continued his workout. After he finished, he put the equipment away and wiped down the room, then refilled his water jug. He walked past the training room and saw Kal in there with his headphones on, typing into the laptop.

He nodded in satisfaction. When his brother wanted to focus, he could shut out the world.

He hoped Kal was on the right track. And he hoped Jackson would listen to him. The outcome of that remained to be seen and was out of Rafe's hands. All he could do was be there to offer his support. And he would be. Like always.

Just like his brothers had always been there for him.

CARMEN ADJUSTED HER POSITIONING IN HER CHAIR IN THE nursing supervisor's office, a room she didn't get to occupy all that often because she was typically running a hundred miles a minute going from one end of the ER floor to the other, or hanging out at the desk charting and scheduling. But if she didn't finish staff evaluations today, they were going to be late. And the one thing she wouldn't tolerate was turning things in late. So her nurses had to fill in for her on the floor, and Tess was handling triage duties while Carmen was occupied in the office doing freaking paperwork.

She looked down at her watch. It was two o'clock, and she'd been at this since she'd come on shift at seven this morning. She liked to be up and moving around, and sitting on her butt for this long staring into her laptop was making her eyes cross.

She loved her job, loved supervising the nursing staff, but the paperwork part? Not so much. Fortunately, this only had to be done twice a year and she was almost finished. She only had one more eval to do, and that was Tess's, whom she'd deliberately saved for last.

Tess was her right hand and could do Carmen's job as well as Carmen, which meant she was qualified for a supervisor's position. Carmen knew that Faith Stansfield was moving to Pittsburgh at the end of August, and that there'd be an opening on the ICU step-down floor for a nurse supervisor when she left. Tess had excellent skills and had stepped in for Carmen in a supervisory capacity when needed. She knew Tess could handle the position, and she intended to recommend Tess to replace Faith.

Of course, she wouldn't put that in Tess's performance review, because she didn't want Tess to know about it in case she got turned down for the job. But Carmen knew all the nurses on all the floors, and no one was better qualified for the job than her friend. Plus, Carmen's recommendation held some weight.

She finished Tess's eval and filed it, along with the note suggesting the promotion. The head of the nursing department for the hospital would review her recommendation, and then, hopefully, Carmen would find out soon.

Of course, losing Tess would leave a huge hole in her department, but she'd never hold back any of her nurses from promotion. Her job was to make them all better so that they could rise up.

She looked up when there was a knock at the door. Tess popped her head in. "Thought you could use a cheeseburger and a chocolate milk."

Carmen grinned. One of the other things she loved about her best friend was how well Tess knew her. "Oh, God, it's like you read my mind. Come in."

Tess carried the tray in and set it on Carmen's desk. "I don't want you to think I'm buttering you up, because I'm not. I figured you'd be hungry. So am I."

"Shut up and sit down. Of course you're not buttering me up. Besides, I just finished."

Tess grabbed her own cheeseburger. "You did? That's great. And even earlier than you thought you would."

Carmen took a long sip of the chocolate milk, letting its sweet goodness slide down her throat before answering. "Yes. I'm so happy to have that done with."

"I can't even imagine how tedious that project is. And then

you have to actually do the evals with each nurse. Ugh. We're all such pains in the ass, too."

Carmen laughed. "This is true."

They ate while Tess updated her on the status of their unit.

"Pretty quiet today, all in all. We had a patient come in obviously looking to score drugs. Complaining of a sore shoulder, said it was an ongoing thing from a previous injury and said some pain meds should take care of the problem. No insurance, refused X-rays or an MRI. Doc said his range of motion was fine. Dude didn't even wince once during physical examination."

"So what did you do?"

"We sent him on his way with a referral for physical therapy. And no pain meds."

Carmen took another bite of her cheeseburger, then smiled after she swallowed. "Bet he was pissed."

"He wasn't happy. Told Dr. Lange to go fuck himself."

Carmen laughed. "Not the first time Lange has heard those words."

"True. You don't make it to ER attending without pissing off a few patients. And other doctors, too."

"Lange can handle it, though. And he didn't toss the punk out on his ass, so there's that."

Carmen's phone pinged with a message, so she took a quick look. Her heart did a dance when she saw it was from Rafe.

Still thinking about our kiss. Want to see you tomorrow.

She sucked in a deep breath.

"Wow," Tess said, emptying her glass of milk. "Who was that from?"

After reading the message about five times, she lifted her gaze from her phone. "I'm sorry, what?"

"You are lost in that message. Love note?"

"It's a text from Rafe."

Tess gave her a smirk. "So it *is* a love note."

"Not a love note."

"Right. You were breathing so heavily it got ten degrees warmer in here. What's going on with you two?"

Carmen shrugged and picked up her glass of milk, sucking the liquid up in her straw. "Nothing much, really."

Tess tilted her head and shot her a look. "You are so lying. Tell me."

"Fine. We kissed yesterday."

"Is that it?"

She frowned. "It was a really good kiss, Tess."

Tess shrugged and leaned back in the chair. "I'll be more impressed when you see some action. Like actual sex action."

"I don't disagree with you there. Sex would be nice. We were headed in that direction, but my grandfather came home."

"You should go to his place next time. Then you won't be interrupted by returning grandpas. Or at least I assume you won't be."

She laughed. "He lives with his brothers."

Tess stood and started piling up their lunch leftovers on the tray. "Then I assume his brothers don't interrupt his sex action."

"I would hope not, though I have no idea what goes on over there. His older brother lives with his girlfriend. I would think they respect each other's privacy."

"Good. Go over to his place and jump on that hot man. Then tell me all about it."

Carmen shook her head. "I'll give it some thought. Thank you for bringing me lunch." She took out her purse and handed money to Tess.

"No, my treat."

"You can buy me lunch when we're not on duty."

"Okay." Tess slid the money in her pocket. "And you're welcome. I'll see you out on the floor."

After Tess closed the door behind her, Carmen picked up her phone and read Rafe's text message again. Her fingers hovered over the keypad, uncertain how to reply.

She typed out, *See you tomorrow?* No, that wasn't right.

Delete.

Maybe, *I keep thinking about that kiss, too.*

No, that was terrible.

Delete.

She blew out a breath.

Maybe she should just put it all out there with a *Hey, how about we have hot sex tomorrow.*

Ugh. Delete, delete, delete.

She laid her head in her hands. Nothing felt right. Why was she so bad at this?

She shook her head and typed her response.

Want to see you, too. And that kiss . . .

She ended her text with a fire emoji.

She half smiled at her reply, then hit send before she changed her mind—again.

Perfect.

She tucked her phone in her pocket, then went back to work.

CHAPTER 15

"OH, BY THE WAY, I NEED YOU GUYS OUT OF THE HOUSE tonight."

Jackson and Kal looked up from the backyard of their parents' house. They had spent the day there trimming trees and sweating their asses off clearing the backyard, trying to get the house finished up so their parents could sell it.

"You got a hot date?" Jackson asked.

"I invited Carmen over."

Kal arched a brow. "Next-door neighbor Carmen?"

"Do we know another one?"

"Hell if I know," Kal said. "I can't keep track of all the names of the women you date."

Rafe lifted his chin. He didn't date that many women. Or maybe he had. But that was before. "Yeah, it's next-door neighbor Carmen."

"I didn't know you two were dating," Jackson said.

"We are. Or we just started. I don't know. Anyway, I want some time alone with her, so if you two wouldn't mind . . ."

"I'll take Becks out after she gets off work," Jackson said. "She'll like that."

Kal nodded. "Consider me gone."

He knew he could count on his brothers. "Thanks, guys."

"Now let's get this landscaping done before I die of heatstroke out here," Jackson said.

"See, this is what happens when you get old," Kal said.

Jackson frowned. "Fuck you, little brother. I can outwork you any day of the week."

Kal shook his head. "You poor old man. Need a cold glass of ice water?"

"Actually, that sounds pretty good," Rafe said. "Would you mind, Kal?"

"Yeah, since you're the youngest, and since you just insulted me, you can go grab us all some ice water."

"Normally, I'd tell you both to go fuck yourselves, but since I can go inside and cool off, I'll go make us drinks."

Kal put his shovel down and pulled his gloves off, then went inside.

"I think he baited me on purpose," Jackson said.

Rafe laughed. "Probably. But at least he's getting us a cold drink."

"True enough." Jackson shoved his booted foot on the shovel and into the dirt against the fence line where they'd be putting in new shrubs.

"Hey, speaking of Kal, did he talk to you at work yesterday?"

"About?"

It wasn't Rafe's place to give Jackson a heads-up about what Kal talked to him about, so he knew he'd have to keep it vague. "Work stuff."

Jackson slanted Rafe a warning look. "You know I can't talk about personnel issues with you, Rafe. Even if it's about your brother."

If Kal hadn't talked to him, Jackson would have said no. The shutdown meant he had. "Sure, I understand."

They went back to work for a few minutes. Then Jackson stopped and leaned against the top of the shovel. "Did Kal talk to you?"

Rafe smiled at him. "You know I can't talk about brother-to-brother conversations. Sworn to secrecy."

Jackson grinned and shook his head. "Asshole."

Rafe laughed, and they went back to shoveling.

Kal came out and handed each of them a tall glass of ice water.

"What did you do in there?" Jackson asked. "Take a nap?"

"Maybe."

Rafe downed two gulps right away, cooling his parched throat. Cold water had never tasted so good.

"What were you two laughing about?" Kal asked. "I heard you inside."

"Family and work secrets," Rafe said.

"Nah. He was talking shit about you," Jackson said.

Kal looked over at Rafe, who shook his head. "It's all lies."

"And I made lunch while I was in there. Now I'm going to eat it myself."

At the mention of food, Rafe's stomach grumbled. "You made lunch? What did you fix?"

"Does it make a difference?"

"No," Jackson said. "You know we'll eat anything. But what did you make?"

"Turkey sandwiches with avocado and chipotle aioli, and a watermelon salsa."

Rafe dropped his shovel on the ground. "And we're breaking."

Kal laughed. "Thought you might say that."

They went inside and washed up, then sat at the kitchen table where they'd grown up. It still bore the scars from elbows and forks and fights at the dinner table.

"You think Mom will want a new kitchen table at the new house?" Rafe asked.

Jackson looked down at the table. "Probably. This one's pretty scarred up."

"You're the one who stabbed the steak knife in the wood when we argued over whether we were gonna stay here or not."

Jackson shrugged. "I was fourteen, Kal. And I didn't stab *you*, did I?"

"No, but it was a heated argument that night."

"And as usual," Rafe said, "I had to play the peacemaker."

They both looked over at Rafe.

"I don't remember it exactly like that," Jackson said.

"I remember," Kal said. "Rafe, you were on my side, arguing with Jackson that if he wanted to leave, he could go by himself, because you liked it here and you and me were staying."

Jackson cracked a smile. "And I said I wasn't going without the two of you. That's when I got mad and stabbed my knife into the table."

"Right when Mom walked back into the room," Kal said.

Rafe nodded. "I give her credit for not flipping out. She just pulled up a chair next to you and asked if you were planning to stab one of us, or if there was something else making you mad."

"Yeah," Jackson said, his lips curving into a smile. "She was always so calm. It's one of the things I love most about her. Her feathers are never ruffled."

"Whose feathers?"

Rafe looked up to see their mother walking into the kitchen. Kal got up and pressed a kiss to her cheek. "Hey, Mom. We were just reminiscing about the kitchen table. And Jackson's knife mark in it."

"Oh, that." She laid her stuff on the table by the doorway. "And you think that didn't upset me?"

"You seemed so calm about it," Jackson said.

She slid in the chair next to Jackson. "To you, yes. I cried in my room that night, I was so afraid you were going to leave us."

"Aww, Mom." Jackson put his arm around her and tugged her against him. "I love you."

"Love you, too."

"You're home early today," Kal said.

"Yes. We're closing on the new house this afternoon, so I took half a day off."

Rafe grinned. "Yeah? That's exciting. This place should be ready to go within a week."

"No worries. We actually have someone interested in buying the house already."

"Really?" Jackson asked. "Who?"

"Glen and Paula English's son, Tim."

"I remember Tim from school," Rafe said. "Didn't he move to Orlando after college?"

Mom nodded. "But he just got a new position here. Tim's wife, Stacy, landed a job already as well."

"That's great," Kal said.

"Yes, it is," their mom said. "They're looking for a place near Tim's parents because Paula is going to watch their twins. They know we've been fixing our house up to sell, so Paula asked me how soon it would be ready."

"Not putting it on the market would be ideal," Jackson said.

"I agree," Mom said. "Tim and Stacy will be flying in this weekend, so they're going to come by and look at the house. But it being just around the corner from Paula and Glen's, if it works out and if they like our house, I'm hoping we can work out a deal."

"We'll make sure to have the backyard landscaping finished by then," Kal said.

Rafe nodded. "Not a problem at all, Mom."

"You all have been so good at pitching in to help us make this place beautiful again. I'm almost sad to leave."

Jackson laughed. "No, you're not. You have that big, beautiful house to move into that has everything you've always wanted. The office, the pool, that fancy bathroom."

"You're right. I'm excited about the new house. But I'll still be sad to leave this place."

Rafe figured she'd be sad to leave until she moved all of her favorite pieces of furniture into the new house and had a chance to decorate. Then she'd forget all about this place.

They finished up the yard work around five. Mom asked them if they wanted to stay for dinner. Kal stayed behind, but Jackson and Rafe went home.

The two of them kicked back for a while and played video games. After their team dominated one of the war games, Jackson laid his controller on the table.

"I need to go take a shower. Becks and I are going to eat and see a movie. Then there's a club one of her clients told her about that we're gonna check out tonight."

He appreciated his brother making plans out of the house to-night. "Sounds fun. Have a great time."

Kal had already texted that he was probably going to crash at Mom and Dad's tonight because he and Dad were packing up some things in the garage.

So if Kal had already talked to Jackson about wanting to move out of Station 6, Kal might have a conversation one-on-one with Dad tonight about it. Or maybe he'd wait and go through official channels.

As Kal's lieutenant, it was Jackson's job to mention it to their captain when one of their firefighters was interested in transfer-ring. Then Captain Mathias would bring it to the battalion chief—Dad—who would move things up the chain if they felt that particular firefighter was qualified for a new position.

Rafe was curious as hell about Kal's situation. He wanted his brother to be happy. And if he wasn't content on Ladder 6, it wasn't good for the rest of the ladder team.

Not that there was anything Rafe could do about it other than wait and hope for the best.

Besides, tonight he had a date, and that was what was first and foremost on his mind.

CHAPTER 16

WHAT A DAY. THE ER HAD ROLLED IN ONE EMERGENCY AF-
ter another, ambulances had been lined up to bring in case after
case and Carmen didn't think she'd sat once the entire day.

All she wanted to do was go home, sit in a tub with a glass of
wine and a good book, eat dinner and pass out early.

But she had promised Rafe she'd come over to his place tonight. He'd told her he was going to cook for her.

She could cancel. She could be honest and tell him she was
tired. He'd understand.

She walked in the front door, hung her keys on the rack and
tossed her bag on the table.

"You look beat," her grandpa said as she made her way into
the living room to press a kiss on his cheek.

"It was a long day."

"You relax tonight. I can fix dinner."

"No, I'll take care of it. I'm going to grill you some chicken
and asparagus and tiny potatoes."

"Sounds good. And you mean *us*, right?"

She rested her thigh against the side of the sofa. "Actually,

Rafe asked me to come over to his place for dinner tonight. Unless you think you need me."

Her grandpa's brows shot up. "A date? You have a date with Rafe?"

"Kind of."

"That's great. I like him, bebita. You two are a good match."

"It's just dinner, Grandpa. We're not getting married or anything."

"I need grandbabies." He emphasized the last word with his soulful eyes.

She wasn't falling for it. "Don't look at me. I'm too busy to have babies."

"Well, I'm sure not having them, so it's gonna have to be you."

She laughed. "Then I'll see what I can do somewhere down the road."

"I don't have that many 'down the road' years left in me. How about you see what you can do sooner? Maybe even tonight?"

Her eyes widened. "Grandpa!"

He shrugged. "Just trying to hurry you along."

"How about you let me fall in love with someone first."

"Okay, okay. I'll wait. But I think Rafe is a pretty decent candidate."

She'd reserve judgement on that. After her disastrous first marriage, she didn't trust herself at all where men were concerned. "I'm going to cook your dinner."

She went into the kitchen, put the potatoes and asparagus on to cook and grilled the chicken. Fortunately, it was a quick meal, so she had her grandfather's dinner finished in a hurry. While he was eating, she dashed to her room and jumped in the shower, making sure to shave all her critical parts—just in case they saw some action tonight.

Though she was so tired she might fall asleep right after dinner. *Some hot date you are, Carmen.*

Hey, if Rafe Donovan wanted to date her, he was going to have to deal with the part of her that came home exhausted after a brutal shift. As a firefighter, she figured he'd understand what that was like.

After she dried her hair and applied a little makeup, she put on shorts and a T-shirt, not wanting to appear too fancy, then looked at herself in the mirror.

"Great, Carmen. You look like you're ready for a trip to the grocery store."

Would it hurt that much to step it up a bit, girl?

She huffed in disgust at the mirror. "Fine."

She pulled off the shorts and T-shirt and stared in the closet, finally deciding on a cotton sundress that was casual, but still a little sexy.

But not too sexy. She didn't want to give Rafe the idea that she was going over there for sex.

You want to have sex with him, idiot. What's your problem?

Deciding not to overthink every damn thing, she slid her feet into her comfy white sandals and went downstairs to check on her grandpa. He was watching TV in the living room. She filled his water glass and set it down on the table.

"I'm right next door if you need anything," she said. "And I have my phone on me."

"I can take care of myself, Carmen."

"I'll be back in time to put you to bed."

He looked up at her, glaring. "I can put myself to bed."

"No, you can't, and don't try or you'll fall."

"Whatever. Pop back over at ten and you can help. Then you can go back over to Rafe's."

She frowned. "What if I'm tired and I want to go to bed at ten?"

"Then you're not doing dating right."

Even her grandfather was pushing her toward Rafe. "We'll see. I'll be back at ten. Love you, Grandpa."

"Love you, too, bebita."

At least she had an exit plan if she got so tired she couldn't keep her eyes open.

She walked across the lawn and knocked on the door to Rafe's house. It took a minute, but Rafe opened the door.

He wore jeans and a short-sleeved Henley that fit tight against his amazing chest and shoulders.

"You look incredible," he said, smiling at her but keeping his eyes fixed on her face, which she appreciated.

"Thanks. So do you. Are we going out?"

"No. I just figured since I invited you over to eat, I should maybe not dress like I'm going to the beach. Come on in."

It was a million degrees outside and even more humid than that. The fact he put on a pair of jeans was quite the sacrifice.

She followed him into the kitchen. He had two wineglasses out.

"White or red?"

"White."

"Sweet or not?"

"Hmm. Not."

He went to the fridge and selected a bottle of sauvignon blanc. He pulled the cork and let it sit.

"How was your day?" he asked.

"Intense. Exhausting. I ran from the second I got there until the end of shift."

He swept his hand down her arm. "Those days are brutal. You must be wiped."

"Kind of."

He poured the wine into their glasses and grabbed both of them. "Come on. Let's go sit in the living room."

They took seats next to each other on the comfortable sofa. He handed her one of the glasses.

"Thanks."

"A lot of emergencies today?" he asked.

She liked that he seemed interested in her work. "Yes."

"Come on. Kick off your sandals, put your feet in my lap and I'll give you a foot massage. You can tell me about your day."

"Seriously?" Her feet ached by the end of her shift, and the one thing she always longed for was someone to rub them.

"Totally serious."

She slid out of her sandals, shifted on the sofa and laid her arm against the pillow of the sofa. She rested her feet in his lap, balancing her glass of wine as she did so. He started off rubbing the arch of one foot, gently at first.

She resisted the urge to moan. It felt so good.

"That's nice."

"Good. So did you have ambulances stacked up?"

Oh, that's right. She was supposed to be telling him about her day, but all she could think about was how he was using his amazingly strong hands to rub the soreness out of her aching feet.

"Right. It's like they were lying in wait for me as soon as I got there. One critical emergency after another."

He nodded, using his fist to roll the tension out of the ball of her foot. This time, she did moan, sighed and took a hard swallow of her wine.

She was in heaven, and if he never stopped rubbing her feet, she'd be okay with that.

"I know how that is," he said. "Same thing happens at the station sometimes. It's like you don't even get a second to breathe the entire shift."

"Exactly. You could go weeks with business as usual, and then all hell breaks loose in one day. That's how today was. By the time I got home, I was beat."

He shifted to her other foot, using his same tender massage, then looked up at her. "You could have canceled if you were too tired to come over. You know I would have understood, Carmen."

"I figured you would have. But I made Grandpa dinner and took a shower, and the shower helped revive me a little."

He smiled. "I'm glad you're here."

"Me, too. And thank you for the foot rub. It's helping in ways I can't even tell you."

She hadn't realized how much she needed the emotional support, the fact he listened to her talk about her day. She told her grandpa, of course, but never too much information, because then he'd complain she was working too hard and he'd feel guilty that she had to take care of him and the house, too. So she tried to downplay the grueling hours and the hard days.

She placed her wineglass on the table. "What did you do today?"

"My brothers and I finished up some yard work at my parents' house. It's ready to put on the market now."

"That's great. So when are they moving to the new house?"

"Pretty soon. Kal's there tonight helping our dad pack up the garage. The son of friends of theirs is interested in buying the place, so they might not even have to put it on the market."

"That's fantastic. I hope it sells fast for them. I'm sure your mom is eager to get into her new house."

He used his fingers to press onto the top of her foot, easing the sore muscles there. "She downplays it, but I can tell she's excited about all the features in the new house. Especially having her own private office there."

"Does she do a lot of work at home?"

He nodded. "If she's on call. She always has court files at home. The current house doesn't give her any quiet space to do that. The new place has a nice office where she'll have some privacy to do her work and to take calls."

"Perfect."

Rafe had both of her feet in his hands now, rhythmically rubbing them. She lay back on the sofa.

"I've often thought about doing some renovations to Grandpa's house."

"Yeah? What kind?"

She yawned. "I'd like to reorganize the garage so I can do my crafting in there."

"Crafts, huh? What kinds of crafts do you do?"

"I restore furniture. Or I would if I could find the space to do it. The garage is filled with some of my mom's old things—things I'd like to restore if I had the space. But there's just so much junk piled up in there, and I can never find the time to deal with it."

"Huh. Maybe I can help you out with that."

She yawned again, blinking to keep her eyes open. "You don't have to do that."

"What if I want to."

"You could . . ."

CARMEN JERKED AWAKE. THE ROOM WAS DARK, BUT ONE thing she knew for certain was that she wasn't in her own home.

The last thing she remembered was talking to Rafe. She looked over to where he'd been sitting. He wasn't there now. She heard music coming from the other room. She sat up, realizing he'd covered her with a light throw. She couldn't help but smile at the sweet gesture.

But, dammit. She'd fallen asleep. Like, utterly passed out on him.

She looked down at her watch, realizing she'd been out for an hour. Great.

You are one hell of an exciting date, Carmen.

She got up, folded the throw over the back of the sofa and slid her feet into her sandals. She smoothed her hair and went in search of the music, which was coming from the kitchen. Rafe was in there, sitting at the kitchen island sipping a beer. He smiled when he saw her come in.

"Have a good nap?" he asked.

"I'm so sorry."

"What for?"

"For falling asleep on you."

"Hey. You work hard. You obviously had a tough day. And then on top of that you take care of your grandfather. Your plate is full, Carmen. Never apologize for working your ass off and being tired, okay? Because I get it."

She inhaled on a shaky breath. "Thanks for understanding."

"No problem. Can I pour you another glass of wine?"

"Maybe some iced tea or water?"

"I'll fix you a glass of tea."

"Great, thanks. I'm going to slip into the bathroom. I'll be right back."

"Sure."

She made her way to the downstairs bathroom and closed the door. Once she did her business, she washed her hands and stared into the mirror. Her cheeks were flushed and her hair was mussed and she looked like she'd been asleep all night.

But she also felt very warm and emotional and not sure what to do with herself.

He understood. He wasn't angry. In fact, he'd treated her so sweetly from the moment she'd walked in the door. And that wasn't something she'd ever had before. She looked at her watch. Only nine. Still time before she had to go help her grandpa get to bed.

She leaned over and rinsed out her mouth with some cold water, then fluffed her hair as best she could and left the bathroom.

Rafe had his face buried in his phone, and he'd switched from drinking beer to iced tea. But as soon as she came out, he slid his phone to the side and stood, handing her a glass of tea.

"Thanks." She took a sip, letting the cool liquid slide down her parched throat. "And thanks for understanding."

"It helps that we both work long shifts that can often be intense. I get where you're coming from. If you'd like to call it a night . . ."

She set her glass on the counter. "No, I'd like to stay. We haven't had dinner—or dessert."

"Dessert. I didn't—"

She snaked her hand around the back of his neck. "And by dessert, I mean you and me. Together. We could start out kissing. I really liked that kiss we shared, Rafe. Maybe we could see where it goes from there?"

He wound his arm around her waist and pulled her against him. "Yeah, I definitely want to do that. But first, how about I feed you dinner?"

What she really wanted to do was kiss him. But, admittedly, she was hungry. "Sure."

Apparently, while she'd been asleep, he'd grilled chicken, sliced it up and added it to a tremendous salad that had eggs, croutons, cranberries, oranges and walnuts. He'd also made an incredible raspberry vinaigrette.

Carmen carried their iced teas to the table and then helped Rafe with their bowls and utensils while he brought the salad over. They sat at the table, and Carmen took a bite. Flavor exploded on her tongue. After she swallowed, she noticed Rafe had been watching her. "It's delicious."

"I'm not the best cook, and I know this isn't fancy."

"Seriously, Rafe. This is delicious. And it's hot as hell outside. I love salads in the summer."

He seemed to relax. "I'm glad you like it."

She loved that he'd been nervous about her reaction. "You don't need to worry. You cook just fine."

"It's not rocket science to make a salad."

"And you'd be surprised how many guys won't even do that much."

He chewed and swallowed, then took a sip of his tea. "You talking about your ex?"

"Among other guys I've been with."

"So no guy has cooked for you before?"

She shook her head. "I guess I've picked all the wrong men."

"I guess so. Not that I'm all that, but I can at least put a burger on the grill or make sure you have a decent meal when you come home from work at night."

Who was this guy? He couldn't be human. She might actually still be asleep, and this was all a dream. "You'd cook—for me."

"Hell yes, I would. Why should a woman do all the cooking? That seems antiquated and sexist and totally misogynist. Besides, men cook these days."

She arched a brow. "They do, huh?"

"Yeah. My mom taught all of us to cook. She said she wasn't raising useless sons, and there was no way we were to expect a woman to do housework or cooking. I can also clean a bathroom and mop floors and dust. Which we all have to do at the fire station anyway. Plus all the firefighters cook, too, so being taught those skills by my mom came in handy when we all decided to become firefighters."

She laughed. "I'm sure they did. Remind me to thank your mom."

"I will."

They finished dinner and did the dishes. By then it was close to ten.

"I have to go help Grandpa get in bed. Mind if I run home for a few, then come back?"

"I don't mind at all. Do you need me to come help you?"

"Thanks, but I've got this. It won't take me long to get him tucked in. He just needs a little help maneuvering into bed. I'll be back in about fifteen minutes."

"Not a problem. I'll be here."

"Okay."

She left and dashed across the lawn, using her key to get into the house. Grandpa was already asleep in front of the TV. She gently woke him, then helped him get ready for bed.

She helped position him in bed so he could see his TV. He was doing much better about moving around in the bed. Pretty soon he wouldn't need her help at all.

"How's it going so far?" he asked.

"How's what going?"

"The date, Carmen."

"Oh." She sat on the side of his bed. "It's going well. We're talking. He made dinner. He's nice."

Her grandfather raised a brow. "You gonna spend the night?"

"Of course not. What if you need me?"

He looked over on the nightstand. "I have a phone. And you're right next door. You have to stop worrying so much about me. You're entitled to have a life."

She started to object, but then he glared at her with his disapproving Grandpa glare. He rarely gave it to her, but when he did, she knew better than to argue.

"Fine. I know you can take care of yourself. But that doesn't mean I'll worry less." She kissed the top of his head. "If you need me, you have to promise to call."

"I promise. Now you have to promise to go and think about yourself for a while. Have some fun."

She smiled at him. "I promise. Te amo, Abuelo."

"Yo también te quiero, bebita."

She left the house and hurried back to Rafe's. He had left the door unlocked, so she went inside. It was dark in the entry, so she wandered through the living room and into the kitchen. On the table was a note.

Outside by the pool. Come join me.

She smiled and headed outside. A blast of heat hit her. July in Ft. Lauderdale was brutal.

There were no lights on out here, either, but she heard the splash of water, so she made her way poolside.

Rafe was in the pool, his arms resting over the side.

"Water feels good. Want to come in?"

She looked down at her clothes. "No swimsuit."

"You could get naked."

"What? And have you miss the new underwear unveiling?"

"Oh, I definitely don't want to miss that, after you went to so much trouble to buy them."

He hoisted himself out of the pool, making her eyes go wide.

She was fully dressed. Rafe, on the other hand, was gloriously naked, giving her a delicious view of his magnificent body.

At least until he grabbed a towel.

"Don't cover up on my account."

He laughed and used the towel to dry his hair, seemingly not caring that his body was exposed to her, which she didn't mind at all. He had the kind of physique a woman could stare at for hours.

Days.

Weeks.

Months.

Okay, forever.

Chiseled muscles, broad shoulders, a wide chest, amazingly muscled biceps, the kind of abs you wanted to run your hands over to see if they were even real, and strong, powerful legs.

And one outstanding cock. She'd lick her lips if it wasn't so obvious.

"You keep staring at it, it's going to get hard."

She slanted a half grin at him. "You're the one who got out of the pool naked. I make no apologies."

"Then I guess you'll have to show me the goods to make it even."

"The goods—oh, my fancy, sexy, amazingly awesome new underwear."

"I'm way more interested in the woman wearing the underwear, but sure. We can start with that."

The way he talked to her, like she was the most important person in his universe, made her tingle all over.

She lifted the sundress over her head and tossed it in the nearby lounge chair. Rafe walked over and teased his fingertip over the lacy strap of her bra.

"Purple's my favorite color."

"Is it?"

His gaze collided with hers, turning her insides tingly and needy.

"It's my favorite color when you're wearing it."

"Naked is definitely my favorite color on you," she said. "You should wear it more often, but only when we're alone together."

"So you're saying I shouldn't wear it to work."

She laughed and moved in closer, feeling the heat simmer between them. "Definitely not to work. Too dangerous."

"You're dangerous. To my heart rate." He teased his fingers around the edge of her bra cup, making her breath catch.

She laid her palm on his chest, feeling his heart race. "It's okay, Rafe. I'm a nurse. I'll take good care of you."

"I know you will."

He slid his fingers into her hair, cupped the back of her neck and leaned in to kiss her.

What started out as a gentle kiss quickly flamed into something more passionate.

Carmen felt as if she'd waited a lifetime for this moment, to be alone with Rafe, knowing they weren't going to be interrupted. Or at least she hoped they weren't, because she needed this time with him, to feel the heat of his lips moving deliberately across hers, his tongue exploring the inner recesses of her mouth. She moved into Rafe, the heat of his body aligning with hers. And when he wrapped an arm around her and pulled her flush against him, she shuddered.

He stepped back. "Let's take this inside."

She nodded, knowing they couldn't continue doing this outside, but wishing they hadn't had to stop, not when kissing him had felt so good.

Rafe tucked a towel around his waist, then grabbed his clothes. She followed him inside.

"You want something to drink?" he asked.

She shook her head. "No. I just want to get naked with you."

His lips curved. "I like where your head is." He reached his hand out. "Come on."

She slid her hand in his. He led her up the stairs and down the hall to his bedroom. His room wasn't at all what she expected. He had a great-looking king-size bed, covered up with a beautiful gray comforter. There was a small dresser against one wall and a nightstand next to the bed. The room was tidy and neat, and there was a bathroom attached to the bedroom.

"It smells clean in here," she said.

He arched a brow. "What did you expect? Dirty sock smell?"

"Maybe."

He laughed. "We all keep our rooms clean. And Becks is a compulsive cleaner, so if what we do isn't up to par, she comes in behind us and cleans again."

"That's helpful."

"Yeah. She's pretty awesome." He pulled her against him. "But hey, let's talk about you."

"What about me?"

"I'm glad you're here tonight. I know you're tired."

She smiled and curved her hand over his shoulder, amazed by the muscle she felt. She wanted to investigate him everywhere, map his body like an explorer. "I had a nap."

"So you've got your second wind?"

"I could go all night."

He swept her up into his arms and carried her to the bed. With one hand, he jerked the comforter down to the bottom of the bed, then laid her on top of the sheets.

"Just so you know, I changed the sheets this morning."

"Right, because that was the first thing I was going to ask."

"Was it?"

She laughed. "No."

She rolled over onto her side and patted the spot on the bed next to her. He climbed onto the bed and lay down next to her.

"Before we do this," he said, "I need to know that you're sure about what we're about to do."

She smoothed her fingertips over his jaw. "Very sure. Now kiss me."

He leaned in, then paused. "You like kissing."

"I like kissing very much."

He pushed her onto her back, covered her body with his and put his mouth on hers.

She sighed in utter bliss. He kept most of his weight off her body, yet the feel of him on top of her was delicious. She slung her leg around his hip, aligning her sex with the heat and hardness of his cock. Then she surged upward, rocking her clit against him.

He groaned and slipped one hand under her butt, and as he kissed her, he held their bodies closer together.

She could come like this. It had been too long since she'd been this close to a man's body, since she'd been kissed so thoroughly, since her body had wept with such need for release. She felt like a flower opening for the first time, only this wasn't the first time for her. It was the first in a long, long time, and she was so close to orgasm she felt her climax hovering. All she had to do was rub against him in just the right way.

But not yet. She moaned. "I need . . ."

He lifted his head, his palm resting on her belly. "Yeah? What do you need?"

She stared up at him, lost in the warmth of his eyes, in the desperate desire she saw there that mirrored what she felt. "Everything."

He rolled off her and undid the clasp of her bra, separating the cups to reveal her breasts. He swept his hand over the globes, then teased her nipples with the tips of his fingers until they rose like points.

"Beautiful," he whispered, before leaning over to take one between his lips.

As he sucked, she gasped at the sweet pleasure, arching her back to get closer to his hot mouth.

She was on fire, and when he snaked his hand over her belly, she was melting from the inside out. He teased his fingers along the band of her underwear, then slipped his hand inside to cup her sex.

He began to move his hand, his fingers sure and deft as he found every spot that gave her the most pleasure. She had already been halfway there, and when he slipped a finger inside of her and used the heel of his hand to gently rub against her clit, she came with a lift of her hips and a hard cry of sweet release.

She shuddered against him, holding on to his wrist to keep that momentum going for as long as she could. And it did keep going, much longer than she thought was possible, but the quivers continued to flow through her until she relaxed, still feeling those tiny pulses of her climax roll through her.

She was panting as Rafe bent to remove her panties, then came back up to brush a kiss across her lips.

"When you come," he said, "you really come."

She smiled. "It's been a long dry spell."

"Dry?" He swept his hand across her lower belly, tapping her sex. "Baby, you are anything but dry."

She rolled over to her side. "And now that you've gotten me sufficiently primed, let's keep going."

She palmed his chest, then slid her hand lower, enjoying the feel of his rippling muscles under her hand. His abs tightened when she rolled her palm over them, and she couldn't resist lingering there.

"You're so . . . hard."

His lips curved. "Not just there."

She grinned. "I'm making my way."

When she reached his cock, she closed her fingers around it, feeling it pulse with life against her palm. He surged upward, making her breath catch at the thought of him doing just that while he was inside of her, something she'd endlessly fantasized about.

"Condom?" she asked.

"On it." He rolled over and pulled a box out of his bedside drawer, took a packet out and tore it open, then put the condom on.

"I'm on the pill," she said. "I haven't been with anyone since I was with my ex. After he left I was tested for HIV and STDs and was clear."

He picked up her hand and pressed his lips to her palm.

"I always use condoms." He kissed the inside of her wrist. "I get tested regularly." He moved his lips up along the inside of her arm, causing goose bumps to pop up along her skin. "Last one was three months ago." He finally crossed over and laid his palms on either side of her head, bending down to nibble on her ear, then whispered, "I'm clear."

Never before had a safe-sex conversation been so sizzling. She shivered, then opened her legs as he covered her body with his. "And as long as we're being honest, I've jacked off a lot in the past year thinking about fucking you."

Her sex quivered as he put the tip of his cock at the entrance of her pussy.

"I've touched myself repeatedly with you in my fantasies," she said, "getting myself off with the thought of you just like this, hovering over me, plunging your cock inside of me and making me come."

"Holy shit, Carmen." He thrust inside of her, then stilled.

She felt him swell, and her body responded by tightening, quaking. She wrapped her legs around his thighs and lifted, and then he began to move, slow and easy at first, at the same time kissing her in that way that made her dizzy.

She was lost in the hot male smell of him, the feel of his hardcore body surrounding her as he continued to thrust in, then pull out, only to push his cock deep and grind against her, making her feel as if she were going to come apart right at that moment. But then he eased out and began the sweet torment all over again, drawing her up that ladder right to the edge.

He licked the side of her neck, from her collarbone all the way to her ear, and then he whispered words to her that made her shiver.

"Being inside of you is like being inside of a fire," he said. "You're burning me, Carmen."

She shuddered, so close to the edge she could feel the tremors. She held tight to Rafe, watching the way his face tightened as his movements quickened, and knew he was right there with her.

She hovered there, right at the precipice, her entire body shaking as sweet pulses roared their way to the surface.

"Come on, babe," he said. "Let's go down in flames together."

She let go and dug her heels into the mattress, crying out with the intensity of the orgasm that tore through her. Rafe reached underneath her to cup her butt cheek, his fingertips digging into her flesh as he roared out a groan that only prolonged the force of her climax.

When she settled, she fell to the mattress, feeling as if she'd run a marathon. She was hot, sweaty and utterly depleted. Rafe rolled to the side, then pulled her against him.

He stroked her hair and her back, and she was content to let the silence surround them. This was good, these few moments where no words needed to be said. They didn't need to analyze what had happened. They only needed to catch their breath and enjoy being together.

But she really needed a shower.

She popped her head up and looked down at him. "I'm sweaty."

He opened one eye. "So not my fault."

She laughed, then rolled over him. "I'm going to rinse off." She got out of bed, then paused at the doorway to see if he was watching her.

"You coming in the shower with me?" she asked.

He grinned and rolled off the bed. "I don't know, Carmen," he said as he followed her into the bathroom. "Will I be coming with you in the shower?"

She gave him a wicked smile.

Oh yes. It was going to be a very long night.

CHAPTER 17

RAFE WOKE UP EARLY, LIKE HE ALWAYS DID. IT DIDN'T MAT-
ter if he was on shift or off. He was an early riser.

When he rolled over in the bed, he could smell Carmen's scent
on the pillow next to him. The problem was, she wasn't there.

She'd left sometime before dawn, saying she had to get home
to her grandfather, get him breakfast and drop him off at therapy
for the day.

He yawned, stretched, got out of bed, put on shorts and a
sleeveless shirt and went downstairs. It looked like he was the first
one up, so he made himself a cup of coffee and walked outside.

It was cloudy today, which made Rafe happy, because it wasn't
so blisteringly hot that his feet melted to the patio outside. He sat
near the pool and sipped his coffee, letting the caffeine do its
thing.

He saw some tree limbs from Carmen's backyard leaning over
into their yard. Not a big deal, but he should get a ladder and trim
those so Carmen wouldn't have to do it. And while he was at it,
he should trim the other trees in their yard to give them a neater
look.

He went inside and peeled potatoes, sliced and put them on to boil, then made some bacon and eggs. By that time, Jackson and Becks came downstairs.

"You should know better than to start cooking bacon this early," Jackson said, stealing a piece of bacon while he took a drink of his coffee.

"Hey, that's for breakfast," Rafe said.

"You can always make more."

"No, *you* can make more."

Becks skirted around Rafe and went to the fridge. "You know six pieces isn't going to be enough. I'll do it."

Becks started the bacon while Rafe drained the water off the potatoes and sliced them, then put them in the pan to fry them up. Kal had come home while he was outside. He washed his hands and sliced mangoes. They got out plates and served up breakfast, then took everything to the table to eat.

After last night with Carmen, Rafe had worked up a hell of an appetite and was starving, but he tried not to shovel the food into his mouth.

"So Carmen decided not to stay for breakfast?" Becks asked.

Rafe lifted his head. "Carmen? Uh, no. Why would she be here?"

"Because I saw her tiptoe down the stairs about four a.m. when I woke up to come downstairs for some water."

"Oh."

"Sooo, Carmen spent the night, huh?" Kal asked. "Do tell, brother."

"Or, don't," Jackson said, frowning at Kal. "Because it's no one's business."

"Oops," Becks said, lifting her shoulders in apology. "I'm sorry. I didn't know it was a secret."

Rafe shrugged. "It's not. At least not to me. I don't know how Carmen will feel about everyone knowing."

"It's not like we're gonna put a sign up," Kal said. "Your private business is your own. Except with us, because we're family and nosy."

Rafe laughed. "Don't I know it."

After breakfast, they all cleaned the dishes and wiped down the kitchen. Becks had to get ready to go to her tattoo shop, and then she left. Kal ran off to do . . . something, and Jackson said he was going to buy tires for his truck, so that meant Rafe was alone in the house.

He went into the garage to get the trimmers and took those out to the far part of the backyard. He grabbed the ladder, climbed up and started cutting away the long hanging branches that he could reach from his part of the yard. When he'd trimmed all the ones he could, he put the clippings in the recycle bin. He stared up at the tree, deciding it looked good enough for now.

Then he studied Carmen's yard. He took the ladder and trimmer and went into her yard, figuring she'd never notice he was there.

He was busily trimming the tree when he heard a tap on the ladder. He looked down to see Carmen, glaring up at him with a pissed-off expression on her face.

"Just what the hell do you think you're doing?"

"I started trimming your tree that was hanging over my part of the yard, and noticed it needed it on your part, too. Figured I'd finish the job since I was already hot and sweaty."

She put her hands on her hips. "Oh, you did. Without even asking me."

He didn't see why it was a big deal. "Okay. Hey, Carmen. This tree is in serious need of maintenance. Mind if I handle it?"

"You do realize I'm perfectly capable of handling my business in my own yard."

He'd finished clipping the last of the fronds, so he climbed down and wiped the sweat from his face with the hem of his shirt.

"Where did I say you couldn't handle it? I just said I thought I'd finish the job I started on my side."

She opened her mouth, then closed it, then opened it again. "Fine. And thanks. And next time, discuss it with me first."

"You got it." He pulled her against him and pressed his lips to hers. She gasped, then kissed him back, laying her palms against his chest, making his heart speed up its rhythm.

When he drew back, he said, "First, sorry I got you all sweaty. Second, I had a good time last night."

She swiped her fingertip across his jaw. "First, I like you sweaty. Second, I did, too. Sorry I had to leave so early."

"Me, too." He started cutting through the limbs on the ground. "Oh, and you missed a great breakfast."

"I did?"

"Yeah. Eggs and bacon and fried potatoes and fruit. Oh, and Becks saw you sneak out of the house early this morning, which she mentioned during breakfast, so now everyone knows you stayed over last night."

She shrugged. "I'm not ashamed of having sex with you. Are you?"

He thought she'd be freaked, so her response made him feel good. "Hell, no. I like you, Carmen. I'm happy to be with you."

Her lips curved. "Same."

"Good. How about we go out somewhere tonight?"

"That sounds fun. What do you have in mind?"

"One of the firefighters from our station has a bar and restaurant, and a lot of the crew go there. I thought you might want to meet some of them."

"I'd love to."

She was a constant surprise. She'd fought being with him for so long. Now she was open to meeting the people he worked with—his friends. But if she was down with it, he definitely was, too. "Great. Pick you up at seven?"

"Sounds good. Now get out of my backyard."

He laughed. "Yes, ma'am."

She went back inside, and he finished cutting up the limbs and cleaned up his mess, smiling as he left her yard.

He had a date tonight. Which wasn't new for him, but he really liked this woman. Enough to show her off to his friends.

So maybe he liked her more than he should.

"YOU LOOK PRETTY. YOU GOT ANOTHER DATE WITH RAFE tonight?" her grandfather asked as Carmen came downstairs that evening.

She'd chosen a colorful, kind of tight-fitting dress. But hell, it looked good on her, and she hadn't worn it yet, so, why not?

"Yes."

He grinned. "Good for you. Where you going?"

"Some restaurant owned by one of his fellow firefighters."

Grandpa turned in his chair to face her. "Which means he's having you meet his family already."

"Not his family. His coworkers."

"With firefighters, his coworkers are part of his family. Same thing, bebita."

She rolled her eyes. "It's just dinner, Grandpa."

"I saw he trimmed that giant tree out back today."

She finished putting on her earrings. "The limbs were infringing on their backyard, so he came over to finish the job on our side. No big deal."

"Uh-uh. It was a kindness, Carmen. He didn't have to do our side, but he did. Why are you so resistant to a man being nice to you?"

She straightened, contemplating what he'd said. "I don't know. Tod, probably."

Her grandfather nodded. "He made promises he didn't keep. He hurt you. But Rafe isn't like that."

"How do I know that? Tod was a good guy in the beginning, too. Besides, I'm not looking for a relationship. This is just for fun."

"Fun. Pfft. You should be looking for forever." Her grandfather got up slowly, grabbed his cane and walked slowly into the living room.

Her stomach tightened at the word *forever*. She hated disappointing her grandfather. But this was her life.

Her fears.

She just wanted to have some fun. What was wrong with not wanting forever?

The doorbell rang, so she walked over to open it. It was Rafe.

His eyes widened. "Wow. You dressed up. And you're beautiful."

She smiled, shoving away her conversation with her grandfather as she warmed under Rafe's praise. "Thank you. You don't look too bad yourself. Come on in."

He'd dressed in jeans and a long-sleeved button-down shirt with white tennis shoes. Even casual, he looked amazing, his tan skin appearing even darker contrasted against the white of his shirt. He was so handsome, and as he came inside and she followed behind him, his walk was predatory, his ass so fine. He glanced at her over his shoulder and when he lifted his lips and gave her a wink, her legs buckled a little.

She realized everything about Rafe was lethal to her senses.

It was a good thing her grandpa was home or they'd never make it out of the house tonight.

"Hey, Jimmy." Rafe went over to shake her grandfather's hand.

"How's it going, Rafe?"

"Pretty good."

"Thanks for trimming that tree out back today. I'd get it myself, but I think my ladder days are behind me."

Rafe grinned. "I was happy to take care of it for you. I had some trimming to do out back at our house anyway. Anytime you need something like that done, just call me."

Her grandpa shot her a look, then smiled at Rafe. "Much appreciated, thanks."

"Are you ready to go?" Carmen asked, deciding not to reopen that conversation.

Rafe nodded, then looked over at her grandfather. "Yeah. You all set here, Jimmy?"

"I am. Got my TV going. Then I'll take myself to bed when I get tired."

"Are you sure you can handle that by yourself, Grandpa?"

"Kal's home tonight, Jimmy," Rafe said. "If you need some assistance getting in bed I know he'd be happy to help you out. Want me to text him?"

Her grandfather shook his head. "Pretty sure I've got this. But I'll let Kal know if I need him. Thanks."

Carmen leaned over and kissed her grandfather's cheek. "You call or text me if you need anything."

He patted her cheek. "And you can stop worrying about me. I'll be fine on my own."

"Okay. I love you."

"Love you, too. Go have some fun. Drink. Dance. Have some sex in the car."

"Grandpa!"

Rafe laughed. "Night, Jimmy."

Her grandfather had already returned to watching TV, so he waved them off.

They got into the truck, and Rafe took off.

"I'm really sorry about him. He's . . . I don't know what's going on with him. I think he wants me to get knocked up. He desperately wants grandkids."

Rafe made a turn onto the highway. "I mean, I'd be happy to do my part in practicing making babies, but I don't think I'm ready to actually have any today. Sorry."

She quirked a smile. "The practice part suits me just fine, too. I'm not ready yet, either."

"Then we're in sync."

She was happy he hadn't flipped out over her grandpa's "making babies" suggestion. "We are definitely in sync."

He reached over and slid his hand along her thigh. "Then maybe we'll try out having sex in the truck later."

"Only if you keep the motor running and the air-conditioning on."

He laughed. "You're making my dick hard just thinking about it."

"Good. Keep that thought going."

He took the exit and stopped at the light. "You know, we don't have to go to the bar tonight. I know a nice secluded spot."

"Not a chance. I'm hungry, bud, so feeding me is a priority."

The light turned green, and he made the left turn. "Dammit."

Her lips quirked.

"So, whose restaurant is it?" she asked.

"Tommy Rodriguez. His family has owned it for two generations. Great fish house."

"Awesome."

They pulled into the full parking lot. Tommy's Fish House was lit up with a nice, welcoming sign. The building was a large one-story with an A-frame roof. It was painted bright white with blue accents. And even standing outside, she could hear the raucous sounds of people laughing.

A good sign, in Carmen's opinion. A crowded, loud restaurant meant good food.

Rafe held the door open for her, and she walked inside. A blast of icy cold air hit her, refreshing her instantly.

A pretty blond hostess stood right inside.

"Can I help—oh, hi, Rafe."

"Hey, Soleil. Tommy knows we're coming. He said he'd have a table in the back for the group."

Soleil nodded. "We're just clearing out a large party. It'll be about twenty minutes if that's okay?"

"Sure. We'll be at the bar."

"I'll let Tommy know you're here."

"Thanks."

He put his hand at the small of Carmen's back, leading her off toward the left where the bar was located. They managed to find a small table in the back.

"I'll get us something to drink. What would you like?"

"How about a pinot grigio?"

"Okay. Be right back."

He walked to the bar and she took the time to appreciate the ambience of the place. It was comfortable, the kind of restaurant you could bring your kids to, but also modern and fun and raucous, so easily a date-night restaurant as well.

A couple approached Rafe at the bar and he shook hands with both of them. She recognized Miguel and Adrienne as EMTs who frequented the ER. Then another guy joined them.

Rafe brought them over to their table.

"Carmen, this is Miguel Acosta and Adrienne Smith. They're both EMTs at Station 6. And this is Mitchell Hendricks, a fire-fighter at Station 6."

She stood and shook everyone's hand. "I know Miguel and Adrienne. They often bring patients into the ER. Nice to meet you, Mitchell."

"Hey, Carmen," Adrienne said.

"Good to see you, Carmen," Miguel said. "Outside the hospital for a change."

Carmen laughed as Rafe set her glass of wine on the table.

"Go ahead and take a seat, Adrienne," Rafe said. "There are no other tables here. The guys and I will go linger by the bar."

"Okay, thanks."

Carmen sat, and so did Adrienne.

"It's always in and out for us," Adrienne said to her. "We never get a chance to chat."

"I know. I'm constantly busy."

"Same."

"How long have you been with Station 6, Adrienne?" Carmen asked.

"Five years. Since right out of EMT school."

"You must really like it."

"I do. I love all the people I work with."

"It helps to have a friendly work environment, doesn't it?"

Adrienne nodded. "Sure does."

They chatted for a while, and Carmen enjoyed getting to know Adrienne.

"So, how long have you and Rafe been dating?" Adrienne asked. "Rafe didn't clue us in on the two of you. He's very secretive."

She laughed, not at all offended. "It's new. We're not really dating, just having fun together. We live next door to each other."

"Oh, I didn't know that, either. That's convenient, isn't it?"

"Yes. I've known Rafe and his brothers for several years now. They're all amazing."

"Yes, they are. It's annoying how perfect they are."

She arched a brow. "Perfect? I don't know about that. No one's perfect."

"Spoken like a woman who's dating a guy. That's when you truly learn how imperfect they really are, am I right?"

Adrienne had a point. "You might be right about that. How else do we learn that they leave underwear on the bathroom floor, or the cap off the toothpaste, or the toilet seat up?"

The guys came back, and Rafe put his arm around Carmen. "For the record, I never leave the toilet seat up. My mother would have slapped the back of my head for doing that."

"Same," Miguel said.

Mitchell nodded. "Without a doubt."

A man in his late thirties came over and shook hands with Miguel, Rafe and Adrienne.

"Hey, you made it, Rafe."

"Tommy Rodriguez, this is my friend Carmen Lewis," Rafe said. "Carmen, this is Tommy, who owns this place."

"Buena noches, Tommy. Estoy tan feliz de estar aquí."

Tommy grinned. "¿Tu hablas español?"

She nodded. "Sí."

"¿Y estás saliendo con este chico? Puedes hacerlo mejor."

Carmen laughed.

Rafe shook his head and looked at Tommy. "Estella dijo que se había casado contigo porque sabía que eras tan fea que nadie más lo haría."

Tommy laughed. "That's probably true. My wife, Estella, has a big heart for ugly men like me."

Carmen looked over at Rafe and realized she'd never heard him speak Spanish before. Of course he was Hispanic; she knew that. But somehow, hearing him speak their native language sounded so . . . sexy coming from him.

"You speak Spanish," she said to Rafe.

"Of course."

"I've never heard it."

"Spanish?"

She rolled her eyes. "Of course I've heard the language. Just not from you."

He shrugged. "I don't use it much. My adoptive parents aren't Hispanic, so I kind of lost touch with the language for a while."

"And then he met us," Miguel said. "Tommy and I forced it on him. He caught back up pretty fast."

Carmen smiled at him. "Bueno."

Tommy put his arm around her and led the group to the table. Carmen and Tommy engaged in a flurry of talk in Spanish, which suited Carmen just fine.

Mom and Abuela had immersed her in the language since birth. But her grandfather wasn't Hispanic and only spoke a handful of words and phrases.

She'd missed having someone to talk with in Spanish. There were a few Spanish-speaking nurses at work, but it wasn't the same as family, as someone you could converse with every day.

Tommy sat them at a large table in the back of the room. They were set apart from everyone else, which meant they could be as loud as they wanted to be.

"I'll bring margaritas and beer," Tommy said, as if that was expected and no one needed to order.

"Sounds great, Tommy," Rafe said with a smile. "Thanks."

Rafe leaned over and whispered in her ear. "La próxima vez que esté dentro de ti, te susurraré en español."

Her entire body flamed hot at the visual of him whispering to her in Spanish as he moved inside of her. She responded with, "Quiero eso," to let him know she wanted what he was offering.

He gave her a promising smile, and then the drinks arrived. She opted for a margarita, and Rafe had beer. Then they perused menus, and wow, Tommy's restaurant had quite the diverse selection. Everything from seafood to pasta to burgers to burritos and anything in between.

She decided on grilled chicken. Then salsa and chips and queso arrived, and she got to know everyone as they drank and talked.

She learned that Miguel and Adrienne were moving in together. They'd been secretly dating for almost a year, though according to what Rafe whispered to her, everyone at Station 6 had already known the two of them were together. It was only when things got serious that they had to go to their captain to admit they were a couple, and changes had to be made to their shifts.

"We put it off as long as we could," Miguel said. "We're a good team, and we hate splitting up."

Adrienne nodded. "I'm going to hate having a new partner, but we have to abide by the rules."

"Rules suck," Miguel said. "I mean, as far as us not working together."

"Hey, we're all going to miss having you on our shift," Mitchell said. "But we understand that the two of you had to be out in the open with your relationship."

"Yeah," said Tommy, who'd taken a break to come sit with them. "But we got tired of the two of you sneaking off to the supply closet."

Adrienne let out a shocked laugh. "We never once did that."

"Okay, maybe once," Miguel said.

"Miguel," Adrienne said, her cheeks turning pink.

"It happens all the time in the hospital," Carmen said.

Adrienne's brows rose. "Seriously? I thought that kind of thing only happened on TV shows."

Carmen shook her head. "Oh no. Trust me, it's not just on TV. Doctors and nurses getting it on in a private room, or two residents who are dating and working ridiculously long hours exercising a little stress relief together. Trust me, it happens more than you think."

"I am shocked," Rafe said.

Carmen laughed. "No, you're not."

"Well, I am," Adrienne said. "I don't know how anyone gets any work done. Or who avoids getting caught. It was difficult enough for Miguel and me to try and steal a kiss, let alone do . . .

anything else. Especially with all the Snoopy Sammies of Station 6 following our every move."

Mitchell laughed as he poured more beer for everyone. "That's because we knew what you two were up to, so we gave you a hard time."

"Thanks, Mitchell," Miguel said.

Mitchell winked. "Anytime, buddy."

"Okay, I won't miss you," Miguel said.

"Yes, you will. Who will laugh at your lame jokes?"

"The crew on second shift."

Carmen could see that these people got along very well. It reminded her of her team at the hospital. Having people you trusted and liked was so important when you had to work so closely together.

Dinner arrived, and it was delicious. The grilled chicken was bursting with flavor, and if she hadn't eaten so many chips with salsa, she probably would have cleaned her plate. But between the chips and the margaritas, she was only able to eat half.

Fortunately, Rafe seemed to have a hole in his stomach, because he ate all his food, then the rest of her plate, too.

"Hungry?" she asked.

He smiled. "Always."

She switched over to water after dinner, and she noticed Rafe did as well, which made her happy. Not that she was monitoring how much he was drinking, but since he was driving, she liked knowing he'd only had two beers and he'd spread those out over a few hours.

Tommy seemed to be in no hurry to get rid of them, even though they were monopolizing a pretty great space. In fact, a few other people arrived, and he made room for them as well. Kal showed up late with his date, a beautiful brunette named Yvette, and Jackson and Becks came in, too, as well as firefighter Ginger Davidson and her husband, Kyle.

"Did my grandpa text you earlier?" Carmen asked Kal when he arrived.

Kal shook his head. "No, but I called to check on him. He said he was going to bed and he didn't need anything."

That's what she liked so much about the Donovans. They were always so thoughtful. "Thanks for doing that, Kal."

"No problem."

Then it got loud, and everyone was talking over one another. Adrienne and Miguel left, and Mitchell took off not long after. She and Rafe moved over to where Jackson and Becks and Kal and Yvette were sitting. Ginger was deep in conversation with Yvette, and Kyle and Kal were talking about something having to do with some video game that was way over Carmen's head.

"Did you all eat dinner?" Carmen asked Becks.

Becks nodded. "Jackson and I grabbed a bite near the beach after I got off work. But we've eaten here before. Tommy and Estella make great food. What did you think of it?"

"It was amazing. If I hadn't stuffed myself full of chips and salsa and queso, I'd have probably licked the plate clean."

Becks laughed. "I know what you mean. It's both an awesome and terrible place to eat."

Carmen nodded. "I can see the pitfalls."

This was the most she had talked with Becks since they had their run-in during her grandfather's fall so long ago. The guys had all come over to help, and Becks had come as well. Carmen had been stressed to the max about Grandpa and had acted like a total bitch to Becks for no reason whatsoever. She'd apologized but still felt like it hadn't been enough. And since then, she'd been so embarrassed about how she'd acted that she'd been avoiding Becks.

"Listen, since we're here, I want to say again how sorry I am."

Becks frowned. "About what?"

"About how I acted that night when everyone came over to help take care of my grandfather."

"Oh, I never even think about that, Carmen. Don't worry. I've let it go. You should, too."

Becks was much more forgiving than Carmen would be. She held grudges. Which she knew was wrong, but she couldn't help it.

"Thanks. You're nicer than I am."

Becks laughed. "I doubt that. You apologized. I knew you were upset. It's no big deal."

"Well, thanks. I feel marginally better now."

"Good. We should be friends, since we live next door to each other. And we're dating brothers."

"That's true." Though she still wasn't sure about the whole dating thing. She intended to take that one step at a time.

"Rafe is a great guy," Becks said. "I've known him since I was a kid."

She'd almost forgotten that Becks was part of their homeless group.

"What was he like back then?"

Becks shifted to face her. "Just a typical kid. I remember him being quiet at first, until he got to know all of us. We arrived about the same time. He and I bonded as the new kids, hung out together a lot. We both liked to read, so he'd chill in my tent, and we'd read anything we could get our hands on. Newspapers, comics, any books that we could find."

Carmen's heart tugged at the education that was denied to them for so long. So many children took for granted what these kids didn't have available to them. "I'm sure it was hard."

"It was, but we managed. And then after he got comfortable, he was always active, running around, kicking soccer balls and playing football. It was like he had all this energy that he didn't know what to do with."

Carmen smiled. "I can see that, even now."

Becks nodded. "He does like to stay busy, doesn't he? Between his job at the firehouse and going to the gym and working with kids at the community center, I don't know when the guy finds time to sleep."

"Wait." Carmen frowned. "The community center?"

"Yeah. The one for at-risk youth. He volunteers his time there just to hang out with the kids. Talks to them about his upbringing. Where he started versus where he's at now. He wants them to know it doesn't matter where you begin. That it's important to have a goal, to see a future for yourself. I've gone there with him a few times to hang out and talk to them as well. But I really like listening to him tell his story to these kids. He's incredibly inspiring."

Huh. She had no idea.

She looked over at him, at the way he laughed and had a deep camaraderie with the people he worked with. It appeared that he had close ties with these people, that he considered them friends, maybe even family.

She understood that, considering his background. Being a firefighter, having that bond of brotherhood meant something deeper to him. Beyond the family he'd made with the Donovans, these were all his brothers and sisters.

She admired that. And appreciated that he thought enough of her to include her in this special circle of friends and family.

Obviously, she had a lot more to learn about Rafe Donovan.

CHAPTER 18

RAFE WAS MAKING BEDS IN THE SLEEPING QUARTERS when Kal came in and sat down on the mattress.

He shot a glare at his brother. "If you're gonna plant your ass where I'm working, you can help."

"Fine." Kal got up and helped Rafe change the sheets.

It got quiet, which meant Kal had something on his mind. Rafe waited, moving around the room in silence with his brother.

"I talked to Jackson about the job change."

They had moved to another bed. Rafe looked up, then around the sleeping quarters. They were alone. "Okay. What did he say?"

"That he wasn't surprised. He knew I was unhappy; he just didn't know why. So we talked it out."

"And?"

"He said he'd approve the transfer if I qualified for the class."

Rafe felt equal parts elation and anxiety. But he wasn't going to say that to Kal. So he grinned. "That's great. How did he feel about it?"

Kal shrugged. "He was fine with it, as long as I was happy. Then he asked if I was sure this was what I wanted."

Rafe straightened and looked across the bed at Kal. "Is it?"

"It's not like I just pulled the idea out of my ass. I've been thinking about it for a long time. The TRT has been on my radar for at least a year."

A year. Damn. "And you never told us about it?"

Kal shrugged. "I needed to be sure about it before I brought it up. Leaving you guys isn't exactly going to be easy. We've been a team practically our entire lives."

Rafe came around and sat on the bed. Kal sat next to him. "We're still gonna be a team, Kal. The three of us. Always. That'll never change, no matter where you go or what you do."

The thought of them being separated made him ache inside. But he knew it was coming. Maybe not with work, but someday, they'd all move on with their lives. He hadn't expected it to be right now. But he'd never do anything to hold Kal back from what he wanted.

"Yeah. Still, you know what I mean. We've always been together. Since we were kids."

"I know. It'll be tough not seeing you on Ladder 6 every shift."

"But you'll see me on the news doing amazing rescues."

Rafe rolled his eyes. "Whatever, wonder boy."

The alarm sounded. It was a full alarm, which meant both truck and ladder as well as EMTs, so they hustled into the bay and climbed into their gear.

The call was three miles away, so it didn't take long to get there. It was a three-car wreck right on the overpass, and it looked bad. One car was pushed against the edge of the bridge and appeared to be pretty smashed up. An SUV was crushed behind it, and a pickup was wedged in between the two of them.

"I'm concerned about structural here," Jackson said as they all climbed out. "We'll need to concentrate on stabilization."

"I'm calling the city." Captain Mathias had driven in with them and was already on his phone.

Jackson nodded. "We need to assess injuries first and see who we can extricate before this goes sideways."

It looked like a couple of the occupants had already climbed out of their vehicles.

"Hendricks. Find out who belongs where and see who might still be inside," Jackson said.

Hendricks nodded. "You got it."

"Brokaw, Smith, see if they need aid," Jackson instructed.

John Brokaw was starting his new shift replacing Miguel Acosta. He was two years into his EMT duties, which made Adrienne his senior.

The EMTs ran over to care for the victims who were free of the wreckage.

"The rest of you, let's get in there and see what we're dealing with," Jackson said.

Rafe went over to the compact car that was balancing precariously against the edge of the bridge. There was a teen girl at the wheel and a little boy who looked to be about eight or nine in the back seat. Both were conscious, both looked scared as hell.

"You okay?" he yelled, since all the windows were rolled up.

The girl gave a quick nod. "I am, but I think my brother's hurt. Can you get us out?"

She started to unbuckle her seat belt, but Rafe held up his hand.

"I need you both to stay right where you are and not move at all for now."

The look of fright in her eyes told him she understood what he was saying. She laid her hands in her lap. "Okay."

The little boy was huddled up in the back seat against the far door, crying. "My arm hurts. I want Mom."

"We're working as fast as we can to get you out of there," Rafe said. "Try not to move, okay?"

"Please hurry," the girl said, her voice trembling.

"What's your name?" he asked, simultaneously trying to see if he could extricate them without moving the vehicle any closer to the edge of the bridge.

"I'm Ariel. That's my brother, Andy. I don't know what happened. It wasn't my fault. Someone hit me from behind, and the next thing I knew, the car was smashed against the edge of the bridge."

"Are we gonna fall over?" Andy asked.

"No. We're not going to let that happen," Rafe said. "My whole team is working to get you two out of here. Your job is to relax and not move."

"We'll try, won't we, Andy?" Ariel said.

Andy gave a short nod.

Rafe took a deep breath. He needed to get the kids out of there. The back end of the vehicle was crunched against the truck. Side doors were smashed in, and the other side was caught against the edge of the bridge, so they couldn't open any doors. Rafe was concerned about making any movements to the car, since the barrier was already cracked. The slightest movement could compromise the barrier and send the vehicle right over the edge of the bridge.

Jackson came over. "Tell me what we've got."

"Two in the vehicle, seem to be no major injuries. Kid in the back is complaining that his arm hurts. Both are alert, though. We need to get them out."

Jackson nodded and signaled for Hendricks and Davidson, who came over.

"We have to stabilize the vehicle. Get the chains and some chocks so we can hold it in place."

"You got it," Hendricks said.

Jackson took a look at the occupants. "Rafe, you okay to stay with them for now?"

He nodded.

A couple more trucks had arrived to help with the scene, so

Rafe felt confident he was right where he needed to be—with these kids.

Hendricks and Davidson came over with the chains, hooked them to the undercarriage and attached them to the fire truck in case the car decided to slide. Rafe felt a lot more secure about the vehicle now.

He walked the kids step-by-step through extrication so they wouldn't be scared. Ariel seemed way more concerned about her little brother than herself. And Andy appeared to be focused on everything that Rafe and his team were doing.

"I wanna be a fireman when I grow up," Andy said.

"You do?"

"Yeah. I was a fireman for Halloween last year."

"Pretty cool, kid. It's a great job and an important one."

"Do you get to rescue people and stuff?"

Making sure Andy stayed occupied instead of worrying was important, so Rafe kept him talking. "Hey, I'm doing that right now, aren't I?"

Andy's eyes lit up. "Yeah. You're rescuing me and Ariel."

"Sure am. And you'll be able to tell all your friends at school about it."

"Cool."

Ariel laughed.

Once the other team moved the SUV out of the way, they had access to one side of the car. They finished stabilization, cut off the door and extricated the kids.

A quick assessment by the EMTs showed Andy had a broken arm and both kids had some cuts and scrapes, but it could have been much worse. They were both going to be taken to the ER for an evaluation, and Ariel was able to call her parents, who were going to meet them at the hospital.

"Will you come with us?" Andy asked Rafe as the EMTs prepped to load him into the ambulance.

The kid was obviously scared to death.

Rafe looked at Jackson, who nodded. "Go ahead. We'll take care of things here, and you can ride back with the ambo crew."

"Thanks." He was relieved to be able to ride with the kids. Though Andy's injuries appeared to be minor, he wanted to be sure.

They arrived at the hospital and were taken into the ER. Carmen was there, and she immediately took charge, assigning Ariel and Andy to rooms next to each other. The kids' parents had arrived and looked very worried.

Rafe gave the parents an update on what had happened with the accident. He wasn't a police officer, but he gave them his take on the accident scene.

"It appears one of the vehicles slammed into the back of Ariel's car, shoving her into the guardrail at the bridge."

Ariel's mother, Glenda, raised her hand to her throat. "Oh my God. We're so lucky she didn't go over."

He didn't tell her just how close it had come to that. "She was so brave and really worked hard to keep Andy calm."

"She's a good kid," Ray, Ariel's father, said, sliding his hand through his hair. "But damn, I think I just got fifteen new gray hairs."

"Don't worry," Rafe said. "They're both going to be fine."

He went in to see Ariel, who was busily texting on her phone. She looked up and smiled. "Hi, Firefighter Donovan. Thanks again for hanging out with us."

"Telling all your friends about your big day?"

He saw her blush. "I am. Hey, would you take a selfie with me?"

"Sure." He leaned over and smiled while she snapped a pic.

"Awesome. Thanks."

"You're welcome. You did good today. You were very brave."

"Thanks. I was totally scared out of my mind. I don't know if I'll ever want to drive again."

"You will. The next time you and your friends want to go somewhere, you won't even think about it."

"You think?"

"Yeah. It wasn't like you did anything wrong. It was just . . . bad timing. And those things are rare. So don't let it spook you, okay?"

She nodded. "Okay. Thanks again for saving our lives."

He felt a pang in his stomach. "You're welcome. Drive safe."

"Oh, trust me, I will."

He stepped into Andy's room. Carmen was in there checking Andy's vitals. She gave Rafe a brief smile but then put her professional one back on for Andy's parents.

"The doctor will be in to talk to you shortly, but they're going to set the break and put a temporary cast on until the swelling goes down, then he can see the orthopedic surgeon for a more permanent cast in about a week."

Carmen leveled a brilliant smile on Andy. "And you, young man, get to choose whatever you want to eat from the menu."

Andy's eyes widened. "Really? I can have chocolate ice cream if I want it?"

Carmen looked over at Glenda and Ray. Glenda nodded. "I'd say you've earned some chocolate ice cream."

"Awesome," Andy said, smiling a wide gap-toothed grin.

"If I'd known that was all I had to do to earn chocolate ice cream, I'd get stuck against a bridge, too," Rafe said.

"I don't know, Mr. Donovan," Andy said. "It's pretty scary."

Rafe laughed. "You're right about that. I was scared, too."

"You were?"

"Sure I was. I didn't want anything to happen to you. You're a future firefighter, you know?"

"That's right. I am. I'm gonna be a fireman someday, Dad."

Ray looked over at Rafe and smiled. "So you've told me. I couldn't think of anything better for you, Andy."

"I'll leave you all alone. It was nice meeting both of you." Rafe shook hands with Ray and Glenda, then went over to Andy and laid his hand on the kid's head. "Be good."

"I'm always good."

Ray coughed and Rafe grinned.

He left the room, and Carmen followed him out.

"Big day so far, I see," she said as he went with her to the main desk.

"Yeah. I rode in the ambo with the kids to make sure they were all right."

She was charting, and she lifted her gaze to his. "That's sweet. They're good kids."

"They are. It was a rough wreck, and the way they were pushed up against the guardrail . . ."

She laid her hand over his. "You were worried."

"Like you wouldn't believe. It could have gone badly."

She squeezed his hand. "But it didn't. You saved their lives."

"The whole team did. I just needed to be here to . . . I don't know. Follow up. Make sure they were really okay."

She nodded. "Sometimes certain cases grab hold of us, hit us in the heart. We can't help it."

"Yeah." He shifted his gaze at the rooms where Ariel and Andy were. Andy was chatting with his dad, and Ariel was talking to her mother. They appeared to be a good family. He was glad to have played a part in reuniting them today.

Carmen looked at her watch. "I'm due for a lunch break. Do you have some time to grab a bite with me or do you need to go?"

"I have time. My EMTs got another call, so my ride back to the station left me. I'm kind of on my own for the moment, unless the truck gets a call and they have to swing by and pick me up."

"Great. I'll meet you in the cafeteria in five."

"Okay."

He radioed Jackson that he was still in the hospital and would take his lunch with Carmen. Jackson said that was fine and that they were going to go on a scheduled training run after lunch, so they'd swing by in about an hour to pick him up unless they got a call.

He headed down to the cafeteria. Since it was after one, the normal hospital lunch crush had mostly cleared out, which suited him just fine. He waited at the entrance for Carmen. His heart did a lurch, as it always did whenever he laid eyes on her. She was wearing her scrubs, which were dark blue and had pockets, and she wore purple tennis shoes. Her hair was pulled back into a high ponytail, and she looked freakin' sexy as hell. And, sure, every other person in the place dressed similarly, but to Rafe, she was the only one he saw.

She walked through the doorway and came up beside him.

"Did I mention how gorgeous you are today?"

She snorted out a laugh. "You're funny."

"Dead serious. Totally hot."

She shook her head. "No, you look hot. And people are staring at you."

He glanced around and saw he was getting some looks, especially from women. He hadn't even noticed. Of course he was in uniform, though he'd left his turnout gear in the truck. He shrugged. "I've only got eyes for you, babe."

"Good to know. Also, I'm having a chicken salad sandwich and some chips."

He grinned at how she blew off his compliment. "Sounds great to me."

They loaded up their trays, and Rafe added a bowl of fruit and a candy bar. Carmen had an employee card on her lanyard, so she swiped for both of them.

"Thanks for lunch," he said.

"My pleasure. Thanks for having lunch with me."

They found a table and sat. Rafe dived into his sandwich, then took a couple of strong gulps of his ice water. He'd developed a thirst working that scene. It was only after his second cup that he could finally concentrate on his sandwich.

Carmen watched. "A little dry in the throat?"

"We focus when we're working a scene, and being fully geared up at the end of July makes it hot as fuck out there."

"Don't you hydrate while you're there?"

He nodded. "Yeah. I emptied my water canister on scene."

She shook her head, then smiled. "Then drink up, dude. I have enough people passing out on me in the ER. I don't need to add you to the list."

"Aww, you care. That's sweet."

"Of course I care. All my treatment rooms are full today. Do you think I want to deal with having to hydrate you via IV in my hallway? It'll look bad for my stats."

He laughed. "I'll be sure to refill my ice water so I don't disgrace your department."

"That's thoughtful of you." She sipped her soda and slanted a snarky smile at him.

When they finished, they walked out of the cafeteria and headed toward the elevators.

They got on the elevator by themselves, and Rafe looked all around.

Carmen frowned. "Checking for safety violations?"

"No. I was looking for cameras."

"As far as I know there aren't any. Why?"

He turned and backed her against the wall of the elevator, his gaze heated and direct, wanting to make sure she knew his intent. "Because I want to kiss you."

To her credit, she didn't shove him away. "You think this is like television, and no one will interrupt us?"

"I have no idea what you're talking about. But we're talking and not kissing."

Now she did push him away and looked at her watch. Then she selected the button for floor seven. The elevator doors opened on the main floor where the ER was located, then closed again.

He gave her a questioning look.

"Just go with it," she said.

"Hey, I'm with you on this ride. Wherever you go, I go."

The doors opened again, and he peeked his head out. The entire floor was vacant. There was an obvious construction site to the right, everything covered by plastic sheeting. But no one appeared to be working up here today. And there were empty, darkened rooms to the left.

She grabbed his hand. "Come on."

She led him into one of the vacant rooms and closed the door. "I need to be back on the floor in ten minutes."

He grinned and approached her, lifting the hem of her scrub shirt. "I can do ten minutes."

"I was just thinking we could kiss."

"Yeah? I was thinking of a lot more than that." His gaze shifted to the bed. It was unmade, but it would do.

She laughed. "I don't know about you, but I don't have any condoms on me. I'm on the pill, but . . ."

He nibbled her neck as he walked her backward toward the bed. "We can do a lot of fun things besides fucking, Carmen."

"Oh, really? Care to elaborate?"

"Yeah." He slid his hands in her hair and put his mouth on hers.

She met his kiss with a pent-up passion. They didn't have a lot of time for slow kissing, for tasting and teasing, but he wanted her to know how much he'd been thinking about her. He took one of those sacred few minutes to thoroughly taste her lips, to delve his tongue inside her mouth and get her as riled up as he felt. And when she moaned against his lips, he knew she felt it, too.

He massaged her breasts through her scrub top and bra, wishing he could take the time to get her naked, to suck on her nipples until she was writhing underneath him. But since he didn't, he slid his hand inside her pants and panties to cup her sex. She moaned and arched against his hand, letting him freely stroke her softness until she whimpered, driving against him until he was the one throbbing.

He released her mouth and positioned her on the bed so her legs dangled over. He leaned over her and smiled while he undid the drawstrings of her scrubs, then drew them down her legs. He kissed her belly, her hips, and pulled her underwear down her legs, letting it dangle at her ankles.

She was panting, and the only word she whispered was, "Hurry."

He spread her legs as much as he could, cupped her butt cheeks in his hands and put his mouth on her. He flicked his tongue all around her sex and clit, drunk on the sweet scent of her.

"Ohhh, yes," she said, lifting her hips to give him access.

He was so hard he ached to be inside of her. But this was for Carmen, and he was going to enjoy the hell out of it. She was sweet and salty, and he loved being this close to her, tasting her heat and feeling her body move against him with wild abandon. That he could give her this pleasure, even briefly, was such a damn turn-on his balls throbbed with it.

When he felt her body tighten, he pressed harder with his tongue around her clit.

"Oh yes, that's it," she said.

She released, reaching out for him. He grasped her hand, and she squeezed his hand as she shuddered through her orgasm.

He gave her a minute to come down from her climax, then licked her thigh, kissed her hip and helped her get her clothes back on.

Carmen took in a deep breath, her eyes still gleaming with

sparkling desire as she smiled at him. She cupped his face and kissed him. "That was amazing. You're amazing."

He grinned. "Glad you think so."

She reached down to rub her hand back and forth over his hard cock. "Now it's your turn."

"I know you need to go back."

She glanced at her watch, then undid the zipper of his pants. "I've got a few minutes."

He cupped her butt and drew her against him. "I'm so hard right now it won't take more than that."

She maneuvered him so he leaned against the bed, then crouched down and drew his pants and boxer briefs down. His cock jutted out, hard and aching. She swirled her hand around the tip, rubbing her thumb over the pre-come that spilled there. Watching Carmen on her knees in front of him made his balls tighten. And when she leaned forward and flicked her tongue out to tease his cockhead, he swore he could lose it right there.

But oh no. He wanted the good stuff. He wanted her sweet, hot mouth on his cock.

And when her lips surrounded him and she drew him into her mouth, he felt like he might die from the agonizing suction, the heat and wetness of her lips and tongue. And oh, fuck, then she took him fully into her mouth and his cockhead hit the back of her throat and he was going to lose it right now.

Hold on, man. This felt too damn good, and he needed just a little longer.

But Carmen cupped his balls and gave them a gentle massage, and that was all it took.

"Oh, fuck, yeah. That's gonna make me come."

She grasped the base of his cock and pumped, taking his cock deep while she used her mouth to squeeze him like a vise. That was all he could handle. He uttered a guttural groan as he lost it, spurting come into her mouth. She took it all, and damn if she didn't make him sweat as he watched her throat work as she swallowed.

After he was empty, he panted hard, holding on to the bed rail for support. Sweat pooled at his lower back, and he could sure use a few minutes to recover. But he knew time was at a premium for Carmen, so he pulled her to stand and kissed her.

"That was fun," she said, licking his lips. "And I know it's rude as hell to come and go, but I really do have to go."

He rested his forehead against hers. "I know you do."

They both dashed into the bathroom to clean up. Carmen ran her fingers through her hair, then refixed her hair into a ponytail and popped a breath mint, handing one to Rafe.

"Thanks," he said. "Are you off tomorrow?"

She shook her head. "Not until Wednesday. Then I have two days off in a row."

"I have Kelly days coming up, which means I get a few extra days off shift. Maybe we can take a little trip together."

She nodded. "We'll see what we can work out. I have my grandpa to consider."

"Oh, right."

"I'll see what I can do, okay?"

"Sure."

They walked to the elevator, and she pushed the button. When it opened, she selected the main floor. He stood next to her, and what he really wanted was to pull her in his arms to kiss her, but the doors opened on the fifth floor, and a few people got on.

Too bad. He couldn't seem to get enough of her.

As the elevator continued to fill with people, they leaned against the back wall, and she slanted a knowing smile at him.

They got out on the main floor, and she stopped in front of him.

"I'll text you," he said.

She nodded, looked around and reached her fingers out to his. That briefest touch of their fingertips was a tease, but it was all they were going to have.

For now.

"See you later," she said.

"Okay. Bye, Carmen."

He watched her walk away, already aching for her.

Damn, he had it bad for her. And that brief touch was going to have to hold him until Wednesday.

CHAPTER 19

"YOU'RE SURE YOU'LL BE OKAY?"

Carmen's grandfather gave her that look, the one he always gave her when he thought she was treating him like a child.

"We've had this conversation before."

"No, we haven't. I haven't left you overnight before."

Again, that steely stare, and she knew she'd pushed him too hard.

"I fend for myself just fine when you're at work, child. I think I can handle an overnight with a friend helping me out. What? You don't trust Theo to help me if I need it?"

"It's not that. It's just . . ." She should shut up. She smiled. "You'll be just fine."

Carmen hadn't been separated from her grandfather since she'd moved in four years ago. So leaving him for a couple of days was going to be extremely difficult. She knew Grandpa had made great improvements with his therapy and was able to do many more things for himself, but he was continually working on that weakness on one side.

Still, he was out of the wheelchair most days now and using

his walker and his cane. He made his way over and stopped in front of her, then looked down at her. "I'm more capable than you give me credit for. I never miss a therapy appointment, and I'm getting a lot stronger. So you need to stop treating me like an invalid, like I can't do a damn thing for myself."

There was more to this than just taking a trip, than just her questioning his ability to care for himself. She pulled a kitchen chair out and motioned for him to sit in the one next to hers. When he did, she asked, "What's really going on?"

He lifted his chin. "Nothing's going on that I can't handle myself."

"Grandpa. Talk to me."

"It's stupid."

Okay, so there was something else. She just had to be patient about it, because pushing him too hard would make him resistant to talking to her. "Nothing about you or how you feel is stupid. And we've always been able to talk about anything."

She waited, because she knew that sometimes he had to let things mull around in his head for a bit before he was willing to share with her. So she sipped on her ice water and scrolled through her phone.

"There was this lady."

Her head shot up. A woman? He'd never mentioned dating anyone.

"Okay," she said, not wanting to lead the conversation. He'd get to it when he got to it.

"We met at bingo. She thought I was too slow stamping my card, so she helped me out. We met several months ago. Her name is Felice. She's beautiful. She's a widow, too. Same age as me. She has one son who lives in Texas, and two grandchildren.

"So we started meeting up regular at bingo. We got along well. We've had dinner a few times. I've been to her house to play cards."

Grandpa had been busy when she hadn't been looking.

"We were having a good time, and then I invited her over here for dinner. She said she was going to Texas to see her son last week and we'd talk about plans when she got back. But after she got back last week, she said she didn't think we should see each other anymore."

Carmen frowned. "Did she give you a reason?"

He shook his head. "I didn't ask."

"So you just said okay and that was it? You both went your separate ways?"

"I guess so."

Something wasn't right about this. "Maybe it had something to do with her visit with her son. How long ago did her husband die?"

"Couple of years ago."

Hmm. "Maybe she told her son about you, and her son was upset about her dating someone. And maybe that made her upset, which is why she pulled away from you."

"You think so?"

Carmen shrugged. "I don't know, Grandpa. But if you just walk away without asking her, you'll never know, will you? You should at least ask her for a reason. And then let her know you still like her. If nothing else, you two could still be friends."

His mood seemed to brighten. "You're right. I shouldn't have just left things the way they were. I'm kind of rusty at this."

Carmen could relate to the rusty part. "We both are. But if you want someone in your life, you have to put yourself out there. You have to risk being hurt."

"Maybe you should listen to your own advice," he said.

She leaned back. "What? I'm dating."

"And at the same time trying to use me as an excuse for not taking a short vacation with Rafe."

She started to object, then thought about it for a minute. Was that what she'd been doing? Was she purposely using her grandfather as a reason for not having a life all this time? For not getting out there after her divorce? Rafe had said much the same thing to her, and she'd acted insulted. But now that her grandpa had said it, she felt terrible.

Okay, but she was dating now. She and Rafe were having fun together. They were taking a trip together.

Maybe she should take her own advice and put herself out there, stop being so afraid. It wasn't like she was going to fall in love. She and Rafe were both just out for some fun. And oh, that man was some fun.

"Fine. I'm going. And you're going to talk to Felice. Deal?" She held out her hand.

Her grandpa shook it. "Deal. And I'm going to be all right. Theo will be here with me. We're adult, capable men. I have my phone with your number. Theo has your phone number. I promise if there's a problem, we'll call you."

She got up and leaned over to kiss his cheek. "Thank you."

Now she could pack and get ready to leave without worrying about him. She and Rafe were driving down to Miami today. Rafe had booked them a room at a hotel on the beach. They'd have dinner, spend the night and be back by tomorrow night.

It would be a short trip, but since Carmen didn't get away much—or ever, for that matter—she was so looking forward to it. She packed a small bag with the things she needed and took a shower, put on a pair of red shorts and a cream sleeveless shirt and slid into her sandals. She grabbed her sunglasses, and by the time she came out of her room, Rafe had arrived and was sitting in the kitchen talking to her grandfather.

She took a moment to admire his darkly tanned legs. He wore navy blue board shorts and a gray sleeveless shirt that showed off his muscled arms. His sunglasses were propped on his head, pushing back his thick, dark hair.

Just looking at him made her body tingle all over. Maybe it was the anticipation of all that alone time they were going to have together. Until now, it had been in short supply. They were going to have almost two days. She couldn't wait.

She walked into the kitchen. "Hey."

Rafe looked up and laid a dazzling smile on her. He stood. "Hi. You look nice."

"So do you."

He took the bag from her hand. "Are you ready to go?"

She nodded, then leaned over to give her grandfather a hug. "Call me if you need anything?"

"I won't need anything. Go and have some fun."

"I will. Te amo, Abuelo."

"Te amo, bebita."

Rafe took her hand in his, and she saw the warm smile spread across her grandfather's lips. They headed outside, and Rafe tucked her bag into the back seat of his truck. Then he grasped her around the waist and brushed his lips across hers.

"I'm looking forward to having you to myself for a couple of days," he said.

Her body flushed with heat. She pressed her hands to his chest. "Me, too."

She climbed into the truck and buckled her seat belt, unable to quell the burst of excitement.

She was going on an adventure with a very hot man at her side.

RAFE HADN'T BEEN TO MIAMI SINCE HE AND HIS BROTHERS had taken a weekend trip several years ago. Not that much had changed. It was livelier and a lot more crowded than Ft. Lauderdale. He liked the beaches here, and the nightlife. Plus, down here he could be totally alone with Carmen. And hopefully, she could take some time to relax.

She seemed to have unwound some on the drive down. He could tell from her body language, the way she leaned back, rolled into the tunes on the radio and grooved in her seat. They'd talked some, Carmen had sung a little, and it had actually been a pretty mellow drive. Just the way he'd wanted it to go. He needed her to de-stress so she could get into the time off.

"Ready for some fun?" he asked as he exited the highway.

She turned to him and smiled. "More than you know."

He wasn't yet convinced she was all-in on this excursion, but he planned to make it relaxing and entertaining for her.

"Or we could just check in to the hotel and you can nap for twenty-four hours or so."

She laughed. "I'm sorry I was so quiet. I've been in my head."

"Second thoughts about this trip?"

"No. My grandpa got dumped by his girlfriend, so I'm worried about him."

Rafe took a right-hand turn, then frowned at her. "I didn't even know he had a girlfriend."

"Neither did I. But I guess they met at bingo and have been hanging out for a few months. She's only been a widow for a couple of years, and she went to visit her son in Texas recently. I get the feeling her son doesn't approve of her dating."

"Huh. I imagine that can be tough on kids who lose a parent."

"I'm sure it is. I just hate to see Grandpa so upset about it. It's clear he really likes this woman."

"Did you discuss it with him?"

"Yes. I told him to talk to her, to let her know how he feels about her."

He nodded. "Good advice."

He pulled up in front of the hotel and turned off the engine.

Carmen turned to him. "Seriously? This is right on the ocean. And fancy." Carmen had expected they'd stay a couple of blocks off the beach. Not a place like this. She could hear the sound of the ocean, and all that tension she'd held inside started to melt.

He crooked a smile. "You deserve fancy."

"But—"

Before she could argue further, he got out of the car and came around to her side to let her out.

"Fancy and expensive, Rafe."

He held out his hand, and she slid out. "You deserve fancy and expensive. And I hardly ever spend my money on anything fancy and expensive. Besides, it's only one night."

She sighed and looked up at the COMO Metropolitan. "Art deco. Gorgeous."

"Yeah, I thought you might like this one." He gave his keys to the valet and grabbed their bags.

The interior was white and bright with some old-world charm. It was lovely, with modern touches that made her curious about this place and the entire area.

He gave his name and his credit card at the front desk, then they headed up to their room.

The room was bright and open—and it was a suite, with a living room and a separate bedroom. The walls were a calming seafoam green, and she couldn't get over the incredible ocean-front views. She wandered into the bathroom, gaping at the deep soaker tub and separate huge shower.

She walked back out and looked at Rafe. "That's it. I'm never leaving."

Rafe shrugged. "Okay, but we might have to get different jobs. Like something illegal that pays well so we can afford this room every day."

She looked around the room again, then out the oversize windows that showcased the beautiful Atlantic Ocean. "Worth it."

"Come on," he said with a laugh. "Let's unpack and go explore."

She was on board for that. Though she was definitely making a plan to have a bath in that soaker tub later.

They left the hotel and walked down Collins Avenue, taking in the views of several art deco buildings.

"The architecture on these buildings is phenomenal," she said as they strolled along. "The white guardrails and porthole windows on the hotel make it look like a ship. How cool is that?"

He grasped her hand. "I had no idea you were so interested in architecture."

"I don't know that I am. I'm just in love with the art deco design. I love everything about the décor from that time period. When I'm restoring old furniture and I can find an old art deco piece? I'm in heaven."

"The buildings are nice," he said as they walked along. "Not sure I'm all-in for pinks or peaches. They're pretty, but they don't seem to hold my attention as much as the black and white."

She nodded, loving that he was engaging with her rather than just along for the walk. "I agree. I'm much more engaged by the stronger tones of black and white, or silver and cream colors. Those pull my attention more than the muted tones."

They walked the entire route, discussing various aspects of the buildings, then stopped for lunch. They both ordered lobster rolls and had beers to wash them down.

After they ate, they walked back to their hotel and changed into their swimsuits. The day was hot, and the walk had been long, so Carmen was looking forward to lounging by the water.

When they reached the lobby, Rafe looked at her. "Pool or ocean?"

No contest. "Ocean."

He grinned. "My thoughts exactly."

Sure, the pool would be nice and much more private, but when you had an entire ocean in front of you to play in, why would you pass that up?

Rafe rented a cabana for them so they could have shade if they wanted it. Carmen pulled off her cover-up, then fished in her tote bag for the sunscreen. She sprayed it on Rafe's back, happily rubbing the sunscreen onto his muscled back and shoulders. Then, even though he could obviously do it himself, she sprayed it on his smooth chest and rubbed it in.

"That feels good." He gave her a hot look. "I like your hands on me."

"I like my hands on you, too."

"Too bad we're outside and not up in our room. I'd put my hands all over you."

She sighed. "Yeah, too bad."

She turned and lifted her hair up so he could put the sunscreen on her back and shoulders. It definitely took him a while to get the spray rubbed in. Not that she minded in the least.

They settled in on their chairs, and Carmen pulled out the book she'd started the other night. She read for a while, then a hotel waitress came over to see if they wanted drinks.

"I'll take a mojito," she said.

Rafe nodded. "Same."

She went back to her book, a romantic suspense that she was really enjoying a lot. Their server brought their drinks and set them on the table in their cabana. Carmen took a sip. It was tart and sweet and absolutely decadent.

"Feeling a little more relaxed?" Rafe asked.

"Definitely more relaxed. Thank you for suggesting this getaway. If I was at home, I'd be doing laundry and scrubbing toilets."

"This is a little more fun than scrubbing toilets."

She laughed and took another sip of her drink, dropped her book into her bag and settled back in her chair. Next thing she knew, she was being jolted awake by the sounds of squealing children. She had no idea how long she'd been asleep. She reached over for her drink, realizing it was empty. Had she finished it, or had Rafe done that? She glanced over and saw that he was lying back in his chair. Was he sleeping? His dark sunglasses covered his eyes, so she didn't know.

"Rafe. Are you awake?"

"Yeah. Just chillin'."

Sweat pooled between her breasts and down her back, so she was ready to cool down.

"How about a dip in the water?"

He sat up and straddled the chair. "Let's go."

She loved how easygoing he was, how he was always game for anything. He never once balked or said he didn't want to do something. Was he always this easy, or was he just trying to please her?

Maybe she shouldn't be so suspicious. He had never once acted like Tod. He wasn't anything like Tod, so she should stop comparing him to her ex-husband and start treating Rafe like . . . Rafe.

And just have some fun with a hot, sexy, totally nice guy.

WATCHING CARMEN SPLASH AROUND IN THE OCEAN MADE Rafe wish he had a camera on him. She wore a skimpy coral bikini that showed off every inch of her beautiful golden skin, including the globes of her fabulous ass.

She dove into the water and came up, sweeping her hair away from her face and laughing as the waves knocked her back. She was strong, though, and held her own against the force of the ocean. Rafe swam over to her and pulled her into his arms. She wrapped her legs around his waist and locked her ankles around his back.

"This feels great," she said. "I was getting hot."

"You are hot."

She laughed and tilted her head back. He let go of her, though her legs stayed wrapped around him. This way she could float in the water without being swept away. He let her drift that way for a while as he dug his feet in the sandy bottom and held on, making sure they both didn't get dumped by a wave.

When she let go of his back and swam off, he followed. They

made their way to shore and sat at the water's edge, the waves lapping at their feet.

She tilted her head and looked at him. "Are you bored?"

"Bored? No. Why?"

"We're doing nothing. You strike me as the kind of guy who always has to be doing something."

"I do?" He laughed. "I'm fine with kicking back. You can't run all the time. Eventually, you'll crash."

"So true." She pulled her knees to her chest and rested her chin on her knees, staring out over the water. "I go all the time. At work, at home. I never take time to just . . . do nothing. I haven't taken a vacation in . . . God, I don't know when the last time was I took a trip or got away."

Now he was even more glad he'd suggested this. She was wound up tight and needed the downtime. "Then sitting here just watching the water is exactly what you need, isn't it?"

"I guess it is." She leaned against him. "Thanks for bringing me here."

"Thanks for agreeing to come. I know it wasn't easy for you."

She sighed. "I worry too much about my grandpa. He even said that to me."

"He told me that while you were getting ready this morning."

She straightened and gave him a surprised look. "He did? What did he say?"

"You really want me to tell you?" He probably shouldn't. She was relaxed, and he wanted her to stay that way.

"Yes, I want you to tell me."

"He said you spend too much time taking care of him and not enough time taking care of yourself. That you've essentially given up your personal life to look after him, so you're spending twenty-four hours a day being a nurse, and it pisses him off. He wants you to be his granddaughter, not his caretaker."

"Ouch. I didn't expect that." She grimaced.

"He seemed to have some pretty strong opinions about the matter."

"Clearly. I guess I need to sit down with him and talk about those opinions."

"He really is stronger than you think he is, Carmen."

"Maybe he is. Maybe I was so devastated when he had his stroke that I've overlooked the strides he's taken in his recovery. But then he'll backslide and have some medical crisis and I'll fall apart all over again."

He put his arm around her and tugged her close. "I understand what he means to you."

"He's everything. He's all I have left of family."

"Yeah, but at the same time he's an adult man who had a medical crisis. And he's done everything he can to recover from his stroke. He's gotten stronger, he goes to therapy, he's even trying to date."

She shifted to face him. "And you think I'm holding him back."

"I didn't say that."

She paused, studying him. "But you think that I am."

"It's not my business to interfere in your relationship with your grandfather, Carmen."

"I'm asking for your opinion based on your observations."

He wasn't sure this was the best conversation to get into when they were supposed to be relaxing and having fun. But he'd opened this can, so he was going to have to spoon out the contents.

"I think you hold him back. That you don't let him do enough for himself. That you might be hindering his recovery."

Her lips clamped tightly together, she turned and faced the water. She didn't say anything for a long time, and he knew he'd pissed her off.

Way to go, Rafe. When would he learn to keep his thoughts to himself on delicate subjects like this?

Though, he'd told Carmen that he was always honest. Didn't he owe it to her to be honest about this, too?

"You're right," she finally said, digging her toes into the wet sand, her gaze focused on the horizon. "I'm too close to my grandfather. I'm afraid he'll have another stroke, or fall and break something, so I smother him with my attention and my medical knowledge to the point that I'm probably driving him crazy—and in doing so, I'm likely hampering his recovery."

She finally shifted to face him. "Thank you for being honest with me."

Okay, so she wasn't mad. He picked up one of her hands and covered it with both of his. "I think you love your grandfather and you'd do anything to keep him safe. That's not a bad thing. But yeah, you're probably too close to the situation and you don't see that maybe you've been keeping him a little too safe."

"So what do you suggest?"

"Back off a little? Let him handle things on his own, like bathing and cooking and getting himself to bed. My guess is if there are some things he's uncomfortable doing on his own, he'll ask you to help him. But giving him some space will go a long way toward making him feel more independent and confident in his abilities."

She nodded. "You're right. I'll start doing that."

"I think you'll notice a change in him right away, too."

"I hope so." She leaned forward and gave him a soft kiss. "Thank you."

"Anytime." He got up and hauled her up to stand. "Now, let's go clean up and have dinner and some fun tonight."

She hit him with a bright smile. "I'm so ready for that."

So was he. He intended to make sure he rocked her socks off tonight.

And he wasn't just talking about dancing.

CHAPTER 20

AFTER SPENDING TIME IN THE SUN TODAY, CARMEN WAS exhausted. They went up to their room and took a shower together, enjoying each other's bodies at length in the oversize stall. After Rafe gave her an explosive orgasm that left her weak-kneed and shaking, she lay down on the bed and ended up passing right out. When she woke, she felt disoriented, and it took her a minute to remember she was in this glorious room with the spectacular view. Rafe was snoozing next to her, so she rolled to her side and enjoyed the other beautiful view.

Awake, he was gorgeous. Asleep, he was equally devastating, his features relaxed, his long, dark lashes resting against his cheeks and his lips slightly parted. His breathing was slow and even. And, bonus—he didn't snore. What more could a woman want in a guy?

She smiled at that and leaned in to brush a kiss against his brow. He blinked and opened his eyes, his lips curving. He didn't wake up grumpy, either, another point in his favor. Instead, he drew her close to his body, making her wish they could just stay in tonight.

"You fell asleep," he said, smoothing his hand over her hip.

"You fell asleep, too."

"I laid down on the bed to be close to you. And then I was gone. You wore me out."

She scraped a nail across his jaw. "Poor baby. If you don't have the energy to go out tonight, we could order room service."

Before she knew what was happening, he'd grabbed her and rolled her on top of him, his hands roaming down her back to cup her buttocks.

"I've got plenty of energy."

She felt the hardness of his cock underneath her, sparking her own renewed energy. She dragged her clit against his firm flesh.

"Fuck yeah, babe," he said, grasping her hips to roll her back and forth across his cock.

Despite their earlier fun in the shower, she was ready, and now. But she wanted him inside of her when she came. She slid off of him to grab a condom from the box on the nightstand, opened the package and slowly rolled the condom on his cock, enjoying the heated look in his eyes.

"Get on me," he said, his voice low and loaded with need.

She straddled him, and he held on to her hips while she slowly slid down his shaft, her pussy pulsing as he filled her. And then she stilled and felt her body grip him tight. She waited out those spasms that could send her over. She felt him throb, too, and she leaned forward, bracing her hands on his chest, and lifted, watching his chest rise and fall with the effort it took him not to let go.

"Do you feel that?" he asked, and she knew he meant the way their bodies were so in tune with each other, the way whenever she quivered, he pulsed.

"Yes. I think my pussy was made for your cock."

He sucked in a breath and drove into her. "You feel right to me. Whenever I'm inside of you, it's like I was made for you."

The words he said were powerful, evoking emotions she wasn't ready to face just yet. So instead, she focused on the physical, lying flat to grind against him, lifting and falling over and over until she burst into a million pleasure stars. She dug her nails into Rafe's shoulders and cried out with her orgasm. He thrust deeply, then shuddered, taking her mouth in a blistering kiss that made them moan against each other's lips as she rode out a massive wave that threatened to consume her.

She lay there on top of him, unable to move, barely able to catch her breath. Rafe smoothed his hands over her back, and she would have been content to stay like that all night.

"I made dinner reservations," Rafe finally said.

"Uh-huh. Sure. I don't think I can move."

"Okay. I'm good like this."

She smiled. He would be fine if they didn't go out, because that was Rafe's personality. He was easygoing and happy to do whatever she wanted to do. But he'd gone to all this trouble to bring her down here and show her a good time. So she intended to drag her ass out of bed. She slid off him and went into the bathroom. He followed behind her, and they cleaned up and got dressed.

Carmen was glad she packed a nice dress, because Rafe told her they were going dancing after they had dinner tonight.

"Where are we dancing?" she asked as she finished her makeup in the bathroom while he brushed his teeth.

He spit out toothpaste and rinsed his mouth. "It's a surprise."

"Fun." She put on her short red dress that flared a couple of inches above the knee and gave her room to move around. Then she added gold heels.

Rafe had already gotten dressed and was waiting in the living area when she walked out. He was dressed in black slacks and a white button-down shirt. She realized she'd never seen him so dressed up. He looked damn fine.

When he saw her, his gaze roamed over her appreciatively.

"You look amazing," he said. "That dress, Carmen. You are stunning."

She couldn't help but smile. "Thank you."

He drove them to the Mandarin Oriental hotel and let the valet park the truck. They went inside the beautifully ornate hotel, then took the elevator to the restaurant, La Mar.

"I've heard of this place," she said. "Impressive."

He tucked her hand in the crook of his arm and smiled down at her.

The view of Biscayne Bay and the Miami skyline was stunning. Rafe gave his name, and they were seated right away at a gorgeous table overlooking the water. Fortunately, there was a nice cloud cover because the sun hadn't set quite yet, but it was working its way down, and it was a spectacular array of orange and red.

Their server—Alejandro—handed them their menus. They both perused the wine list and settled on a bottle of Gewürztraminer.

Carmen looked out over the water, at the lights coming up over the city now that the sun had set.

"So this is how the rich people live."

Rafe laughed. "I don't think we're rich just because we're having dinner here."

"I don't know. I don't generally come to Miami to have dinner at a fancy restaurant."

"Think of it as a vacation."

She shifted her gaze to his. "I don't generally come to Miami to take a vacation, either. Or have dinner at a place like this."

Their server brought the bottle, opened it and poured a small amount into Rafe's glass. He lifted it and sipped, then nodded at the server, who filled their glasses.

Carmen took a sip. It was bright with just a hint of lingering sweetness. Perfect.

"What if you were rich?" Rafe asked. "Where would you live?"
She frowned. "What?"

"Just pretend you're suddenly rich. What would you do?"

"Oh. I don't know. I've never even thought about it."

Rafe took a sip of his wine, his long fingers seemingly incongruous with the delicate stem of the wineglass. "Come on, Carmen. You've never played the 'what if?' game?"

"Never. I tend to keep my feet firmly on the ground. Don't you?"

He shook his head. "Nah. When my brothers and I were homeless, we'd all play the 'Someday, when we're rich' game. We'd tell each other what our dreams were when rich parents adopted us, or when we'd come into some spare money to buy a lottery scratcher that would net us a million bucks."

"I see. And what were your dreams?"

"When I was a kid? That I'd buy a boat and my brothers and I would sail to South America. We'd fish, and then when we got to the end of South America, I'd buy us a mansion and we'd live there forever."

She nodded and took a swallow of her wine. "Big dream. Nice one, too."

"I thought so. What's yours?"

"I told you I never—"

"So think of one. Right now. If you found yourself suddenly wealthy, what would you do?"

She tried never to think beyond her means. That only set her up for disappointment, wanting things she couldn't have. But it was just a game, and a game couldn't hurt her.

"I'd set my grandfather up so he could be comfortable for the rest of his life. A new house, completely ADA compliant so he wouldn't have to worry about things he couldn't reach, or the potential for falling. He'd have twenty-four-hour-a-day assistance. A chef, a housekeeper, a nurse's aide if he ever needed one."

She poured more wine into her glass and took another sip.

"But what about for you?" Rafe asked.

"I don't need anything."

"Need is irrelevant, Carmen. What would you *like* to have? What are your dreams?"

She'd never talked to anyone about her dreams. Her totally unattainable, ridiculous dreams.

"Come on," he said. "This is just for fun. Nothing written down. Just between you and me. I told you mine."

He had. And it had been a beautiful dream.

Their server came, and they placed their dinner order, plus appetizers.

Carmen took another swallow of wine and stared out at the water.

"Come on," Rafe said. "Let's hear it."

He wasn't going to let it go, so she took a breath and exhaled.

"I've always wanted a big house. A big, bright, brand-spanking-new house. Not a mansion or anything, but something I could call my own. Something I could raise kids in. My forever home. Tod and I lived in an apartment. A crap apartment that was built in the eighties and constantly needed something or other repaired. We were saving money for a house that we never ended up buying. Then we got a divorce. After the divorce I moved in with Grandpa, and as you know, the house needs some work—which you've done for me, and I so appreciate it."

"But your dream is to have a new house."

She nodded. "Someday. Maybe."

"It's an attainable dream, Carmen. Unlike a boat to sail to the tip of South America."

She laughed. "Hey, it could happen. Never discount your dreams."

"I would like to have a boat someday. I think I've outgrown the South America part."

"So you're not planning to run away?"

"No. I'm firmly planted in Ft. Lauderdale. Probably forever."

Hearing him say that made her stomach dance with butter-flies, though she had no idea why. He wasn't hers, and they weren't a forever couple, so where he decided to plant his forever flag made no difference to her.

Fortunately, their server brought the appetizers. They shared lobster and crab ceviche that was simply to die for.

"I could eat this over and over again for the main course," she said, glad that she and Rafe had shared an appetizer. Otherwise, she'd have pigged out on this ceviche.

But when Alejandro brought their dinner, she realized she might still be hungry, especially when her branzino was set in front of her. The smell alone made her stomach growl with hunger. And with the rice and vegetables to accompany it, she knew she'd never be able to finish it.

Rafe had the fish stew, and they ended up sharing their dishes.

The flavors were spectacular. Her branzino was moist and delicious, and Rafe's fish stew was out of this world.

"I'm going to have to try to make that fish stew," Carmen said after their server had removed their plates.

"If you do that, I'm coming over for dinner."

She laughed. "I'll make it for you. Or at least my version of it. I like to try my own take on different foods I've sampled and enjoyed."

"Yeah? How does that work out for you?"

"Generally pretty good. They may not taste exactly the same, but I add different flavors to make it my own."

"So you like to experiment." Since they'd both declined dessert, he handed his credit card to the server. "Try new things."

"Of course. Keeps me from getting bored. I don't like to cook the same things over and over."

"And I don't like to eat the same things over and over. See how well matched we are?"

She laughed. "Like we're meant to be."

As they left the restaurant, Carmen rubbed her stomach. "I need to walk five miles to burn off that dinner."

"I've got a better idea."

They got into the car, and he drove out of the area. Carmen spent her time looking out the window at all the scenery, at the people who were out at night wandering around. Since it was summer, there were even more tourists populating the streets of Miami.

They ended up back at the hotel. Rafe handed off the truck to the valet. She thought they were going upstairs, but then a car came for them.

"No place to park where we're going," he said.

"Okay." She was enjoying this mystery.

The drive didn't take long. The first thing she noticed was all the people. Then the music. Latin music. Loud and boisterous, making her want to move, to dance. The driver stopped, and Rafe got out, holding his hand for her. She scooted out of the vehicle, and the music grew louder.

"Little Havana?" she asked.

Rafe smiled and nodded, and Carmen's nerve endings fluttered with excitement. They walked past clubs where musicians played drums and trumpets, and all she wanted to do was stop and listen and dance. But she also wanted to see everything, experience all that Little Havana had to offer. There was so much color, so much culture offered up by this group of exuberant, beautiful people.

They finally stopped at Ball & Chain, a vibrant, clearly hot venue, noted by the number of people milling about both inside and outside. Her body was already swaying to the music while they stood outside waiting to get in.

Rafe took her hand and skirted them around the ridiculously long line, making his way to the door where two bouncers were checking people in.

One of the guys obviously knew him.

"Hey, Rafe."

"How's it going, Carlo? Busy night."

"Crazy busy," Carlo said. "Just you and your girl here?"

Rafe nodded. "Yeah."

The guy motioned with his head. "Go on in."

"Thanks, buddy."

"Anytime."

As they walked inside, the music grew louder. Carmen took it all in. People smashed together dancing, so much color, from the lights on the ceiling to everyone's clothes to the band to—everything. The smell of sweat and alcohol fueled her, and she felt nothing but utter joy.

She turned to Rafe. "I can't believe you got us in here."

He shrugged. "It helps to know people. I've known Carlo since he lived in our neighborhood. We stay in touch, so I know he works at this place."

So useful. And Carmen was deliriously happy that they were here.

Rafe worked them toward the bar, which was crowded with people. But these were her people, so everyone was laughing and drinking, and they had no problem hustling their way in, where they ordered mojitos and watched the bartender flip bottles and entertain them while mixing drinks.

"Think you can flip a bottle around your back and catch it in midair?" she asked Rafe.

"I can totally flip a bottle around my back."

She cracked a smile. "So can I. What you're saying is between the two of us we'd have a huge mess to clean up."

"Yup."

The bartender served them their mojitos. Carmen took a sip. It was sweet and delicious, and the mint revived her senses.

They moved away from the crowded bar. Luckily, a couple got up and left their table just as she and Rafe were passing by, so they took a seat right near the dance floor.

Carmen drank her mojito and wriggled in her seat as she listened to the energy of the salsa music.

Rafe got up and hauled her out of her seat. "Let's go."

"We'll lose our table."

"That's okay. You want to be on the dance floor, don't you?"

"More than anything."

He grinned. "Then let's dance."

"Now you're talking."

She took several long swallows of her drink, finishing it off, which she knew would go to her head in a hurry, but she didn't care. Not when the music called to her. Rafe held on to her hand while he led her into the middle of the crush of people on the floor. She figured they'd each move separately to the music, which would have been fine with her. What she hadn't counted on was him taking her into his arms and leading her into a rhythmic salsa dance, spinning her and using his hands to guide her.

Wow. Rafe could dance. She watched his movements, the way he moved his hips and feet and the confident way he turned her as if he'd been doing this his entire life. He was perfectly at ease on the floor, grinning at her as he spun her around and even dipped her a few times, which made her laugh.

By the time the song ended, she was drenched in perspiration and utterly satisfied. They even got a few claps from the other couples around them.

They stayed out there for two more songs. By then Carmen was dehydrated and desperate for water, so they left the dance floor and went back to the bar for a drink. They both got water to drink.

"You can dance," she said.

He shrugged. "A little."

She laughed. "More than a little. You're amazing."

"You can move, too."

"Thanks. Where did you learn to dance like that?"

"I dated a dancer once. She gave me a few lessons."

"More than a few, I would imagine."

"On my days off, I'd meet her at the club where she worked. She gave lessons, so rather than just sitting around and watching, I joined in."

Smart guy. "It paid off."

"Yeah, she was good at her job."

She sipped her water and enjoyed standing under the cool air-conditioning. "Why did you two break up?"

"She was only in Ft. Lauderdale for a short gig. She was moving on to Orlando, then to St. Petersburg. It was never anything serious for either of us. Just fun. But she was really sweet. Last I heard, she was dancing for an off-Broadway show."

"That's awesome."

"Yeah, it is. I hope she ends up on Broadway. That was always her dream."

Carmen liked that Rafe had nice things to say about one of his ex-girlfriends. So many men only talked shit about their exes. "Then I hope her dream comes true, too."

He looked at her and smiled. "She'd like you."

"She would? Why?"

"Because you like to dance."

She laughed. "I definitely don't dance as much as I used to."

He swept her hair away from her face. "You're beautiful when you dance. Your whole body moves to the music. I like watching your hips sway."

"You had your own hip action going out there."

He leaned in and brushed his lips across hers for a brief kiss, then said, "I can show you some hip action later."

She had just cooled off, but his words ignited a fire deep inside of her. "I'm counting on it."

They went back out on the floor and danced again, taking occasional breaks to have cocktails and water.

Carmen was having the time of her life. She hadn't danced this much in years. The crowd was friendly and boisterous and drove her enthusiasm. Who wouldn't have a great time dancing with all these people?

By one a.m., though, her feet were throbbing and she was more than ready to leave.

She sat in the chair and kicked her right shoe off to rub her foot. When Rafe came back from the restroom, he crouched down in front of her.

"Done, princess?"

She gave him a nod. "So done."

He stood and held out his hand. "Come on. I'll call a car for us, and we'll head back to the hotel."

She slipped her shoe on and winced, deciding that maybe these heels hadn't been the best idea. All she wanted now was to get back to the hotel, take her shoes off and go to bed.

But as they waited outside for the car, she leaned against Rafe's shoulder and thought about what a wonderful time she'd had tonight.

And she had Rafe to thank for it.

CHAPTER 21

IT WAS LATE BY THE TIME THEY GOT BACK TO THEIR HO-
tel. And by her limp, Rafe could tell Carmen was totally done
with wearing her shoes. He knew exactly what she needed.

She kicked off her shoes when they got into the room and fell
into the chair.

"Want something to drink?" he asked.

"Water would be great."

He went down the hall and filled their ice bucket, then came
back and poured water and ice into a tall glass and handed it
to her.

She took a sip and smiled up at him. "Mmm, thanks. I think
I sweated out all the water in my body on the dance floor."

"And made your feet sore."

"Like you wouldn't believe. I'm on my feet all day at work,
and they never hurt. A few hours in these damn heels, and I may
never walk again."

"I've got a solution for your sore feet. A nice soak in that tub."

Her eyes lit up. "I do want to try out that sexy bathtub."

"I'll get it running for you."

She stood. "I'll get naked."

Those were his three favorite words. He went into the bathroom and turned the water on, getting it to the right temp. He found some bath bomb stuff on the side of the tub and sniffed it. It wasn't overpowering, just a subtle lavender scent. He walked out to find her wearing only hot pink satin panties.

Ignoring how damn sexy she looked, and his first inclination to throw her on the bed and kiss her all over, he said, "You want one of those bath bomb things in there?"

She turned and nodded. "Ooh, yes, please."

He unwrapped a bomb and tossed it in the water, watching it fizz.

Carmen came in, gloriously, beautifully naked, her hair piled on top of her head. There were so many things he wanted to do with her, but right now her comfort was most important.

"It looks fantastic," she said. "Thanks for thinking of it."

"I figured it might make your feet feel better."

He held out his hand and helped her climb into the tub. She settled in against the back of the tub with an *ahhh* sound.

"This is perfect."

"I'll leave you alone to enjoy your bath."

She narrowed her gaze. "Where do you think you're going?"

"Into the other room."

"No, you don't. Get naked and get in this tub with me."

He cocked a brow. "I think if I get in the tub with you, it won't be very relaxing for you."

"But you can rub my feet. And that *would* be relaxing."

He wanted Carmen to have whatever she asked for on this trip, so if that's what she wanted . . .

He went into the other room and stripped out of his clothes, then came into the bathroom, liking the way her gaze traveled over his naked body. Since the faucet was high up in the center of the bath, he stepped into the tub and settled back on the opposite end of her, taking her feet and propping them on his stomach so they'd stay submerged in the hot water.

"Now the bath is perfect," she said, sliding farther down and closing her eyes.

He began to rub the soles of her feet, gently at first to massage the entire foot, trying to figure out where her feet were sore. The problem was, she made moaning noises everywhere he touched. And because she kept making sexy moaning sounds, his dick got hard. Which meant his dick stood at full attention now and he was rock-hard and aching and Carmen was in foot rub nirvana and had no idea he was completely turned on while rubbing her feet.

Great. Now she was gonna think he had a foot fetish when really it had to do with the sounds she was making. Though she did have really cute feet. He lifted her toes out of the water to see her toenails had been painted a pretty coral color. He teased his fingers between her toes, and she giggled—and moaned again. He rolled his eyes and suffered in silence, then fisted his hand and kneaded it into the ball of her foot.

"Oh, God," she said. "That's so good."

Then she started rubbing his chest with her other foot, teasing his nipple with her big toe. He'd never had this kind of foreplay before, and he wasn't a foot guy, but he had to admit he was hella turned on, so whatever Carmen wanted to do to him, he was game for it.

And when her foot slid down to his lower belly and connected with his hard cock, her eyes drifted open and she gave him a lazy smile.

"So, rubbing my feet turns you on?"

He continued to massage her foot. "No, you moaning turns me on."

"I was moaning?"

"Yeah. A lot. Sex moans."

She laughed. "I was not giving you sex moans."

"The hell you weren't. Apparently, foot rubs make you hot."

She extricated her foot from his hand, then crawled across the tub to sit on his lap. She swiped her finger down his chest. "Well, who knew foot rubs would be such a turn-on for me?"

"I sure didn't. But I'm damn happy to be in the tub with you right now."

He grasped her hips and slid her across his aching cock. She drew in a gasping breath and reached up for the wall for support. "I like how that feels."

"I like how you feel. Hot and wet against me." He wanted to slide inside her like this, but not without a condom on. Which was going to pose a problem, because he was rock-hard and he needed her.

But this wasn't about him, and he could ease *her* ache. He reached between them and slid his hand across her sex, making her moan again, and this time because it really was about sex. Her slick folds made his balls tighten as he teased her clit, then slipped a couple of fingers inside of her.

She gasped. "Rafe. Yes. Fuck me with your fingers."

God, she was killing him.

She rode his hand, rocking against him with abandon while he watched her body writhe in a sexual dance. When she reached down and wrapped her hand around his cock, he groaned.

"Oh, fuck yeah," he said. "Make me come with you, babe."

It wouldn't take him long. Watching her ride his hand and his fingers nearly broke him. Especially now, as she stroked his cock, twisting her hand around his shaft while she looked down at him, her gaze lost in a haze of pleasure as he fucked her with his fingers. His balls locked up tight against his body as he prepared to lose it.

And when her pussy squeezed his fingers in spasm and she threw her head back and screamed out with her climax, he let go, groaning out his own orgasm as he spurted into her hand, shoving his shaft forward over and over again until he emptied completely.

She fell on top of him, her body heaving breaths. He withdrew his fingers and wrapped his arms around her so he could hold her until they both came down from that magnificent high.

It took a while, but when she finally raised up to look at him, she had a satisfied smile on her face.

"I've never had a bath like that before."

"Same. And now the water's getting cold."

They got out and rinsed off in the shower. Carmen towel dried her hair, and they went into the bedroom and climbed under the covers. Rafe pulled Carmen next to him.

"I had a great time," she murmured, followed up by a yawn.

"I'm glad. Me, too." He stroked her hair. "Too bad we have to go back tomorrow."

"Yeah."

"We could run away."

She let out a soft laugh. "Oh, sure. Neither of us has any responsibilities. No one would notice we were missing."

"It would take them weeks to figure out we were gone. Since nobody loves us."

She drew circles on his chest with the tip of her finger. "Exactly. We're so unloved. We could be halfway around the world in your sailboat by then."

"Wait. My sailboat? Don't we have to win millions of dollars first?"

"Oh, right. I guess we'll have to go get a lottery ticket in the morning. Then we'll get the sailboat."

"Because we're guaranteed to win, us living a charmed life and all."

"Right. Charmed. That's us, Rafe."

That was the last thing she said before she fell asleep.

Charmed.

He felt pretty charmed right now. This had been a damn fine day. Hell, ever since he'd hooked up with Carmen.

He didn't even need to become a millionaire or have that sailboat anymore to feel like he had everything he ever wanted.

CHAPTER 22

CARMEN WAS IN HER OFFICE CATCHING UP ON REPORTS
while eating her lunch when there was a knock on her door.

"Come in."

Tess popped her head in. "Can I have lunch in here?"

She smiled at her friend. "You don't even have to ask."

Tess walked in with her sandwich and a soda. She closed the
door behind her, then slid into the chair across from Carmen's
desk. "We've been slammed all day with patients, you've been
buried in here with paperwork and we haven't had one damn
second to catch up since you came back from your trip. I need
details. So, start spilling."

"Details on . . . ?"

Tess cocked her head to the side and gave Carmen a "don't
bullshit me" look. "You know what I'm talking about. Miami.
You and Rafe. Come on, Carmen. I need to know how it went.
You didn't even text me when you got back yesterday."

"Weren't you and George both off together yesterday?"

"Yes. So?"

"So, I didn't want to bother you when you both had a day off together. You mentioned going to the beach. Alone time with your husband, you know? No way I was going to interfere with that."

Tess rolled her eyes. "My husband and I get plenty of alone time together. You, on the other hand, had your first alone time with your boyfriend. I stared at my phone all damn day waiting to hear from you."

"You did not."

"Okay, fine. Not the entire day. George and I hit the beach. We ate at a great restaurant. We went home and then we had wild monkey sex. After we showered the sand off, of course. And no, I wasn't looking at my phone during any of those times. Does that make you happy?"

Carmen laughed. "Deliriously. You do have an amazing marriage, you know."

Tess lifted her shoulders and offered up a giddy smile. "I do, don't I? I'm damn lucky and I know it. Now tell me about your trip to Miami."

Now that she'd made Tess wait for it, she supposed she should spill some details. Not all of them, of course. But some. "We had a great time."

"And?"

"And, we had a great time."

"Come on, Carmen."

"Fine. We drove down, checked into an amazing hotel—the COMO Metropolitan. Very art deco. Supremely gorgeous. We had a suite with a living room and stunning views and the most amazing bathroom ever. It was totally decadent."

Tess chewed and swallowed and grinned, all at the same time. "Awesome."

"We went for walks, we went to the beach, we ate amazing food, we went dancing. Oh, and Rafe can dance. I mean he can really dance well. I danced until I couldn't move my feet. It was exhausting and exhilarating."

"Wow. It sounds like you had an incredible time, honey."

"I did. We had fun together. And we talked—about so many things. From the inane to the really serious. It wasn't just doing things, you know? I couldn't have asked for a better vacation. I didn't want to come home."

"Aww. It sounds like you really connected with him."

Did she? She supposed she did. But she didn't want to think about that, not when their time together had been so good. "We had fun."

"So you said. What about the emotional connection?"

"I don't know, Tess. I'm trying not to do that."

"Do what? Get involved? Care about someone? Fall in love?"

Fall in love. The words alone caused her heart to clench, and then sent shivers down her spine. "I don't know."

"Tell me what bothers you about it."

She stared at her salad that lay untouched. She'd planned to eat, finish her review of reports and then walk out on the floor for the afternoon. Now she'd lost her appetite and her motivation.

"I had such a wonderful time with Rafe. He's kind and considerate and fun and sexy, but you know, I was in love once, and love turned on me. I'm not sure I can ever trust it again."

Tess wrinkled up the paper from her sandwich and stuffed it in the bag. "Okay, I totally understand where you're coming from. But is it fair to lump all men—Rafe, especially—in with your ex-husband and what he did to you?"

"Of course not. But I can't help how I feel." She paused, letting that emotion wash over her. Real feelings surfaced, and they were the ones she wanted to avoid the most. "I'm scared, Tess."

Tess gave her a nod of sympathy. "I know you are, honey. But denying yourself a chance to experience love again is only letting your ex win. Do you want him to keep screwing you over for the rest of your life? If you end up alone and lonely, then he wins. Again and again."

She hadn't thought of it like that, but what Tess said made a lot of sense. She'd cocooned herself after her divorce, wrapping herself up in her hurt and anger and misery, refusing to open herself up to the possibility of ever falling in love again because she might get hurt.

But what would happen if she did give love a chance? She might get hurt again? What would happen if she didn't get hurt? She might end up happy. Which would be the biggest screw-you to her ex. And that would totally be worth it.

"You know what? You're right. I haven't been giving myself a chance. It's time to end that. Things with Rafe might wind up going nowhere at all, but I should at least open myself up to the possibility."

Tess nodded and stood. "That's right. You'll never know if you don't try."

Carmen got up and came around her desk, then pulled Tess into her arms. "Thank you for always forcing me to see my truth."

Tess grinned and squeezed her hand. "Well, you know me. Pushy, pushy, pushy."

"That's why I love you. Now get your ass back to work."

"Yes, ma'am. You coming out onto the floor later?"

"As soon as I finish reading through the reports. You did great while I was gone, by the way."

Tess's eyes shined with happiness. "Thanks, boss. I'll see you out there."

After Tess left, Carmen went back to her desk and checked her phone. There was a text message from her grandpa. He told her he had a date with Felice tonight, and she'd be picking him up at six for dinner, so he wouldn't be home when she got there.

A date, huh? Carmen smiled at that. *Good for you, Grandpa.*

He'd done great while she was gone, and he'd had no issues at all. She'd been worried about him for nothing. And he'd obviously fixed things with Felice, since the two of them were going out tonight.

She had another text message, this one from Rafe.

BBQ and swim party at our place tonight. Can you come over after work?

Her lips curved and she sent a reply.

I'll be there.

She checked her watch. She still had five hours on shift, but she knew those hours would go fast. And then she'd get to see Rafe.

Now that she eliminated hesitation over her emotions, she had a new plan to put into action.

She couldn't wait.

RAFE HAD GONE TO WORK OUT A LITTLE LATER THAN usual today, then had stopped at the community center to work with the kids this afternoon. Having the extra days off shift always gave him time to catch up on things in his life he hadn't had time to attend to, and this was one of them.

He'd shot hoops with several of the twelve- and thirteen-year-olds, remarking to them how tall they were getting. Jamal had long, lanky legs and a good stride, making it hard to keep up with him on the court. By the time they'd played for an hour, Rafe was ready to drop.

"What's the matter, old man?" Jamal asked, looking as if he could do this all day. "Trouble keepin' up?"

The kid had barely even broken a sweat, while Rafe leaned over, bracing his hands on his knees, sucking wind. "Okay everyone. Water break."

Jamal smirked.

Luisa Rodgers, the manager of the community center, walked

over to him while he guzzled down what felt like a gallon of water. "They love when you visit."

"Right now they love kicking my butt."

She laughed. "That, too."

He noticed the kids had carried on without him. "How are they all doing?"

"Good. They like coming here, and it gives them something to do, especially now, during the summer months when school is out."

"It looks like you have a lot more kids this summer than usual."

Luisa nodded. "It seems that way. Which is a good thing. We want the kids to feel comfortable coming here, to know they have a place to hang out with other kids their age, and still have adult supervision."

"Which is a lot better than being on the streets and getting into trouble."

"So true. And since it's free for all the kids, it doesn't matter who they are. No one has to fill out paperwork, so they can just walk in and have a good time."

That's what was so important to Rafe. He wished he and his brothers had a place like this when they were homeless. He knew some of the kids here had no other place to go. And while the community center didn't provide food or shelter, it was air-conditioned, and gave the kids an avenue to learn social skills, to read, to watch TV and play video games. Anything to keep them from feeling isolated or alone.

"You provide a great service here, Luisa."

She smiled. "It's the community that provides the service, along with people like you who are interested enough to dive in and engage with the kids. They know people care about them, and that's vital."

"I definitely care what happens to them. All of them."

"And it shows." She looked down at her phone, then back up

at Rafe. "I'm sorry to leave you, but I have a meeting coming up, if you'll excuse me."

"Go ahead."

He followed Luisa inside the main room. Some of the kids sat in the lobby hanging out, typing on their phones. He wandered into the library to see a group on computers. Computer activity was monitored so that kids couldn't go places they shouldn't, but they still had access to explore and learn. And then there were all the books. He saw several kids sitting and lying on the floor reading. One of the things he loved about the center was that anyone could grab a book, lie on the floor and just read. No one was going to yell at them about it. There were bean bag chairs and rugs and comfortable chairs spread throughout the library. There were workstations with computers, and netbooks they could check out, too. There were gaming consoles as well, and, along with the gym, there was no reason for any kid to ever get bored here.

Plus, they offered water and juice to drink. Other than needing to eat, a kid could spend an entire day here.

Rafe wondered what it would take to provide food for the kids during the summer months when school wasn't in session.

It might help kids who wandered aimlessly without parental guidance in the summer. If they could provide low-cost meals to the kids—even sandwiches for lunch—they might be able to keep the kids here, and out of trouble, for the day.

He checked his phone and realized he needed to hightail it out of there.

He hit the gym on his way out to say goodbye to the kids he'd played basketball with, promising to stop in on his next day off.

"Try to work on your endurance," Jamal said. "Maybe you can keep up with me."

Rafe laughed. "Yeah, I'll see what I can do."

After he got into his truck, he made a few calls to some of the members of the community, and some people who knew other people that were higher-ups in the community, to see what they could do about providing summer lunches for the kids. Several were on board with the idea, and they agreed to meet with him next week to talk about it. He'd get Becks and his brothers involved, too, because he knew they'd get shit done.

Now that he had that plan rolling, he stopped at the store to buy supplies for the barbecue tonight. He'd already talked to Jackson and Kal, who were picking stuff up as well, so he grabbed chicken breasts and thighs along with the ingredients to make his sauce.

All the brothers made their own versions of their favorite barbecue sauce, which usually worked out great when they had parties, because then everyone got to try something different. Of course, Rafe thought his was the best—a little spicier than what his brothers made. He couldn't wait to try it out on Carmen to see what she thought about it.

He drove home. Jackson and Kal were already there, crowding up the kitchen with their shit.

"I see you're already making sauce and rub," he said as he unpacked his groceries.

Jackson shrugged. "You're late. You snooze, you lose, man."

"Yeah," Kal said. "Where've you been?"

"I worked out and then I spent some time at the community center."

"How's it going over there?" Kal was chopping onions but stopped to look up at him.

"Good. What do you guys think about offering lunch there? Like sandwiches in the summer for the kids."

Jackson looked at him and nodded. "It's a great idea. It would keep the kids there for the day who wanted to stay. How would you get funding?"

"I made some calls today, and there are several organizations interested in helping out. I'll have to talk to Luisa about it first, see if maybe she could apply for grants or find if there's any money for it. But you know how it is with kids. They're constantly hungry. And if there's a way to keep them occupied all day, at least in the summer months, it would go a long way toward keeping them out of trouble."

Kal waved his cutting knife at Rafe. "I think it's a kick-ass idea."

He was glad his brothers agreed with him and didn't think it was a stupid suggestion.

Now he just had to shove them out of the way so he could find some room to make his barbecue sauce.

He put a saucepan on the range and added oil and sautéed onions and garlic. Then he tossed in the rest of the ingredients, including his secret spicy ingredient, and let it all simmer for a while. He took a taste and grinned. "Oh yeah, perfect."

"You'd like to think so," Jackson said, looking over his shoulder. "But, sadly, it's not as good as mine."

"Or mine," Kal said, not even bothering to look at them.

"I guess we'll find out later."

"We should do a blind taste test and see which sauce everyone likes the most," Rafe suggested.

Jackson nodded. "I'm down with it."

"Same," Kal said, coming over with a spoon to dip it in Rafe's sauce. "It's good. But I'm afraid it's not gonna be good enough to win."

Rafe wasn't the least bit affected by the shit-talking from his brothers. He knew the games they played, trying to get into his head. His sauce was the best and he'd win the taste test tonight. "You're both losers. And I'm gonna prove it."

Bring on the party.

CHAPTER 23

CARMEN ENDED UP HAVING TO STAY AN EXTRA HOUR AT work to finish up with a patient, so she hustled home to shower and get dressed and make a dish for the barbecue.

There were already cars parked in the driveway, and she heard music and the sound of people laughing coming from the backyard. But she went in through the front door, which was unlocked.

Becks was in the kitchen with Jackson, the two of them working side by side at the island. Becks smiled when she saw her.

"Hey, Carmen."

"Hi. I know I'm late."

"No one's ever late," Jackson said. "We're glad you made it."

"I hope you haven't already eaten."

"Things move pretty slowly around here," Becks said. "We've just been drinking, and the guys are grilling. I made margaritas and there's beer and wine. What would you like?"

Happy to hear that she hadn't missed dinner, she slipped the salad she'd made into the fridge. "A margarita sounds awesome."

Jackson took a plate outside, leaving her in the kitchen with Becks.

"I had to work past the end of my shift at the hospital, then come home and shower and dry my hair and . . . well, you know."

Becks laughed as she poured ice into a glass. "I do know. I actually closed the shop early today, but I still had to come home and shower and do the hair thing, and then I wanted to make a side dish. I mean, it's not like we can get out of the shower and, voilà, we're ready like guys are. It takes us some time."

"Right? It's so annoying. I should just buzz all my hair off and save myself an hour every day."

Becks handed Carmen her margarita. "Yeah? You'd look hot that way."

Carmen laughed. "I was joking. Mostly. Except on days I'd like to sleep in."

"I can relate."

Rafe came through the back door with an empty plate and smiled when he saw Carmen. "Hey. I didn't know you were here."

"I just got here. Becks fixed me a margarita, so we've been chatting."

"Oh, good." He went to the sink to wash the empty plate.

Becks leaned over and whispered to her. "Watch this."

Carmen had no idea what was about to happen.

"Hey, Rafe," Becks said, "Carmen told me she's thinking about buzzing all her hair off and going bald."

Rafe dried the plate, then walked over to her. "Yeah? If that's what you want to do, you'd look hot that way. And think of all the time you'd save getting ready for work."

Carmen gave him a shocked stare.

Becks arched her shoulders and smiled.

"I've gotta go check the chicken. Come on outside when you're ready." He gave her a quick kiss on the lips, then left.

Carmen laughed. "He says that now, until I come home bald someday."

"He's got it bad for you."

"Why do you think that?"

"Because he's telling you that he's going to like you no matter how you look. A lot of guys wouldn't do that."

"You think?"

"Please. You know how superficial men can be. Women, too. We value ourselves based upon our partner's looks." Becks climbed up on the chair on the island to sit next to Carmen. "It might not be right, but it's how it often is."

Carmen took a sip of the margarita Becks had made for her. It was salty and delicious. "True. Our attraction to someone is based on their looks, at least at first, until you form a deeper connection."

"Exactly. Which is why I'm telling you that Rafe cares about you. His feelings for you have gone beyond the 'Hey, I'm dating a beautiful hot woman' to 'I care about this woman and I'd proudly walk beside her, bald or not.'"

She hadn't thought about that. She took another sip of her drink. "That's sweet. But I'm not shaving my head."

Becks laughed. "Good call. You have amazing hair. I mean, you'd look hot as hell without it, too, but unless it's a fashion statement you want to make, you should keep it."

Carmen got up and grabbed the pitcher from the fridge to refill both their glasses. "I think it's settled, then. What else should we decide on now? World peace? The next presidential election?"

"Oh, funny. How about this weird battle the guys have going on about barbecue sauces?"

"Barbecue sauces? I haven't heard about this. Fill me in."

Becks told her about the contest the brothers had concocted.

"Seriously." Carmen teased her fingertip around the condensation on the glass. "And then what happens? Does the winner get anything?"

Becks shrugged one shoulder. "Bragging rights, I guess. Brothers. Who knows what goes on in their heads?"

Carmen rolled her eyes. "You know, sometimes I'm sad that I didn't grow up with siblings. Other times—not so much."

Becks raised her glass and tilted it toward Carmen. "You said it."

Carmen toasted with her.

The door opened, and Jackson popped his head in. "You two hiding in here?"

"Maybe," Becks said. "Or maybe we're just having girl time."

Jackson paused. "Oh. Okay. Well, do whatever makes you happy, but just know that I miss you."

"Okay, babe. I love you."

"Love you, too."

He closed the door, and Carmen turned to Becks. "He wasn't about to demand your presence out there, was he?"

"No. He's sweet that way." Becks laughed. "Come on. We don't want to deny the boys our awesomeness. Let's go outside before they start crying."

Carmen grinned. Considering they didn't have the best start to their friendship after Becks had moved into the house with the guys a few months back—which had been entirely Carmen's fault—she really liked Becks a lot. She was outgoing and friendly and had a wicked sense of humor. It was no wonder Jackson had fallen in love with her.

They took their drinks and walked outside. The wind had picked up, and Carmen noticed the cloud cover. She smelled rain in the air and hoped the guys would be able to finish the barbecuing before it started to storm.

No one seemed to mind the wind. There were people in the pool playing volleyball, and a few folks sitting by the water. Carmen recognized Miguel and Adrienne. Adrienne spotted her and waved, so Carmen waved back.

Rafe was over by the grill along with Jackson and Kal. The three of them appeared to be concentrating on what they were doing, so instead of bothering him, Carmen followed Becks out to the pool area. They took seats by a couple who Becks introduced as Callie Vassar and her husband, Aaron, both firefighters. She also met firefighter Ethan Pressman and his wife, Penny, who she was surprised to learn was also a nurse, albeit at a different hospital.

"I work in labor and delivery," Penny said. "How about you, Carmen?"

"ER."

"Oh. Tough job. Admirable."

"So is yours. But babies are the best."

"I love it. I've been doing it ever since I graduated nursing school. I wouldn't want to do anything else. In fact, I was just talking to Callie about her labor and delivery experience since she recently had her little boy."

Carmen shifted her glance to Callie. "Oh, you're a new mom?"

Callie nodded. "Yeah. Max was born a few months ago."

"How thrilling for you. Congratulations."

"Thanks. It's like I learn something new every day, and I'm still a little nervous."

"A little?" Aaron put his arm around his wife's shoulders. "She's bought at least ten books on babies and child-rearing. She watches videos all the time. When she was pregnant we signed up for all the classes, both pregnancy and newborn."

Aaron looked over at Ethan. "All. The. Classes."

Ethan laughed. "You just have to go with it, dude. When Penny was pregnant with Byron, we did the same thing, even though she already knew everything."

Penny shrugged. "It's different when you're on the other side of the process."

"It really is," Carmen said. "I don't have kids, but my grandfather has been ill and in and out of the ER several times. You would think being an ER nurse I'd be totally calm in those situations, knowing what to expect."

"And you're not," Penny said. "Because it's different when

you're not the one in charge, and when someone else is leading care either for you or for someone you love."

Carmen nodded. "Exactly."

"It's the same thing being a firefighter," Ethan said. "When you're off duty and you see something happen, like a car accident or a fire, you want to take charge, but you can only do so much. You have to yield to the fire crew or police that arrive on scene, even though you know what needs to be done."

"So you're not allowed to pitch in and help?" Carmen asked.

Rafe had come up behind her. "No. We're not on duty, and we're not geared up. And it's not our scene to work, so we have to back off."

Aaron nodded. "If we're first on the scene, we can offer aid, but of course we generally don't have the equipment to either put out a fire or extricate someone from a vehicle, so all we can do is call it in and do whatever we can to assist the victims until fire or police arrive."

"That must be so frustrating," Becks said.

"Very," Rafe said.

Carmen tilted her head back to look at Rafe. "Has it happened to you before?"

"It's happened to all of us before. We can't just drive by an accident or a fire where no one has showed up yet. We always feel compelled to stop and see what we can do to help."

Carmen nodded, knowing how they all felt. "As an ER nurse, I've stopped a time or two when I've come upon an accident. But it's not like I have the full supplies of the ER at my disposal so I can help someone who's injured. I just do what I can to assess the situation and wait for help. I understand how you all feel."

Callie shifted in her chair. "The way I look at it is that whoever is in that car or who might be in that building is at least getting first responders who know something and can maybe help them right away. We might not have hoses hooked up or be able to pull them from the wreckage, but we can call it in and offer immediate assistance."

"And that's pretty damn good, if you ask me," Rafe said.

Carmen squeezed his hand. "Yes, I suppose it is."

"Okay, now that you've all patted yourselves on the back, how about we drag our self-congratulatory asses into the house for some barbecue?"

They all looked up to find that Jackson had come over to stand next to Rafe.

"Oh, like you don't feel the same way?" Rafe asked.

"Didn't say that. You know damn well I feel the same way. I'm just hungry, so let's go eat."

Carmen couldn't wait to dig into all the amazing-smelling food.

"Don't forget that we have to judge the sauces," Becks said as they made their way into the house.

"Oh, right. Will they tell us who made what?"

Becks shook her head. "No. It's a big secret. Then we vote."

Carmen gave Becks a look of disbelief as she opened the door and they walked inside the house. "Wait. We don't get to know whose sauce is whose?"

"No."

"Well, that's bullshit."

Becks gave a commiserating look in return. "I know."

As Carmen entered the kitchen and saw the amazing spread of chicken and ribs and the three sauces lined up, she decided she was going to be honest.

She supposed she had no choice, since she had no idea which sauce belonged to which brother.

This should be interesting.

CARMEN TRIED ALL THREE SAUCES. SHE DABBED THE first onto her ribs. It was bold, with just a touch of vinegar flavor.

The second was sweet, with a honey and brown sugar flavor, and was delicious with the chicken thighs. The third was amazing. It had a seriously spicy kick and went well with both the ribs and the chicken.

All three of the sauces were unique and outstanding.

She noticed Rafe eating and wandering the crowd. Watching, no doubt, to see what everyone was sampling. He did his fair share of eating, too. She saw him go inside to refill his plate twice—no, three times. Or was it four? She'd lost count. And each time he came outside, his plate had been loaded. He finally sat next to her.

"Are you sure you've had enough to eat?" she asked, looking down at his plate. "What is that? Your fourth serving?"

"Third. And I might go back for more."

She shook her head. "It was all delicious."

"And did you decide which sauce was your favorite?"

She pulled her plate to the side as if him looking at it would reveal her thoughts. "I'm not telling you that. I have to vote."

He laughed. "You're not gonna tell me?"

"Of course not. That would be cheating."

"In what way is that cheating?"

"I . . . I don't know. But I'm still not telling you. Now go away."

"You want me to go away? Like I can't even sit with you now? Do you think I'm sending you some psychic vibes that might sway your vote?"

She rolled her eyes. "Now you're being ridiculous."

"You're the one who told me to go away."

"You're the one who asked me which sauce I was voting for." She narrowed her gaze at him, just to prove her point.

His lips twitched.

"I swear to God, Rafe Donovan, if you laugh at me right now, I'm dumping this plate in your lap."

He stood. "Okay. Fine. I'm going away."

As soon as Rafe left, Becks slid into the chair next to her. "Were you two fighting?"

"He asked me what sauce I was voting for."

Becks gasped. "That son of a bitch."

"I know." She continued to track him as he made his way to the door.

"So what did you think of the sauces?" Becks asked.

"I thought they were all incredibly good. And all totally different. I have no idea how I'm supposed to vote on the best one."

Becks sighed. "Same. One was tart, one was sweet, and one was spicy. And I loved all of them."

"Agreed. So basically, we're screwed."

Carmen finished off the last of her chicken, dipping it in the spicy sauce, her tongue exploding with the flavor. She swallowed and took a sip of her margarita, pondering the dilemma. "We could stuff the ballot boxes."

"Vote for all three?"

"Yes. Then we'd know we weren't hurting anyone's feelings."

She laughed. "That would be cheating."

Carmen shrugged. "I know. Which would be terrible, wouldn't it?"

"Yes." Becks sipped on her drink. "But honest, right? We did like all three sauces."

"This is true." Then a thought hit her. "I wonder if everyone else feels the same way, or if they all have favorites."

Becks grinned, catching on to Carmen's idea.

It didn't take long, based on conversations with everyone there, to find that there was a consensus that everyone enjoyed all the sauces equally. And when Becks and she suggested they may want to stuff the ballot boxes, everyone thought that was a perfect plan.

By the time plates had been tossed into the trash and all the leftover sides had been tucked away in the fridge, the votes had been cast. To keep it fair, Penny Pressman and Adrienne Smith were going to count the votes while everyone else waited outside.

Rafe cradled his beer between his hands as he sat with Carmen. Jackson and Becks and Kal sat with them.

"You actually look nervous," she said.

"I'm pretty sure I'm gonna win."

"In your dreams, asshole," Kal said.

Jackson sighed. "I feel sorry for the two of you losers."

"You do realize this is just a friendly contest," Carmen said.

Rafe looked at her as if she'd just sprouted two heads. "You didn't grow up with my brothers and me. This is serious shit, Carmen."

"Seriously serious," Jackson said.

Becks looked over at Carmen and just shook her head.

Carmen shrugged, at a loss to understand. "Serious barbecue sauce competition."

"Well, yeah," Kal said. "We take everything we compete at as if it's an Olympic event."

Growing up together must have been fun for these guys. If fun was a constant competition.

The door slid open, and Penny and Adrienne walked out.

Rafe took her hand. "This is it," he said, his gaze riveted to the women.

Adrienne grinned. "It's a three-way tie."

Jackson, Kal and Rafe all looked at one another.

"What the fuck?" Rafe asked. "How the hell could it be a tie?"

"A tie?" Jackson asked. "What the—a tie?"

Kal looked at everyone as if there'd been some kind of conspiracy. "Nuh-uh. You're lying."

"Maybe we all liked all your sauces," Becks said.

Jackson narrowed his gaze. "I smell a setup."

Becks looked shocked. "A setup? What do you mean?"

"I . . . don't know." Jackson dragged his fingers through his hair. "How the hell could there have been a tie?"

"Does it matter?" Penny asked. "The sauces were all amazing. I know I couldn't choose just one, so I voted for all three."

Penny looked at the guys as if she dared them to complain about that.

"I did the same thing," Callie said. "I mean, I liked them all, so I voted for all of them."

"Same," Carmen said.

Rafe frowned. "You did what? You voted for all of them?"

"Of course. Which one was yours?"

"The spicy one."

"Oh, I loved that one," Carmen said.

"But not enough to single it out."

She rolled her eyes. "I loved all of them. They were all so unique and incredibly flavorful. I just couldn't choose, Rafe. I'm sorry."

"Huh. I guess that's okay."

"It's not okay," Kal said. "Now none of us can claim to be champion."

Becks patted him on the back. "You poor baby. I'm sure the three of you will find something else to compete over."

Jackson laughed. "Probably."

"Likely by shift tomorrow would be my guess," Mitchell said.

Rafe shot a glare at Mitchell. "Hey, we're not that competitive."

"Oh, you aren't?" Callie asked. "How about the last run time? Jackson was supposed to be timing *us*, and instead I ended up in charge of the stopwatch so he could run against the two of you for best time."

"Really, Jackson?" Becks asked.

Jackson shrugged. "It was just so I could stay in shape."

Rafe coughed and muttered, "Bullshit."

Carmen laughed and got up to go put her glass in the dishwasher. She ended up filling a tall glass with ice and water, having had enough margaritas for the night. She had to work tomorrow, so she needed to start clearing her head. She rinsed the dishes in the sink and loaded those into the dishwasher, then started cleaning off the kitchen counter and stove.

"What are you doing in here?"

She turned around and saw Rafe standing behind the island.

"Cleaning."

"You're a guest here. Guests don't clean."

"No, I'm your girlfriend. And girlfriends pitch in to help. Since I got here late, this is me helping."

She turned around and continued to wipe the counters. Suddenly, a pair of arms surrounded her. Rafe kissed the side of her neck, causing goose bumps to skitter along her skin.

"Girlfriend, huh?" he asked.

She realized as soon as she said it that he might think it was a big deal. Or that maybe he'd react negatively. Obviously his arms around her and him kissing her neck was the opposite of a negative reaction.

And she liked it. A lot.

"Your charms don't work on me when I'm cleaning," she said, dropping her head back to lie on his shoulder.

"They don't?" He lightly bit down on that spot between her neck and shoulder that never failed to make her quiver.

"No. I'm very focused right now."

He turned her around and kissed her, and she lost all thoughts of cleaning the kitchen. They hadn't had much alone time tonight, and now that they were in the kitchen by themselves, and his hands were sliding with ease along her back, all she could think about was him touching her.

She palmed the island for support while he explored her mouth with his tongue, making her dizzy and weak and desperately wishing that all these people would leave soon.

When he broke the kiss, she was breathing heavily. She swiped her thumb across his bottom lip. "Who knew cleaning the kitchen was a form of foreplay?"

His lips curved. "I need to get all these people to go home."

Happy to hear that he was on her same wavelength, she nodded. "Soon, hopefully."

"Yeah, real soon."

Jackson opened the door and came in, Becks following right behind him, so Carmen reluctantly stepped back, and Rafe helped her finish with the kitchen. Within the next hour, the party broke up and everyone left. Since Rafe and Carmen had cleaned the kitchen, Jackson, Becks and Kal had decided they'd take care of the grill and pool area.

"I should check on my grandpa," she said to Rafe after the others went outside to clean up.

"I'll go with you."

"Thanks."

They walked across the lawn, and Carmen noticed a strange car in the driveway.

"Hmm," she said, frowning. It was after eleven.

"One of your grandfather's friends?" Rafe asked.

"No. I know all their cars."

She unlocked the door and went inside. Other than the kitchen stove light, which Grandpa always left on for her when she was out late, all the lights were off, which typically meant he had gone to bed.

She started toward his bedroom, but Rafe grasped her wrist.

"Didn't you say he had a date tonight?"

"Yes."

"And didn't she pick him up?"

"Yes."

Rafe looked at her, his head cocked to the side for emphasis. It took her a few seconds to comprehend what he wasn't saying out loud.

Then her eyes widened. "Oh. You think she's in there with him."

"Probably."

"Huh." He had never brought a woman over to spend the night before. Then again, he hadn't been feeling as spry as he'd been feeling lately, so maybe . . .

"If he had a problem, he'd let you know, Carmen."

She stared at the closed door, trying to decide how intrusive to be. How intrusive she'd want her grandfather to be if the situation were reversed. He probably wouldn't appreciate her banging on his door or just walking in on him if he was in the middle of . . .

Well, she wasn't going to visualize that.

"You're right. I'll just leave him be. If he needs me, he'll let me know."

Rafe smiled. "I imagine he's got the situation in hand. Or elsewhere."

She shook her head. "Rafe."

Rafe took her hand and led her down the other hallway toward her bedroom.

"Where do you think you're going?" she asked.

"To your bedroom. To get you naked and see if I can make you come without making you scream."

She followed him, giving him a look. "That seems entirely unfair."

"Yeah, but I'll have to be quiet, too."

She could already imagine the things she'd do to him. "No matter what I do?"

"No matter what you do."

One corner of her mouth lifted. "Oh, you're on."

Fortunately, her bedroom was at the other end of the hall. For some reason, she found herself being more quiet than usual, which was ridiculous. If, in fact, her grandfather was busily engaged in . . . whatever, the last thing he'd be doing was listening for whatever it was she was doing.

Still, she closed her bedroom door gently, then locked it.

Rafe was right there, pressing her body against the door, his body aligning with hers.

"Shouldn't we get away from the door?"

"I thought this was a challenge," he said.

"You're mean."

"No, I'm not. I'm determined to win."

He swept his hand over her collarbone, between her breasts, cupping one and giving it a gentle massage, waking up her desire in a fury of passionate need.

And when his hand drifted lower, lifting up the hem of her shirt, she let out a short moan.

"Shh," he whispered, covering her lips with his, kissing her slowly, deliberately, taking his time to explore her mouth in a way that did nothing to quell her whimpers and moans, especially since his hands continued to roam freely over her body.

He lifted the bottom of her shirt, and his warm hand palmed her stomach, his fingers teasing the hem of her shorts before delving inside to cup her sex.

She broke the kiss, panting. "Rafe."

His gaze was heated, his cock hard against her hip. "Carmen." He continued a slow, sensual exploration of her sex with his hand, making her unable to process what she'd been about to say.

He had her, right here against the door, so near to an orgasm that her hips rose against his hand, demanding he give it to her.

And when she climaxed, it was so intense she fought to hold back the loud cries that wanted to escape her lips. Instead, she fisted her hands in his shirt and bucked against his hand, so not content to whimper softly as she rode out the powerful waves until she finally fell against him.

He picked her up and laid her on top of her bed, stripped off his shorts and underwear along with his shirt, watching as she wriggled out of her clothes and threw them on the floor. She pointed to her nightstand drawer, and he smiled at her, a wide, grateful smile as he pulled out a condom.

"I'm glad you're prepared."

"Always."

He put the condom on and spread her legs, then leaned over the bed and slid inside of her.

"Like silk," he said, his hands pressed on either side of her as he began to move. "Hot, liquid silk."

His words made her quiver; she lifted her hips to draw him closer, deeper, needing that connection between them that always seemed to drive her right into orgasm.

And when he cupped his hand under her butt and lifted her, rubbed his body against hers, she was there, ready to go off.

He knew it, too. She was sure he could feel it. They were always so in sync, their bodies seemingly made for each other. Which was ridiculous, of course, but in the moment, in this moment, all she could do was respond to Rafe's movements, to her own body, and to the emotion overwhelming her.

And when she tightened and released, he let out a guttural groan and shuddered against her, making her climax intensify until she let out a cry she couldn't hold back. He swallowed the sound by kissing her deeply, swamping her senses with the taste of his lips and tongue.

He pulled up, staring down at her with such dark depths of emotion in his eyes, communicating without words just how damn intense that had been.

She was panting, looking up at Rafe and wishing she could stay like this, with him giving her that utterly satiated, sexy look. Then he gave her a crooked smile.

"You made noise."

Now it was her turn to smile. "You made more noise than I did."

He disengaged, then pulled her up and off the bed. "Did not."

They went into the bathroom to clean up. He wrapped his arms around her and kissed her, a warm, emotional kiss that made her want to pull him into her bed and wrap her body around his for the night.

But that wouldn't work. Not with her grandfather there. Grandpa already had them half headed to the altar, and she wasn't about to give him more fodder.

So they got dressed, and she inched open her bedroom door. Rafe moved up behind her.

"Sneaking me out the front door?" he whispered in her ear.

She laughed and turned to face him. "Kind of."

He kissed her again, and then they slid out of her room to the front porch.

"Thanks for the barbecue tonight," she said.

"Thanks for dessert."

She swept her finger across his lips. "Truly, my pleasure."

He kissed her, and she knew he meant for it to be a short goodnight kiss. But she was leaning against the door, and he moved into her, and she couldn't resist sliding her hand against his chest. And then she was lost in him again, and before she knew it he had closed the front door and they were kissing long and deeply and there was no way she was going to let him go.

He broke the kiss. "Back to your bedroom?"

She nodded. "Definitely."

So much for sneaking him out of her room. Maybe just one more round, then she'd have him leave.

CHAPTER 24

RAFE AND THE CREW OF ENGINE 6 WERE CURRENTLY IN competition with Ladder 6, doing hose drills. It was backbreaking, sweat-inducing work, but he was determined that their team would win.

They came in two seconds behind Ladder 6.

Dammit.

"Should have run faster, Rafe," Mitchell said as they caught their breath at the end of the drill. "You were lagging."

Rafe faced off against Mitchell. "Oh, I was the one lagging? You could barely heft the hose onto your shoulder. You must have eaten too many ribs last night."

Ginger walked by. "I ate hummus and salad for dinner last night, and I kicked both your asses."

Rafe glared at Ginger, then looked over at Mitchell, who shrugged and said, "She did."

"Yeah, she did. Shit."

Mitchell clapped him on the back. "The barbecue was great, man. No regrets. Except we ran like slugs out there. I probably shouldn't have eaten that fourth plate."

Rafe laughed as Mitchell walked away.

Well, hell. He probably shouldn't have stayed up half the night making love to Carmen. Then again, he thought about the way her body had moved under—and over—his, the sounds she tried so hard not to make, the way she'd come apart for him time and time again. The way they'd both collapsed—finally.

Totally worth it. He wished he hadn't had to leave her before dawn. She'd been wrapped around him, one leg across his stomach, her head on his shoulder. Despite it being hot-as-fuck summer, waking up to Carmen's body against his was something he could get used to.

The alarm sounded, and he ran for the truck bay, slid into his turnout gear and boots and climbed into the truck. Ladder 6 was also responding.

"Report of three-alarm fire at a six-story apartment," Jackson said. "Stations 23 and 16 also responding. Smoke reported from the third floor."

"That sounds like a clusterfuck," Rafe said.

"So we'll need to do evacuations," Ginger said. "And set up on the floor below the fire."

Jackson nodded. "We'll do our assessment as soon as we get there."

They were the first on scene. Captain and battalion chief had also come on scene, so they would direct the project. The building was old brick, and Rafe saw flames. Not good.

They entered the lobby of the apartment. Building manager was already there, and people were walking out from the stairwell.

"Lock out the elevators," Jackson said to Mitchell and Ginger. "We don't want anyone getting stuck."

Mitchell and Ginger nodded and hurried off to the elevators. As soon as both elevators got to the main floors, they'd lock them down to make sure no one else could get on.

Jackson opened up the key box to get access to all the apartments in case they had to evacuate someone or assist with removal.

Once elevators were shut down, Jackson got with his team. "Ladder team set up outside and start putting water to those flames. The rest of you set up on two and drag hose up to three. The backup teams will start evacuations."

Rafe nodded. "You got it, Lieutenant."

Rafe had Mitchell, Ginger and Tommy with him. They went out to the truck and grabbed their gear, then entered the stairwell. When they got to the second floor and chocked the door open, they unlocked the standpipe that would provide the water they needed. Rafe unscrewed the cap off the standpipe with his wrench and attached the elbow. They flushed the system into the stairwell to rid the pipe of debris, then moved up the stairwell and made their way to the third floor.

"Mask up," he said. "Smoke's heavy up here."

They propped the door and laid the hose down the hallway. Fortunately, it appeared as if there were no people up here, though his team knocked on all the doors anyway, announcing themselves as the fire department and listening for sounds of people inside. Grateful that there were no answers, they walked their way closer through the thickening smoke.

It was easy to find the apartment where the fire was located. The orange glow was obviously visible under the doorway.

"We're at the fire," Rafe said into his mic.

"Fighting it outside as well with ladder team," Jackson reported. "Take it down carefully and let us know if you need backup."

"You got it."

"This is gonna be ugly," Mitchell said.

Rafe nodded, still remembering what it was like to be knocked out by the blast from the back draft. He didn't want a repeat of that, so he intended to be cautious as they entered the apartment.

When they made sure the hose was laid out, he got on his mic.

"Charge the hose."

They waited for water to fill the line. When it did, they soaked the door, then opened it.

The room was fully engulfed. They doused it with water and made their way inside. It was already apparent to Rafe that the flames had gone through the ceiling and into the floor above. Rafe reported that to Jackson, who said he'd send another team in and call for more backup. They already had the other teams checking floors and making sure there was sufficient air in the lobby in case they needed to resupply.

Rafe's team could only work one apartment at a time, so they cleared the main room and moved into the next, putting the fire out in the kitchen, the hallway and a small bathroom. The entire apartment was an inferno, so they took their time to make sure the fire was fully extinguished.

With the hoses pouring in from the open windows from the ladder team, they had this under control. At least on this floor. Rafe heard on his earpiece that the fire had spread to the north side of the building, so the other stations were battling it there.

Rafe's stomach dropped as they doused the flames in the master bedroom and he surveyed the scene. It was clear there was a body in the bed.

Shit. Clearing an empty apartment was one thing. Finding out someone hadn't made it? That sucked. Hard.

"We've got a body in the master bedroom," Rafe reported.

It took Jackson a couple of seconds to respond. "I'll notify the coroner and the fire marshal."

"I hate this part of the job," Ginger said, her hand on his back as he led with the hose.

"Same," Rafe said.

They didn't have time to stop. They moved into the other bedroom and extinguished the fire in there, but Rafe's thoughts continued to linger on the person in the other room who hadn't made it out.

They did another walk-through, making sure there were no other hot spots, then moved into the hallway and entered the adjoining apartments. There was a small fire in one that they put out easily. The fire hadn't yet made it into the apartment on the other side.

With the fire out, they could go in and start checking walls for flare-ups to make sure nothing would reignite.

They went downstairs to unload their air tanks and put on fresh ones just in case new flames broke out.

"Everything okay up there?" Jackson asked.

Rafe nodded, still feeling the effects of finding the body, but shoving it aside for now. He had a job to do. "Fire's out. We'll head back up to check for hot spots."

"Okay. We won't send the coroner up there until all the smoke is cleared, but the fire investigation team is on their way."

He nodded and grabbed his pry bar. His crew went back upstairs, poking through the debris and the walls, making sure the fire hadn't reignited.

Mitchell and Tommy were working in the main living area. Ginger was in the kitchen, and Rafe told them he'd work the bedrooms. He steered clear of disturbing the area around the body in the master bedroom, because he knew the coroner and the fire investigation team wouldn't want that space disturbed.

He made his way into the smaller bedroom. Nothing in there, and he breathed a little easier.

They finished their walk-through, then Rafe notified Jackson.

"Noted," was all Jackson said. "Is it clear up there?"

"Yeah."

"Coroner and fire investigation team are on their way up to you."

Rafe waited for them. He led them to the bedroom where the body was located, then waited to make sure no new fires broke out while they did their jobs, listening in as the coroner indicated it was a smaller adult body and likely female.

Damn.

She'd been all alone in here with no one to help her.

They should have gotten here in time to save her.

Once the body was bagged and removed, Rafe and his team walked down with them.

All three stations were waiting as the coroner's crew wheeled the body outside. Rafe and his team walked behind them. It was somber and quiet as they watched them load the body into the coroner's van.

"You okay?" Jackson asked. Kal was next to him.

"I'm fine."

Jackson nodded, knowing he didn't want to talk about it. Not right now.

"Let's pick up and get out of here."

They learned from a few of the people who lived on the same floor that the woman lived alone, worked the late shift at a restaurant and slept in most mornings. That's all they knew at the moment since the investigation team would have to determine the cause of the fire.

It took another couple of hours to clean up and roll hoses, put all their equipment back in the truck and coordinate with the other stations and do a final walk-through of the entire apartment complex to make sure nothing else was going to spark up again.

When they finally made it back to the station, Jackson asked Rafe to write up a report about the scene in the apartment so he could add it to his own. After he showered and scrubbed down the grit from the fire, writing the report took Rafe several hours. He didn't want to leave out any details, because he knew this one had been big, and he wanted to make sure he got it all in there. He only stopped to eat dinner, then went back to work. He read through it several times, then asked Ginger, Tommy and Mitchell to read it over to make sure he hadn't missed anything.

They all called it good, but he wanted to go over it again. He remembered a few fine details, so he added those in and then turned the report in to Jackson.

They ended up getting another call. Fortunately, it was a minor car accident with no injuries, so they weren't on scene long.

By the time they got back, Rafe figured he'd crash in his bunk, but he couldn't sleep, couldn't handle the darkness. Every time he closed his eyes, all he could see was the charred remains of that apartment and that body in the bed.

Had she cried out, or died of smoke inhalation, unaware of the fire breaking out around her?

Too many damn questions.

He got up and went into the main room. It was empty, so he grabbed a bag of chips and a water and turned the TV on. He found the sports channel, though he wasn't really tuned in to the scores or what the commentators were reporting on. It was just talking. Noise. Exactly what he needed right now. Something, anything, to drown out the visuals in his head.

Jackson slid onto the sofa cushion next to him.

"Can't sleep?"

"No."

Jackson looked at the TV for a few minutes, then over at Rafe.

"Wanna talk about it?" he asked.

"Not really." Rafe continued to stare at the TV.

"It might help."

"Probably. But not tonight. It's too raw for me right now, Lieutenant."

Jackson nodded. "Maybe tomorrow, when I'm your brother again and not your lieutenant."

"Maybe."

"Okay." Jackson stood and left the room.

Rafe continued to stare at the TV, not really sure what he was even watching.

He didn't care, either. As long as he had noise, he'd be good. Sleep would come later.

Much later.

CHAPTER 25

CARMEN CHEWED ON A RAGGED FINGERNAIL AND STARED out her kitchen window. Though she had no idea what she was even staring at. It wasn't like staring at the side of Rafe's house was going to provide any answers to all her questions.

She hadn't seen Rafe for three days. Three long days. And she didn't understand why.

After his last shift she'd called and asked him over for dinner with her and her grandfather. He'd politely turned her down, saying he had "things to do" that night. But when she'd gone out to the grocery store, his truck had been in the driveway. And it had stayed in the driveway the entire night.

She'd texted him the next day from work asking him if he was okay. He'd given her a three-word answer: *I'm fine, thanks.*

He hadn't asked her how she was or in any way engaged her in conversation. Just that vague three-word answer. And then she hadn't heard from him at all that day. He'd been on shift the next day, so she knew she wouldn't hear from him, but she still texted him to see if everything was all right with him.

This time, no reply at all. She had often texted him when he was at the station, and he'd always replied to her.

So today she had the day off, and so did Rafe. And she intended to get to the bottom of whatever was going on with him.

"You're sure staring a hole in the Donovans' house."

She pulled her attention away from the window and onto her grandfather, who sat at the kitchen table playing solitaire.

"I am not. I'm looking at the weeds I need to pull around the side of the house."

Grandpa gave her the side-eye. "No, you're not. You're wondering why you haven't seen your boyfriend in a few days."

She pivoted and leaned against the counter, crossing her arms. "And how would you know that?"

"Because you've been moping, and because I haven't seen that boy around here, and you haven't gone over there. Simple deduction."

"Okay, fine, Sherlock. There is something going on. He's been quiet and withdrawn and isn't answering my text messages."

"Maybe he's busy."

"And maybe he's ready to move on. Maybe he's seeing someone else."

Her grandfather shook his head. "Why does your mind go there first thing? You know Rafe is nothing like Tod."

She didn't know that. Okay, she did. But she couldn't help but have those thoughts. Or maybe he was losing interest in her.

"You should go over there and talk to him."

"I don't know. If he wanted to talk to me, he'd call or text or come over. He obviously doesn't want to see me."

"It could be that something's wrong and you need to go find out what it is."

And get her heart broken? No, thanks. She turned back to the sink she'd been scrubbing before her mind had started to wander.

"Carmen."

"What?"

"Go talk to him. You'll drive yourself crazy until you get answers."

She lifted one shoulder in a half shrug. "Maybe."

"Now."

"Fine." She rinsed the sink and dried her hands. "But only so we don't have to keep talking about it."

Grandpa was looking down at his cards. "Whatever you think is best."

Oh, right. As if he hadn't manipulated the entire conversation.

She went into her room, freshened up a bit, then headed out the front door, feeling ridiculous because her pulse was racing.

What was the worst thing that could happen? He'd slam the door in her face? She didn't think Rafe would do that, but then again, who knew with men? They were entirely unpredictable, and often untrustworthy.

She sucked in a deep breath, released it, then rang the doorbell.

And waited.

No answer. Maybe he wasn't home. His truck was there, but it was the only vehicle parked in the driveway. Maybe he'd gone somewhere with one of his brothers.

Finally, though, the door opened and Rafe stood there. He looked unkempt and awful, like he hadn't slept in days.

"Oh. Hey, Carmen."

"Rafe. Are you okay?"

"I'm fine."

She waited for him to invite her in. He didn't, which only irritated her more. But she was also concerned about the state of his appearance, so the caring side of her was having a deep war with the part of her that was very pissed off at him.

"Mind if I come in?" she finally asked.

"Sure." He stepped aside and held the door for her.

She walked past him, waiting for him to shut the door. He raked his fingers through his hair. "I was playing a video game."

As if that explained him completely ignoring her for days.

She followed him into the kitchen.

"Want something to drink?" he asked.

"No, thanks. I'm good."

"Okay."

He stood there, leaning against the kitchen island, as if he was waiting for her to do something or state her business.

So. Irritating.

"Rafe. You haven't spoken a sentence to me in three days. You haven't called or texted me. What's going on?"

He looked down at his bare feet. "Nothing. I'm fine."

He smelled like he hadn't showered. His hair was a wild mess, he had beard stubble all over his face and his shorts and T-shirt were wrinkled as if he'd slept in them. In short, he was a hot mess. And that just wasn't like Rafe at all.

Worst of all, there were dark circles shadowed under his eyes. Something was definitely wrong.

She stepped up to him and laid her hand on his forearm. "You're not fine. Tell me what's going on."

"I already told you. It's nothing." He pulled his arm away and went to the fridge to grab a beer.

"Rafe. It's not even noon."

"So?"

She took the beer from his hand and placed it on the counter. She retrieved a glass from the cabinet, filled it with ice and water and handed it to him. "So . . . talk to me."

She saw the misery on his face. He took several deep swallows of the water, then laid the glass down. "It's a long story."

"I've got the time." She grasped his hand, grabbed the glass of water and led him into the living room. She pulled him down on the sofa so he was seated next to her.

Then she waited, wanting to give him the time to open up to her.

For a couple of minutes he didn't say anything, just stared down at their hands clasped together.

"There was a fire the other day at an apartment building. I covered lead along with some of my other team members. We got into the main apartment where the fire had broken out, extinguished the flames. Found one person in the master bedroom, dead."

She squeezed his hand. She'd seen fire victims in the ER before. It was devastating. She couldn't imagine what he'd seen there.

"It was a young woman. We didn't get there in time to save her."

"Oh, God. I'm so sorry, Rafe."

He looked up at her, his eyes filled with tears. "We've had fatalities on calls before. I don't know why this one bothers me so much."

She rubbed his arm. "Chances are she was already gone before you even arrived on the scene. You know that, right?"

"Yeah, I've been debriefed and talked to the counselor and the chaplain. That's what they both told me. Doesn't make it any easier to swallow." He dragged his fingers through his hair. "I still see her in my head when I try to sleep. Every time I close my eyes, she's right there. I can't make it go away."

"And you probably won't be able to. Not right away. Not for a while. But eventually, it'll pass."

He frowned at her. "So what am I supposed to do?"

"Live with it. It's part of your job. Sometimes we lose people. And sometimes it's horrible."

He looked defeated. "It fucking sucks."

"Yes. It does. That part of it does definitely suck. But how many lives have you saved, Rafe? How many people have you pulled out of the wreckage of a vehicle? How many people have you saved from a burning building?"

"No clue." He shrugged, as if that didn't matter.

It did matter. It was everything. She needed to make him see that.

"When your mind wants to go to that dark place, think about the lives you've saved instead of focusing on the one you lost."

"She was twenty-one, working the night shift at a restaurant while she juggled college classes. She was just starting out, Carmen. And now her life is over."

Carmen's heart ached for the loss. And for Rafe's pain. "It hurts. I know it hurts. But you can't dwell on this. If you do, it'll destroy you. Look at what you've done the past few days. You're way in your head, babe, and you've got to climb out."

He sighed, then tilted his head to stare at her. "I guess you're right."

"I know I'm right. You forget where I work. I see death every day. Burn victims, missing limbs, paralyzed victims, suicide attempts, domestic violence, gunshots, drug overdoses. You name it, it comes through my ER."

He rubbed his thumb over hers. "How do you deal with all of it?"

"At first I didn't. My first year in the ER, I came home and cried nearly every day. And then, thanks to a very kind supervisor on my floor who taught me well, I learned to steel myself, to not get emotionally involved. I was no good to my patients if I fell apart. I was no good to their families if they saw me crying over what happened to the people they loved. My job is to see to their care. My job ends when I walk out the door at the end of my shift. I'll never last as an ER nurse if I take it home with me every day. It'll end my career. I had to learn that fast."

She rubbed his arm. "You have to learn to leave it at the station at the end of your shift, too, Rafe. Or it'll take you, piece by piece, until there's nothing left of you. And then the job you love will end up becoming the job you hate."

He finally straightened and shifted to face her. "But how do you *not* feel?"

"I didn't say I don't feel anything. I have empathy for all my patients. I just don't have an emotional attachment to any of them. My job is to help them, to provide care for them to the best of my abilities. But I don't get involved with them, with their lives or with their emotions. My patients need me to be damn good at my job, and that's what I give them. They don't need someone to love them. They need someone to help make them well.

"Your victims don't need you to fall apart. They need you to put out the fire, pull the ones who are alive from a smoky building, rescue them from the wreckage of a vehicle, or the countless other things you do every day. That woman who died the other day? She has family to mourn her. It was an awful tragedy. But . . . you saved other lives that day by putting out that fire. Other families will be able to move back into that building and go on with their lives because of what you did. That's the part you have to focus on. The other part? You have to let it go."

He nodded. "You're right. Thanks for talking me through it."

"You're welcome. But I still think you need to continue the counseling, because it's not going to go away in a day."

He raked his fingers through his hair. "Yeah. I guess so, since this one seems to be lingering."

She nodded. "It will. Until you get to the place where you can accept it and move forward."

"I guess sometimes this will happen."

"It happens to all of us who care for people. It happens to me sometimes and I have people that I go talk to. Our jobs aren't easy."

He blew out a breath. "Thanks. I needed to hear that."

She swept her hand over his jaw. "I'm glad I could help."

"Yeah, more than you know. I guess I need to take a shower. And eat."

"You go shower. I'll fix you some food."

"You sure?"

She nodded.

"Thanks. I won't be long."

"Take your time. You might need to do some extra scrubbing. You kind of smell."

He smiled, and good God, it was nice to see that smile on his face again.

He stood and sighed, then disappeared upstairs.

Carmen went to the fridge, pulled out some eggs, a ham steak and fruit. She threw the ham steak into the skillet to start frying. While that was cooking, she sliced some strawberries and added blueberries and blackberries to a bowl. Then she cracked the eggs and whisked them in a bowl, set it aside and sliced some green peppers and onions. When the ham was done cooking, she chopped it up, mixed it with the eggs and vegetables and tossed them all in the skillet together to whip up an omelet. She added cheese at the end, folded it over and slid it onto a plate, then put the fruit salad into a cup.

She heard the door open, and Rafe came downstairs looking a lot more like—Rafe. He wore a clean pair of navy shorts and a powder blue tank.

He came up next to her. "You made an omelet?"

"I did." She handed him the plate. "You smell a lot better. And you shaved."

"Yeah." He took the plate from her, then looked around. "You're not eating?"

"I had a big breakfast with my grandfather this morning. I'll eat some of this fruit."

She sat with him at the kitchen table, happy to see him devouring the omelet and the fruit while she casually scooped up some of the fruit salad.

"This is really good," he said in between mouthfuls.

"Glad you like it." She'd also poured him a large glass of mango juice, which he greedily emptied, making her wonder when he'd last eaten a decent meal. Now she was happy she'd made the omelet oversize.

When he finished, he took his plate to the sink and cleaned up all the dishes, something that made Carmen think he might be on the mend, especially since he nudged her out of the way when she tried to help. He told her to go sit and relax.

Once he was done with cleanup, he grabbed another glass of juice and came to sit beside her.

"So, what have you been up to?" he asked.

"Mostly being pissed off at you."

He cocked a brow. "Yeah? Why?"

"You were in pain and you blew me off."

He shrugged. "I internalize when I'm upset."

She shook her head. "That's not going to work for me, Rafe. The last guy who held secrets from me was my ex, and it was because he was fucking someone else."

Rafe gave her a look. "Carmen. I'm not with anyone else."

"And how was I supposed to know that? I called you to invite you to dinner at my house, and you said you were busy. I texted you and you ignored me. Put yourself in my place. If the shoe was on the other foot, what would you think?"

He started to answer, then stopped. "Okay, you have a point. But how many times do I have to tell you that I'm not your ex? I'm never going to act like him, or treat you like he did. So stop comparing me to him. That's not fair."

Now it was her turn to blurt out a reply, and then hold back for an instant as his words sunk in. "You're right. I've been holding you to this low standard left by my asshole ex for way too long. And for that, I'm sorry. I won't do it again."

He nodded. "Thanks."

"But you can't shut me out when you're feeling shitty. We

won't have a relationship if we don't communicate with each other." She swept her hand along the side of his face. "It can't only be the good times we share, Rafe. We have to be willing to share the bad ones, too, you know?"

He took her hand and pressed a kiss to her palm. "Yes, I do know. I should have let you in. I'd have felt a hell of a lot better a hell of a lot sooner if I'd just come to you and told you what happened. I'm sorry, Carmen. It won't happen again."

She felt the sincerity in his words and in his apology. Words hovered on her tongue. Important, monumental words that scared the hell out of her. She wasn't ready to say them. Not yet. Not until she was certain she was going to hear them back.

"Thank you. Are you feeling better?" she asked.

"Much."

"Good. So how about that invitation to have dinner with my grandfather and me? It's still open. And Felice is coming over tonight."

"Oh yeah?" He leaned back against the sofa. "And how's that going?"

"Surprisingly well, actually. She came over the night I invited you. She's very sweet."

"I'd love to come over for dinner. Thanks for inviting me— again. And for forgiving me." He pulled her onto his lap, his fingers splaying over her hips. "Now. Is there anything I can do to make it up to you?"

She laid her palms on his chest, realizing how much she'd missed the feel of his strength and heat, and never failing to be surprised at how fast he could fire up her desires.

"Where's the rest of the fam?"

"Becks is at work. Jackson is having his truck detailed. Kal is doing a training session."

Knowing that they were alone sparked her up. She realized it had been days, and she needed him inside her.

"Then yes, Rafe. Sex. Right now. Right here. I need you."

She suddenly found herself flipped over onto her back on the sofa. Rafe kneeled between her legs, his hands on her knees, spreading them apart.

"I need to get a condom."

She was throbbing, aching for him. "Then go. And hurry up."

After he left, she shimmied out of her shorts and underwear. She was about to take off her tank top, but he had already gotten back.

"That was fast," she said.

He dropped his shorts and boxer briefs, his cock erect and painfully beautiful. "I missed you the past few days."

"Same." She pulled off her tank and bra, tossing them to the floor.

Rafe slipped on the condom and lowered her to the sofa.

She wrapped her legs around his hips. "I don't need foreplay. I'm ready for you now."

"That's good, because I'm rock-hard and aching for you," he said. He slid inside her with one thrust, making her gasp from the searing intensity of the way her body responded to him.

He bent his head to kiss her, and she whimpered, not able to get close enough to him as he moved within her. She dug her heels into his back as he drove deeper, harder, seemingly needing this as much as she did. The leather sofa soon grew slick with their sweat as they slid together in wild abandon, lost in each other and in the sensations. The way he touched her, moving his hands over her breasts, down the side of her rib cage, then gripping her hip as he rolled against her.

His tongue flicked against her earlobe.

"Me encanta estar dentro de ti."

I love being inside you.

His whispered words sparked an orgasm so intense she nearly

cried from the pure joy of it. But instead, she cried out his name and surged against him, shaking as her climax rolled on and on.

He thrust hard and came, his entire body vibrating with his orgasm, his fingers digging into her flesh as he pulled her tight against him, his face buried in her neck.

She panted, catching her breath, for the first time since she seemingly lost her mind with lust, suddenly aware that they were only a short distance from the front door. And she was totally naked and utterly stuck to the leather sofa.

"We need to get unstuck," she said.

He lifted his head and looked down at her, smiling. "I don't know. I kind of like being stuck to you."

She splayed her palms on his chest. "I mean my ass is stuck to the sofa."

"Okay." He disengaged, then stood, helping her up.

She grabbed her clothes and dashed into the downstairs bathroom to clean up. She really needed a shower, but that wasn't going to be possible right now. She grabbed a washcloth and went into the living room to wipe down the sofa. When she was done, Rafe was leaning against the doorway.

"What are you doing?" he asked.

"Wiping down the sweat from the sofa."

He laughed and shook his head. "Want something to drink?"

"A tall glass of ice water would be amazing."

"Sure." He pushed off the wall, and she followed him into the kitchen, tossing the washcloth into the laundry room on her way.

He handed her a glass of ice water. They sat at the kitchen island together. She took several sips of the water. "Thank you," she said.

"No, thank you." He leaned over and kissed her. "For the talk, mainly, but the sex was pretty damn good, too."

She laughed. "You're welcome."

Now everything was better. At least she hoped it was better for Rafe. She certainly felt like things had been somewhat resolved. She knew he wasn't going to forget what he'd been through or what he'd seen right away. Or ever. But hopefully, he'd start to tuck the nightmare away and understand that he saved lives all the time, and look at the more positive aspects of his job now.

She cared about him. She loved him.

At some point, she was going to have to tell him that. But for now, those words could wait. It wasn't like either of them was going anywhere.

CHAPTER 26

"HEY, WHO BOUGHT FLOWERS?"

Rafe was just coming down the stairs and glared at Kal. "Leave those alone. They're mine."

Kal cocked a brow at Rafe. "Someone sent you flowers?"

"No, dumbass. I bought the flowers. For Carmen." He sat down at the kitchen table to put on his tennis shoes.

"Oooh. Things must be getting serious."

He looked up at Kal and frowned. "Flowers aren't serious."

"Aren't they?" Jackson asked as he came into the room and leaned down to sniff the bouquet Rafe had bought when he'd run out earlier. "I don't remember you ever buying flowers for a woman before."

"You don't see everything I do." But his brothers were right. He'd never bought flowers for a woman before, because he'd never been serious about any woman.

Was he serious now? He sure as hell had had a serious conversation with Carmen earlier today, had opened up to her in ways he hadn't even with his brothers.

Jackson and Kal both had sat down and tried to talk with him about the fire. He hadn't been ready, hadn't wanted to talk about it. He'd been in his head, replaying that day over and over again, wondering what he could have done differently, how he might have saved that woman. And every time he'd come up a failure.

Talking it out with Carmen had been a balm to his soul. She'd reminded him that they didn't win every time, and not everyone could be saved. But they both saved lives every day on the job, and that's what he needed to focus on.

"Your mood has improved, too," Jackson said, coming over to lay his hand on Rafe's shoulder. "You feeling better now?"

Rafe nodded. "Yeah. I was dealing with some shit about the fire the other day. Carmen came over and helped me deal with it."

"I'm glad to hear it. But you know, you can always talk to me or to Kal if something about a fire gets to you."

"I know. I just wasn't ready to face it yet. Losing that woman hit me harder than I realized."

Kal sat down next to him at the kitchen table. "I'm sorry you had to be the one to see that. It has to be one of the worst things to ever go through."

Rafe hadn't opened up before because he hadn't wanted to talk about it. Not until he'd talked it out with Carmen. Now he did. "It was bad. I kept thinking if we had gotten there sooner we might have been able to save her."

Jackson pulled out the chair on the other side of Rafe. "You know that's not possible. She was gone before we ever got up to her floor."

"Yeah, I know that now. Carmen made me see that I need to focus more on the lives we do save, not the ones we lose."

Jackson nodded. "That's some damn good advice."

"Working where she does, I'm sure she knows that better than anyone," Kal said.

"She does. And thanks, guys. I know I can always count on

you to be here for me. And the same goes for both of you. If you need me, I'm here."

"Does that mean you'll buy me flowers?" Kal asked.

Rafe gave a side-eye look at Kal. "Do you want flowers?"

"I don't know. Maybe. Those are pretty."

Rafe shook his head. "Dickhead."

"Prick."

Jackson laughed, then started walking away. "Good to see everything's back to normal now. I gotta go get ready for my date."

"Maybe you should pick up some flowers," Kal suggested.

"Huh. Maybe I should." He pointed at Kal. "You're smart. I never knew that."

"Fuck you."

"Love you, too, bro." Jackson disappeared upstairs.

Rafe stood. "What have you got going on tonight?"

"I'm beat after that training class today. I'm just gonna hang out, fix myself some food and crash."

"How did it go?"

"It was intense. TRT is gonna kick my ass."

"You're gonna love doing this, aren't you?"

Kal leaned back in the chair. "It's like this is what I was meant to do all along. I could tell as soon as we started the training that it was a perfect fit. It's hard, yeah, but I need that challenge."

He could tell from the expression on Kal's face that the Technical Rescue Team was exactly where his brother belonged. "That's great, Kal. When will you make the move from Station 6?"

"I have to go through the full training class and qualification. Then if I get accepted, I'll move."

Rafe already knew that Kal would ace everything once he was committed to something. And Kal was definitely committed to this. "You know I'm gonna miss you."

"Same."

"But I'm damn happy you're gonna do something you love."

Kal grinned. "Thanks. Me, too."

Rafe picked up his phone to check the time. "Okay, I gotta go."

"Have fun. Don't forget the flowers. Unless you wanna give those to me."

"Funny."

He grabbed the bouquet and walked next door, rang the bell and waited. The door opened and an older, very attractive woman answered.

She smiled at him. "You must be Rafe Donovan. I'm Felice Sheffield."

He held out his hand. "Very nice to meet you, Felice."

She looked at the flowers. "Carmen is going to love those. Come on in."

He followed Felice inside. She wore orange-and-white capris, bright orange sandals, and an orange button-down shirt. She had shocking white, curly hair that she wore cropped short.

"How convenient that you live next door," she said as they walked past the living room toward the kitchen. "Jimmy tells me you and your brothers are firefighters."

"Yes, ma'am."

"That's so nice. My uncle was a firefighter and used to tell me so many amazing stories. I admire what you do."

"Thank you."

"I was a mechanic in the army."

He blinked. "Is that right?"

They entered the kitchen. Carmen was at the stove, and Jimmy sat at the kitchen table.

"Hey, Rafe," Jimmy said.

"Hey, Jimmy." He walked over to Carmen with the flowers. "I brought these for you."

She looked at the bouquet of mixed flowers. He didn't really know what she'd like, so he picked out this one because it was colorful and vibrant and it smelled delicious, which reminded him of her.

"These are beautiful, Rafe. Thank you." She kissed him, just a brief brush of her lips across his, but it was the first time she'd kissed him in front of her grandfather, so he figured that was a big deal.

He cleared his throat and stepped away.

"So, Felice was just telling me she was in the army."

Felice went over to the stove. "I met my husband, Ronald, there. He was in charge of large equipment, and I was a mechanic. So our paths crossed quite a bit."

"That's fascinating," Rafe said.

"My stint in the military paid for both of our college educations," Felice said.

"Beer?" Carmen asked Rafe.

"I can get it." He went to the fridge and grabbed a beer while listening to Felice tell the story of her relationship with her husband and how they juggled college while having their son.

"It wasn't always easy, but we made it work." Felice looked over at Jimmy. "You know what it was like back then."

Jimmy nodded. "Tough times. Carmen's grandmother and I didn't have much, but we had our daughter and a small place to live. And I brought enough home to put food on the table, and Maria did some housecleaning when she could, so every little bit helped."

Rafe knew what it was like to have nothing, when even a little seemed like a lot. "But you both made it work."

"We did," Felice said.

"And we were happy," Jimmy said. "You've got to find your happiness no matter where you are in life, don't you, Felice?"

Felice glanced across the room at Jimmy and sighed. "That you do."

Rafe exchanged glances with Carmen. She gave him a knowing smile.

Yeah, Jimmy and Felice had a serious romance going on.

"Anything I can do to help?" Rafe asked.

"No, you sit," Felice said. "Carmen and I have this under control."

"She's teaching me how to make spaetzle," Carmen said.

At his questioning look, Carmen added, "Noodles. German noodles."

"Oh, cool."

"You could put the sausages on the grill, if you'd like."

"Consider it done." He got up and took the sausages out of the fridge. Jimmy went outside with him and helped him get the grill ready.

"You look stronger," Rafe said, noticing how much time Jimmy spent on his feet these days. "Must be all that hot sex you're having. Helps build muscle."

Jimmy choked out a laugh. "No comment."

"But you like her—Felice."

"A lot. More than a lot."

Rafe studied him as he waited for the grill to come up to the right temperature. "So you're in love with her."

"Yeah."

"That's great, Jimmy. I'm happy for you. Felice seems like an amazing woman."

Jimmy stared into the house with a smile before turning his attention back at Rafe. "She is. I think I realized I was in love with her when she took a step away after her son had reservations about us."

"But that's resolved now, right?"

"Oh yeah. He and I got a chance to sit down together. I told him I loved my wife as much as she loved his dad. That there would never be anyone like that for either of us, but that both of us deserved some happiness. He understood that. Felice told me that her son said he couldn't ask for a better guy to look after his mom."

Rafe smiled. "That's a great thing to say. You must have been relieved to hear that."

"You have no idea."

Rafe put the sausages on, then took a long swallow of his beer.

"I want to ask Felice to marry me."

Rafe blinked. "Really? Does Carmen know that?"

"Not yet. I have to talk to Carmen about it first. Make sure she's okay with it. And I need to ask David, Felice's son, too. And then if they both say it's okay, I'll ask Felice."

Rafe blew out a breath. "Big steps, man."

"Don't I know it. But I want her in my life. I want to wake up next to her every day and go to sleep next to her every night."

Rafe turned the sausages, then closed the grill. "I hope it all works out for you, Jimmy. I want you to be happy."

"Thanks. I want the same for you. And for Carmen."

Uh-oh. He wasn't sure where this was leading. He hadn't had a chance to talk to Carmen about his feelings about her, and he didn't want to have the conversation with Jimmy before he had it with Carmen.

He knew how he felt about her. He was crazy about her. Hell, he was in love with her. He probably had been for a while now, but those were big steps. Big feelings.

And he sure as hell wasn't going to tell her grandfather that until he told her.

"Thanks, Jimmy. Carmen and I are doing great."

"But long term . . . where do you see it going?"

He was going to have to tread carefully here. "Are you worried about leaving her behind if you and Felice make a life together?"

He shrugged. "Something like that."

"The one thing I've always known about Carmen is that she

can take care of herself. She doesn't need anyone to hold her hand. Not you, and not me. It's what I admire most about her. I don't think you'll have to worry about her, Jimmy."

"I know I shouldn't, but I wouldn't be family if I didn't. I just need to know she's going to be okay, that all these moves I'm trying to make aren't going to hurt her."

Rafe had to admire the consideration Jimmy took with Carmen's feelings. Family took care of one another, just like Rafe and Jackson and Kal had done when they were on their own. Like the Donovans had done when they'd adopted all of them. So he understood where Jimmy was coming from.

Which meant he was going to have to allay some of Jimmy's fears.

"I'm going to be honest with you, Jimmy. I straight up can't tell you where Carmen and I are going to end up. Not until I have some conversations with her first. But I can tell you that as of this moment, I'm not planning on going anywhere. She's in my life, and I intend to keep her there, as long as she's willing to stay."

Jimmy nodded and grasped Rafe's shoulder. "That's good enough for me. Thank you."

Rafe turned off the grill and loaded the sausages on the plate. They went inside, and Rafe saw that Felice and Carmen were laughing and drinking wine at the counter.

If he knew his woman like he thought, she was getting a bit tipsy.

"Sausages are done," he said.

She turned and grinned. "Fabulous. So is the spaetzle. And we made green beans. This is going to be so good, Rafe."

"I can't wait."

They sat at the table, and Carmen brought the bottle with her.

"Felice tells me she loves to travel," Carmen said, taking another swallow of wine. "And she goes to Europe a lot, to Germany and France and England."

"I've been telling Jimmy that he'll have to come with me," Felice said. "He loves beer and, oh, the beer in Germany is so good."

"We'll definitely have to hit up Germany," Jimmy said. "You know I like my beer."

Rafe was just digging the food. The noodles were different from what he was used to. They were also delicious. "This is really good. I like the noodles."

"I'm so glad," Felice said.

Rafe could see this—this scene as a family. Jimmy, Felice and Carmen sharing dinner together on a regular basis. He didn't know how the living arrangements would work themselves out.

He knew this was Jimmy's house. But Felice had a house as well. If they got married, would they move into her house or would she move in here? And if it was here, would Carmen stay?

He wished he could talk to Carmen about it, but it was up to Jimmy to discuss his future plans with Carmen. He assumed then Carmen would talk to him.

And how would Rafe fit into all of this?

How do you want to fit in, dude? What's your plan for your future with Carmen?

That was the big damn question, wasn't it?

Maybe he needed to focus less on Jimmy and Felice and figure out his own future life plan. Because it was clear as hell that he was done running around with different women. Carmen was it for him. The thought of not having her in his life caused his gut to twinge.

But how did she feel about it? About them?

Ask her, idiot. Tell her how you feel.

He needed to do that. But not while Jimmy was getting ready to upend her life with this whole proposing to Felice thing.

He'd wait. There was plenty of time.

After all, neither of them was going anywhere.

CHAPTER 27

"WAIT. HE WANTS TO GET MARRIED?"

Carmen nodded, trying to focus on the lunch menu in front of her. But Tess tugged on her arm.

"He wants to get married?"

She finally pulled her focus from the menu. "That's what he told me. He wants to propose to Felice."

"Wow. That's big, Carm."

"It sure is."

"How do you feel about it?"

She shrugged. "I don't know. Fine, I guess. Felice is good for my grandpa. He's healthy at the moment. He deserves to be happy."

"But?"

"No *but*. I guess it was just unexpected. I know they've been seeing each other on and off. More on lately than off."

Tess gave her a smile. "Hey, when you get to be the age of your grandfather, you don't have time to waste. When you fall in love with someone and know they're the one, you go for it. Time's precious, you know?"

She supposed she hadn't thought about it that way. When her grandfather had dropped the proposal bombshell on her the other night, she hadn't said much other than *Oh* and *That's great*. She probably should have been a little more enthusiastic on his behalf. He was likely very disappointed in her reaction.

Carmen had wanted to take Tess out for lunch today, for two reasons. One, to get out of the hospital for a break, and two, to give Tess some news.

It was always nice to have that time away, and there were several restaurants within walking distance of the hospital, so they ordered lunch and caught up on their lives.

"George and I are thinking of taking a big trip on our next vacation."

"Yeah?" Carmen took a sip of her iced tea. "What's the plan?"

"Maybe somewhere in the Caribbean. I've always wanted to go to St. Lucia."

"I know you have. You've been talking about it for years."

"I think I've finally convinced him. But money is kind of tight, so we'll see how the savings go."

Carmen grinned. "Well, I think they'll go pretty well for you, considering the news I have."

Tess frowned. "What news?"

"I'll be doing your official evaluation this afternoon, but I wanted to tell you I recommended you for a promotion to nurse supervisor of the ICU step-down unit. And the unit is going to offer you the job."

Tess blinked. "Get the fuck out of here. Seriously?"

Carmen grinned. "Seriously. Congratulations."

Tess put her hand over her mouth, and Carmen could see the tears well in her eyes.

"Do not cry. If you cry, then I'll cry."

Tess got out of her chair and flung her arms around Carmen. Carmen hugged her tight.

"Thank you," Tess said. "This means everything to me."

They hugged like that for a good minute, then Tess fell back in her chair. "I . . . don't know what to say."

"You don't have to say anything. You earned this promotion. You'll make a fine department supervisor, and I'll miss you like crazy in the ER."

"Holy shit. Wait 'til I tell George. He'll die."

Carmen grinned. "No, he'll take you to the Caribbean."

"He will, won't he? Oh my God, this is just the best day ever."

It was. She loved that Tess was getting what she deserved. And that made their lunch together so much better. In fact, they ended up taking a bit longer to eat, which was even more fun.

Then they got back to work. Carmen did Tess's evaluation that afternoon, which was probably the most fun she'd ever had doing an eval. They'd both grinned through the entire thing.

In two weeks, Tess would be moving up to the ICU, which meant Carmen would have to replace her in the ER. No easy task, and something else she'd have to add to her list of things to do. But for today? She was smiling.

And after work she would get to see Rafe. He was off today. They had a date tonight to see a movie. She didn't want to see a movie. She wanted to talk to him about her grandfather.

She pulled out her phone and texted him.

Ok if we cancel the movie and hang out at your place tonight?

He replied a few minutes later.

Fine with me. Everything ok?

She texted back with: *Just want to talk.*

He sent a reply: *Sure. See u tonight.*

He added pizza and wine emojis at the end, making her smile. That's what she needed. Rafe would help her make sense of all the questions she had in her head about her grandpa and his wanting to get married.

She was probably overreacting anyway.

But she ended up counting the hours until her shift was finished. She went home and changed clothes. Her grandfather had therapy today, and then he was going to Felice's house. He'd called her earlier and left her a message to let her know they were going to dinner and bingo tonight. He said he'd text what time he'd be home, or he might stay at Felice's tonight.

She'd ended up texting Rafe to let him know her grandfather was out, so he should come to her place, and she'd text him when she got home.

This way they could be alone in case Jackson and Becks and Kal were around.

She took a shower and slipped into a sundress. It was hot as the seventh level of hell out today, and the fewer clothes she had on, the better. The sundress had skinny straps and was cotton and short and just about perfect as far as minimal clothing went. Besides, it was totally cute with colorful geometric patterns over a white shift. Not that it mattered, since today she was going for comfort over pretty.

She texted Rafe that she was home, unlocked the front door, then went into the kitchen and poured herself a tall glass of wine. She cleaned potatoes and started slicing them to make fries, then made hamburger patties. She was chopping onions and tomatoes when Rafe came in.

"Something smells good in here," he said, coming around to press a kiss to the back of her neck. "Oh, it's you."

She giggled as goose bumps broke out on her skin. "It's the onions."

He continued to kiss along her shoulder. "Beg to differ."

She laughed. "How was your day?"

"Good. I got a summer lunch program finalized for the kids' center."

"You did? How did you manage that?"

"A few grants and some corporate sponsorship."

"That's fantastic, Rafe. What a wonderful thing to do for the community and for those kids." The man was always busy. And what an amazing thing he'd done. She admired him for that.

"Thanks. How was your day?"

"Good. I promoted Tess today, and did her evaluation, which was fun. Other than that, it was a light patient load."

"Nice. I'll bet Tess was happy."

"She was thrilled."

"That's awesome. So what can I do to help you?"

"I thought I'd make burgers and fries for dinner tonight."

"And I thought we were ordering pizza."

She shifted, leaning against the counter, and gave him a sweet smile. "Wouldn't you rather have burgers, with gooey cheddar cheese and avocado, along with homemade fries?"

He arched a brow. "Okay, that does sound better."

"Good, that's what we're having. Grab yourself a beer and go fire up the grill and put some oil in the fryer outside."

"You're so bossy."

She laughed. "You like me that way, because you eat better when I'm bossy."

"I'll accept that."

He fished a beer out of the fridge and went out back, so she finished slicing the vegetables and slipped those in the fridge.

She had to admit she appreciated having Rafe around to help her with dinner. She also liked how comfortable he obviously felt in her house. He never asked permission for anything, always offered to help, did dishes side by side with her and knew his way around putting things away in the cabinets.

Like now, when he came in and got the potatoes and burgers out of the fridge to take outside. It hadn't taken long for Rafe to become an integral part of her life.

She got out the avocados and sliced those, then grated cheese to put on the burgers. She also decided she wanted a salad, so she chopped up lettuce, tomato, carrots, cucumbers and added in some walnuts and cranberries to give it a little kick. She made a vinaigrette and put it in the fridge to cool. By then Rafe had come back in with the fries and the burgers.

She put all the condiments on the table, along with the nice, soft buns she'd bought at the store.

He grabbed the salad and dressing, and now it was time to eat. She was so hungry.

Rafe was obviously hungrier.

It always entertained her to watch Rafe eat. The guy had an appetite. When she invited him over, she knew he'd eat well, so she'd made sure to buy extra. By the time she'd finished her burger, he'd already gone through two, plus a rather large serving of fries and salad.

"I see you've worked really hard on slowing down," she said with a teasing smile.

He glanced over at her. "I did. I only ate two burgers."

She laughed.

It made her wonder what it would be like to have kids with him. What if they had all boys? What would it be like to feed three or four boys with appetites like his? She could only imagine what their weekly grocery bill would be like.

Still, she could well imagine cute little boys with thick heads of Rafe's dark hair and his soulful brown eyes.

Yeah, that giant grocery bill would be totally worth it.

"What?" he asked, startling her out of her fantasy.

She straightened. "Oh. Nothing. I was . . . thinking."

"About?"

Caught in the act. Now she'd have to come up with something. And she knew what she wanted to talk to him about. "My grandfather wants to propose to Felice."

"Is that what he wanted to talk to you about the other night?"

She nodded. "He sat me down and asked me what I thought about her, and then he said he loved her and wanted to marry her."

He dipped a French fry in ketchup and shoved it in his mouth, chewed and swallowed, then washed it down with a swig of beer. "And what did you say?"

"What was I supposed to say? Felice is wonderful, and it's obvious she loves my grandpa. If she makes him happy, what more could I want for him?"

"So you gave your blessing?"

"Actually, no. I was kind of shocked. It's all happening so fast, you know? I think I might have mumbled *oh, really?* a lot at him."

"That's not surprising. But if you love someone, how much time do you need?"

Interesting observation. "I guess. But I called him today after I got off work. I didn't want him to think I disapproved, so I told him he should ask Felice to marry him. Life is short, and it's not like the two of them have another fifty years or anything. They should enjoy their lives together."

"That's sweet. And you're right. People who love each other should be together."

"Yes." She looked down at her plate, suddenly unable to eat any more. She didn't know what was wrong with her other than everything suddenly seemed as if it was changing. She'd been so comfortable here with Grandpa. And now he and Felice would get married and then . . .

And then she had no idea what would happen.

Nothing was certain anymore.

Rafe laid his hand on hers. "What's wrong?"

"I feel . . . unsettled. Like my whole life is changing."

"Because of your grandpa?"

Her unsettled feeling was only partly because of her grand-father. It was also because of her feelings for Rafe. Feelings she was still holding on to, because she was still afraid to tell him how she felt. She hadn't been in love since her ex, and that had been an epic disaster. She was afraid to fall again, afraid if things went wrong she'd never recover.

She felt as if she was balancing on the edge of a cliff, unable to take a step back and unable to take the leap that could mean a possible amazing future—or utter catastrophe.

So instead, here she stayed. Hovering.

"Yes, because of my grandpa," she said, knowing she was lying to him but still unable to admit her feelings. "His decision changes a lot of things about my life."

"Do you know what you need?" he asked.

"No. What do I need?"

"You need some nighttime skinny-dipping."

She arched a brow. "In your pool?"

"Nah. Jackson and Becks are home tonight. I've got something else in mind."

"Really. And what might that be?"

"Let's clean up the kitchen first, then I'll take you on an adventure."

"Okay. Definitely yes." She needed an adventure, something fun to take her mind off all of her serious thoughts. Now wasn't the time to be serious.

It was time to get out of her head—and see what Rafe had up his sleeve.

CHAPTER 28

RAFE COULD TELL CARMEN WAS ALL UP IN HER HEAD about something. Maybe her grandpa and his plans to marry Felice. And maybe it was also something else. He didn't really know, and at the moment, his only intent was to get her to relax and have some fun.

He pulled into the out-of-the-way parking spot and turned the engine off.

Carmen turned to him. "I have no idea where we are."

He grinned. "That's the point."

"I don't even see a beach. Just a forest of bushes."

"Trust me, it's there."

She gave him a dubious look. "You aren't going to kill me and bury my body where no one will ever find me, are you?"

"I bring you to a secluded beach, and that's the first thing you think of?"

She shrugged. "I watch a lot of true crime shows."

He shook his head. After grabbing a couple of beach towels, he got out of the truck and came around to meet Carmen in front.

"It's so dark," she said. "And I don't see lights anywhere."

"I found this beach a few years ago. It's small, but there's enough sand that we can wander out and get in the water. And it's safe. Our local lifeguards know about it and said it's fine for swimming."

She looked over at him. "In other words, your lifeguards also come out here."

He grinned. "That's how I know it's safe." He took her hand and led her through the bushes that kept the beach opening hidden from the public. It wasn't a wide opening, but fortunately, Rafe knew the way. It wound around like a maze for about fifty feet, but then it opened up and they were at a clearing that was nothing but private beach and ocean.

"Wow." Carmen stared out over the small stretch of sandy beach and waves. "This is amazing."

"Yeah."

"I don't think I've ever seen any part of the beach unoccupied like this. I mean, sure, at night, but there's always buildings and hotels and lights. Here there's . . ."

"Nothing."

She lifted her gaze to his and offered up a knowing smile. "Yes. Nothing. No lights, no people around. It's perfect, Rafe."

He knew she'd like it. He led her down to the sand where he toed off his tennis shoes and dropped them on top of their towels. He dug in the sand and hid his keys, just in case someone should happen to walk by, though it was unlikely.

"Let's get naked," he said.

"Are you sure?" She gave him a hesitant look.

He pulled her into his arms. "We could always lie down on the towels and just make out."

"You would be happy doing only that, wouldn't you?"

"I'm always happy to kiss you."

She looked out over the ocean. "It's beautiful tonight."

The moon was half-full, enough to highlight the water, but not enough to put them out in full view of anyone who might happen to come by. Not that they'd be seen. Rafe made sure of that.

When she turned back to him, she said, "I've never skinny-dipped a day in my life."

He smoothed his hand down her back. "You don't have to tonight, either, if it makes you uncomfortable."

"Nothing about being with you makes me uncomfortable." She took a step back and lifted the dress over her hips, then off, letting it drop to the towel. She hadn't worn a bra, so she was left wearing a very pretty shade of coral underwear. She shimmied out of those and took his breath away standing in the silvery moonlight naked.

He shucked his board shorts and pulled off his tank, adding his clothes to hers.

"You look amazing naked in the moonlight," she said.

He laughed. "Babe. Nothing compared to you."

"Well, I'm hot and sweaty, and happy it's dark. Let's get in the water."

He took her hand, and they walked to the water's edge. The water felt cool as he waded in to his waist, but Carmen dove right in, then came up laughing.

"This feels amazing." She dipped back under the water, coming up right in front of him, smoothing her hair back with her hands.

He drew her against him. "You look like a mermaid."

"Yeah? You think I'm here to tempt you out to sea?" She wrapped her legs around him.

"Maybe."

He kissed her. She tasted salty, like the ocean, but her kiss was damn sweet on his lips. He cupped his palm around her neck and dug his feet in the sand to hold them in place as the waves washed over them.

He saw lightning flash off the horizon. He knew it was far

enough away not to be concerned, but he also knew a storm could roll in pretty fast, too.

Carmen pulled her lips from his. "Storm's coming in."

"Yeah."

She rubbed her fingers across his jaw and rocked her hips against him. "I guess that means we should get out of the water."

"Soon . . . ish."

She smiled, then pushed away from him.

They splashed at each other, diving in and out of the water and laughing so hard that Rafe felt like a kid again. It was perfect to be there with Carmen, isolated and free to do whatever they wanted.

He wanted her to play for a while, to let go of whatever tension was tying her up in knots. He wanted her filled with joy, and God, he wanted to keep hearing her laugh.

By the time they walked out of the water, the wind had picked up, whipping all around them, and the lightning was moving closer. Clouds were coming in, too, obliterating the moon. But it was still humid and hot on the beach, so they didn't even need to dry off. They collapsed on the towels, and Rafe lay on his back. Carmen came down on top of him, her nipples rubbing against his chest.

"Cold?" he asked.

"Not at all."

"Your nipples are like tight nubs against me. I thought you might be cold."

"No. I'm hot. Very hot."

She leaned in and kissed him, and suddenly he was hot, too. Very damn hot. He slid his hands down and grabbed a handful of her butt to draw her body along the length of his cock. She whimpered in response and rocked against him. He wanted to rub her pussy, but his hands were covered in sand.

He rolled her off of him. "Come on."

They stood and grabbed their clothes. He shrugged into his board shorts and dug his keys out of the sand while Carmen put her sundress back on. They made their way to the car where he had a cooler and several large bottles of water shoved in ice. He opened one, using it to pour over his hands and to scrub the sand off their bodies.

"That's so damn cold," she said, shivering.

"Need to get the sand off so I can touch you."

They climbed in the truck and he started the engine, cracking the windows open, then pushed the seat all the way back so she could come over and straddle him.

Thunder cracked loudly outside, and lightning splintered the sky a brilliant white. But all he could focus on was the warm, beautiful woman sitting on top of his hard cock. He grabbed a condom from the center console and pulled his shorts down while she lifted her dress, revealing her smooth, sweet sex to his view. He swept his hand along the softness of her pussy, watching the way she threw her head back and writhed against his questing fingers.

"Your fingers are cold," she said. "And I'm so hot."

"Too cold?"

She looked down at him, her eyes blazing hot with passion. "No. It's perfect. Your hand feels good, Rafe. Touch me."

Somewhere in the distance he heard a phone buzz. Maybe on the floor of the car; he couldn't be sure. It stopped, then started up again.

"Yours?" he asked.

She rested her hand on his shoulder and rocked her sex against his hand. "Don't care. Make me come."

He slid two fingers inside of her and used his thumb to roll over her clit.

"Yes. Just like that. Oh, God, I'm coming. I'm coming."

The way her body tightened and convulsed around his fingers

nearly tore him apart. And watching the way she shuddered with reckless joy was the hottest damn thing he'd ever seen.

He withdrew his fingers, and she sat on his thighs. He tore open the condom wrapper and put it on, and Carmen slid onto his shaft. Watching his cock disappear inside her made his balls quiver.

And then she gripped his shoulders and rode him while the skies opened and rain poured down in torrents all around them. Thunder shook the ground while Carmen shook every part of his body as she swayed against him, her sweet heat enveloping him in a haze of pleasure.

He gripped her hips and thrust into her, soaking in her cries of pleasure as she jammed her palm onto the roof of the truck and rode him for all he was worth.

At this moment he wasn't worth much, because there was a storm going on inside the truck, too, and he was about to explode with it. He just had to wait for Carmen.

And when she burst, so did he, shattering along with her as they rode out their own storm together until she fell against him, her entire body shaking with the aftereffects.

"Wow," he managed, listening to her ragged breaths while the storm moved past them.

"Yeah." She nibbled lightly on his shoulder.

One thing was for certain. He was never going to give this woman up. She was his, and always would be. He had to tell her how he felt about her, that he loved her, and how much he wanted her in his life. Like, permanently wanted her in his life.

She rolled off, and they got fully dressed this time.

Carmen finger combed her hair, then pulled down the mirror of the visor. "Wow," she said. "I'm a mess."

"A beautiful mess," he said.

She looked over at him and smiled, then reached for her shoes, grabbing her phone from the floorboard. She stared at it and frowned, scrolled, then her eyes widened.

"We need to go, Rafe. Right now."

He could tell from the sound of her voice she didn't like what she'd read on her phone. "What's wrong?"

"My grandpa is in the hospital."

His stomach clenched. "What happened?"

"I don't know." She looked over at him, her expression one of panic. "We need to go."

He put the truck in gear and backed out of the parking spot, heading to the hospital. Whatever was going on, he hoped it was nothing serious.

CHAPTER 29

"HOW BAD IS IT?" CARMEN STOOD IN FRONT OF THE NEU-rologist, Rafe and Felice right behind her.

"It was a TIA, nothing like the one he had years ago. We've treated him with medication, and we'll monitor him overnight. He's stable and he's showing no other symptoms."

"And what is his prognosis?" she asked. "Do you feel like this is a precursor for another major stroke?"

"Not at all. If he keeps taking his meds—and continues with his therapy, he should recover just fine. They should be transferring him up to a room shortly."

Carmen nodded. "Thank you, Dr. Alou."

She exhaled but couldn't seem to get warm. Her entire body was covered in goose bumps, and her legs were shaking.

"Do you want some coffee?" Rafe asked.

She gave him a short nod. "That'd be great, thanks."

"I'll be right back. How about you, Felice?"

"I'm good, honey, but thank you."

After Rafe walked away, Carmen turned to Felice. "Tell me what happened."

"We were just sitting on my back porch watching the lightning. I have a great view of the ocean, and Jimmy likes that. And suddenly he started talking to me but only gibberish was coming out of his mouth. I asked him questions, and I could tell he was trying to answer me, but nothing of what he said made any sense."

Carmen nodded. "Typical stroke symptom."

"So I called 911 immediately, and an ambulance came. By then he was already starting to come out of it, but I didn't want to take any chances. Plus he was a little shaken up, and he said he didn't remember anything of what had just happened."

Carmen laid her hand over Felice's arm. "You did the right thing. You must have been so scared. I'm sorry I wasn't there."

"Honey, I'm not afraid. Jimmy's a strong man. He'll be just fine. Though I think we need to put him on a better diet. That man eats a lot of junk food. I've been doing some research, and diet can be so important in reducing his chances for a repeat stroke."

She loved how much Felice cared about him. "That's a good idea. We'll talk about that."

"Let's go into the room," Felice said, putting her arm around Carmen. "I know he'll want to see you."

They had been in the waiting room, since the team had been doing tests on her grandfather. As a nurse, waiting outside the room while other medical professionals worked on her grandpa had been so difficult for her. But she also knew the worst thing to do was get in the way of the medical team, so she'd stayed in the waiting area. Now the only thing she wanted to do was see her grandfather, to assess for herself that he was all right.

She passed the main nurses station where she worked in the daytime, saw nurses that she occasionally worked with when they switched shifts. She saw the sympathy on their faces. They also knew how hard it was to be on the other side of the care team. She nodded at them as she made her way into her grandfather's room, then put on her best smile.

"Hey, Grandpa," she said.

He appeared to be in decent shape. Almost his usual self, in fact, though he had some dark circles under his eyes. She took a glance at the monitors, making sure that all his vitals looked normal.

They did, which gave her some comfort.

She leaned over, brushed his white hair from his face and kissed his forehead.

"Hey, bebita. I'm sorry about all this."

"Shh, Abuelo. Nothing for you to be sorry about. How are you feeling?"

"Tired. I want to go home and sleep in my own bed."

"You will soon enough."

He looked up at her with confusion in his sweet eyes. "I don't know what happened. One minute, Felice and I were having a nice conversation about the storm coming in, and the next, I was being loaded up into an ambulance."

She felt for him, for how traumatic this experience must have been for him. "Everything will be fine now. The doctor said you had a ministroke and there's nothing to worry about, and you shouldn't have any repeat episodes."

"That's what he told me. I don't want to go through that big one again. I've worked hard for so long to make it back from that one. No steps backward."

"Eating less fried foods might help keep your cholesterol down," Felice said, coming around to the other side of the bed to squeeze his hand.

"And you'll be the one to keep me on that new diet, won't you, my love?"

Felice leaned over and gave him a short kiss, then pressed her hand to his cheek. "You know I will."

Carmen could hardly hold back the tears. Between her and Felice, she knew they could get her grandfather healthy again.

The door opened, and Rafe walked in. "There's my buddy."

Her grandfather smiled. "Hey, Rafe."

"Just lying around like you've got nothing better to do, I see."

"Well, you know, I like the attention."

Rafe cracked a smile. "Who doesn't?" He handed the cup of coffee to Carmen.

"Thanks," she said.

"So? How you feeling?" Rafe asked.

"Like a house fell on me. Mainly because it's past my bedtime and no one will let me sleep."

Rafe nodded. "Yeah, hospitals will do that to you. Those nurses are so mean."

Carmen frowned. "Hey."

Rafe nudged her with his shoulder. "I didn't say you were mean. Just those other nurses."

One of those other nurses just happened to come in. "We have the transfer papers for your grandfather, Carmen, so they'll be in shortly to take him up to his room."

"Thanks, Steph."

It took another hour to get her grandfather moved and settled into his room, then hooked up to all the monitors and have his vitals taken. By then, Carmen could tell he'd had enough. She'd already sent home an exhausted Felice, who promised she'd be back first thing in the morning.

Once she was sure her grandfather was settled and asleep, she and Rafe left for the night, with explicit instructions to the night nurse to notify her if there were any changes.

Then they climbed into Rafe's truck. She barely even noticed the streetlights as he drove. All she could think of was her grandfather's face in the ER, how vulnerable he had looked, and how she'd been on the beach, out of touch, when he'd needed her the most.

She hadn't even answered her phone when it had buzzed. She'd been so into her own feelings, her own needs, she'd ignored the most important phone call of her life.

"I should have been there," she said.

"What?"

"He had a stroke, and I wasn't there to take care of him."

"He wasn't even home, Carmen. He was at Felice's house."

"But if I had been available, I could have seen to him right away. I could have done something. Maybe they could have both been at the house."

He made the turn onto the highway. "You're not even making sense, babe."

She tucked her hair back behind her ears, feeling as if she was doing this all wrong, as if she had her priorities upside down. She'd been there for her grandfather since his stroke, had helped him get stronger. Lately, she hadn't been there for him because she'd been spending all her time fooling around with Rafe, and now this had happened.

She'd dropped the ball, big-time, and it had cost the one person who loved her without reservation.

She pressed her hand against her stomach, hardly able to breathe as the impact of it all hit her squarely in the center of her being.

"It doesn't make sense."

"What doesn't?" he asked.

"You and me. I can't do this. I can't be with you and take care of my grandfather at the same time, Rafe. I can't spread myself that thin. I have a job that demands so much of my time, and when I'm not doing that, I have to focus on his health. Everything was fine before."

He exited the highway and pulled over onto a side road, put the truck in park and turned to face her. "Before what? Before you and me?"

She turned, too. "Yes. He was fine. He was getting healthy, and

I was taking care of everything for him. And then I slipped. I started going out with you, and spending time with you, and I . . . I lost my focus."

"You couldn't have prevented his stroke tonight, Carmen. You're a nurse. You know that." He reached for her, but she recoiled, pushing herself against the door of the truck.

"I don't know that. How do I know that, when I haven't even been paying attention? Felice knows. She's been paying attention to his diet and his exercise and everything about him. Me? I have no clue, because I've been giving all my attention to you, when I should have been giving my attention to my grandpa."

Rafe started to speak. Stopped. Then started again.

"Look. I get it. You're stressed and upset. You need to give it some time. Get a good night's sleep. By tomorrow—"

She shook her head. "No. Don't patronize me like I'm some idiot. I know what I'm talking about. He needs me. I'm sorry, but he needs me more than you do. I can't do this with you anymore."

"So, what? You're breaking up with me? You can't have both of us in your life so you're dumping me?"

She turned and looked down at her hands. "Yes. I'm sorry. I have to do this for my abuelo."

"This is ridiculous. Come on, Carmen. You don't mean that. What we have together is special. If you need help taking care of your grandfather, I'll be there for you. I'll help you."

"I don't need help. I don't need the distraction."

She raised her gaze to his, her entire body filled with misery. "I don't need you. I can do this alone."

He went quiet and turned to face the street, his fingers gripped tight to the steering wheel. She thought maybe he'd say something else. Instead, the silence was like a giant boulder suffocating her in the truck.

Finally, he put the truck in gear and drove the few miles to their houses. He pulled into her driveway. She unbuckled her seat belt and started to pull the door open, but his hand on her wrist stopped her.

"I love you, Carmen. I kept waiting for the right time to tell you, but I guess there never is a right time. And I think you're wrong about this, but I will never make you choose between family and me. Family always comes first. I know that better than anyone. But if you ever need me, for anything, I'm right next door. All you have to do is ask."

Tears pricked her eyes, and it was all she could do not to burst into sobs right there in the truck. She wanted more than anything to fling herself against him and cry, and ask him to hold her until all of what she felt—the hurt, the fear, the uncertainty—went away.

She needed him. Now more than ever. But she had to do this herself, had to eliminate the one thing from her life that made her lose her focus. And that one thing was Rafe.

So instead, she nodded and slid out of the truck, shutting the door behind her.

She walked into the house and turned on the light, the emptiness of the house making her feel lonely.

Empty.

She didn't have her grandfather here. She didn't have Rafe.

Right now, she had nothing.

She turned off all the lights, went into her room and closed the door.

CHAPTER 30

RAFE SWIPED THE SWEAT FROM HIS EYES AS HE FIN-
ished mowing the last row of grass in the front yard. He turned
off the mower, then glanced over at Carmen's house.

Her car was there, so he knew she had the day off. But it had
been nearly a week since she'd broken up with him, and he
thought that since Jimmy was home and settled, maybe she'd have
called or texted him by now, that she'd have realized she made a
mistake. That she wanted him in her life.

Instead, he hadn't heard a word from her.

Maybe all his feelings for her had been just that—his feelings.
And his feelings hadn't been reciprocated. Because when you
loved someone, they were supposed to love you back.

Had he totally misread that? He'd never been in love before,
so how the hell was he supposed to know how it played out?

Since he looked like a dumbass staring over at her house, he
put the mower away and finished off the weed eating, figuring a
good sweat session in the steamy late afternoon would help clear
his head. When he went inside, Jackson and Becks were in there,
and the house smelled fresh.

"Cleaning?" he asked, swiping his brow with a paper towel.

"Top to bottom," Becks said.

"Looks good. Smells even better."

"Well, we make a fantastic team, even scrubbing toilets." Becks beamed a smile at Jackson, who rolled his eyes.

"Yeah, it's my favorite thing to do on my day off," Jackson said. Becks laughed.

"Oh, and Kal called," Jackson said. "Mom and Dad are doing a mini housewarming party at the new house today and want everyone to come over tonight for dinner."

It wasn't like he had anything else to do, and helping his parents celebrate their new place sounded like a great idea. "Sure."

He went into his room and took a shower, scrubbing the grass clippings and sweat off. When he came downstairs, Becks and Jackson weren't there, so he figured they were cleaning up as well. There was no need to wait for them, so he got in his truck and drove over to his parents' new place. He parked in the driveway and got out, staring at the house that was so foreign to him, not the place where he grew up.

But they'd all talked about it. Mom had been afraid he and his brothers would be upset about giving up the place they'd called home since Josh and Laurel Donovan had adopted them. They'd all assured her that home was wherever their parents lived, which was true. As long as he knew where they lived, he'd have a place to call home. And this place was pretty tight.

They'd moved in a week ago. It was a great house, with a pool and lots of extra space for all the things his mother had coveted for years, like an office and a much bigger, fancy new kitchen.

If anyone deserved to have everything she wanted, it was his mom.

Rafe hadn't had much love during his early years. Hell, his birth parents had barely registered his existence. To them, he'd just been in their way. Getting away from them had changed his life.

So when Rafe and his brothers had gotten caught in that house fire and rescued by Josh Donovan, and then Josh and Laurel had brought them home, Rafe didn't know how to handle having parents who actually took care of him, who cared about how he felt. It had taken him a while to warm up to them, but Laurel was persistent in her affection and had broken down his walls until he couldn't help but need and want the love he'd always been denied.

Now he'd move mountains for the woman he called Mom.

He walked through the front door and found his mother in her office to the right. She was a beautiful woman, with her dark skin, her curly hair, and a body that she kept fit by doing yoga, of all things. He didn't know where she found the time, given how busy she was. But that was his mom, always making sure that she took care of herself as well as others.

"You about set up in here?" he asked as he walked into her office.

She turned and smiled at him. "Just about." She slipped a couple of books into the built-in bookshelf, then hugged him.

It wouldn't matter how old he got, Rafe would always welcome his mother's hugs. For some reason he needed one badly right now, so he lingered a little longer than typical, wrapping his arms around her and holding her tight.

When he pulled away, she studied him. "Something's wrong."

He pulled his lips into a half smile. "Nothing's wrong. I'm fine."

"No, you're not, and I can see it on your face. Come on. Let's go into the kitchen and have something cold to drink. Then you can talk to me."

The cold drink sounded good, but his mother couldn't help him with Carmen.

She poured them some iced tea and handed him a glass. They sat in front of the bay window in the kitchen.

"Have you been in the pool yet?" he asked.

"Every day to swim laps. It's perfect and I love it."

"And you're the one who didn't want to move."

She shrugged. "I take back what I said. I love this house. The master closet is perfect. My office is everything I ever dreamed of, and I know I'll use the pool a lot."

"How does Dad like it?"

"He loves it. The garage is bigger, and he's already talking about building a workbench across one wall, which is what he's always wanted. He and Kal are at the store right now buying . . . I don't actually know what they're buying."

"Probably some cabinets and wood."

"Yes, I think that's what they mentioned." She took a sip of her tea. "So tell me what's going on that's got you upset."

"I'm not upset."

She tilted her head down and gave him the look he remembered so well from when he was a kid and tried to lie his way out of something. It was a very effective look.

"Try again," she said.

"Carmen's grandfather had a mini stroke."

"Oh no. Is he all right?"

"He's going to be fine. But she freaked out. She was out with me when it happened, so she said she should have been with her grandpa, that she could have done something to prevent it. And then she dumped me."

"Ah, I see. It's a natural response to a crisis. She felt guilty because she wasn't with him. Give her some time to come around."

"I don't think so, Mom. She said a lot of things about how we shouldn't have been together in the first place, and how I made her lose her focus and all she had time for was her job and taking care of her grandpa."

"Uh-huh. And this was right after her grandfather had his stroke, right?"

"Yeah."

"Can you imagine how upset she was then? How much that scared her? He's her only living relative, right?"

He nodded.

"Honey, she panicked. And I'm sure you're hurt by the things she said. But you're going to have to find a way to forgive her if you want her in your life." She studied him. "Do you?"

He took a long swallow of tea before answering. "I told her I loved her and that I'd always be there for her. And then she got out of my truck and left me."

"Oh, my sweet boy." She squeezed his hand. "I'm sure that hurt. Do you think she loves you?"

"Yes."

Mom smiled. "No hesitation. That's good. Give her time, Rafe. She's got a lot to process, and her grandfather's health crisis frightened her in a big way. She is probably missing you like crazy right now."

He shrugged. "I don't know. If she didn't see that I could be by her side and help her through all this, what kind of future do we have?"

"Everyone processes a major event like this differently. Carmen's been on her own, just her and her grandfather, for a long time. She's never known any other way. It'll take her a while to realize that she can lean on you when times are tough."

"Or, maybe I can show her that I'm always going to be there for her, no matter what."

His mother nodded. "You could do that. Without pressuring her, of course."

"Well, yeah. I'd never do that."

"Do what you think is best. You know your relationship with her better than I do."

He had a thought in mind. He didn't want Carmen to think he was going to walk away and forget her.

And he wasn't going to give up without a fight. He cared about her too much for that.

So now he had a plan. He just hoped it worked.

CHAPTER 31

CARMEN HAD A MILLION THINGS TO DO TODAY AFTER SHE got off work. She stopped at the store, her grocery list in her hand so she could zoom through the aisles and get what she needed.

Fortunately, Felice had been staying at the house with Grandpa the past week, so she didn't need to worry about him being alone. Though he'd been acting grumpy as hell lately and saying both the women in his life were fussing way too much over him. He said he felt fine, his new meds were working great and he'd like everyone to leave him the hell alone so everything could go back to normal.

As she drove home, she realized her grandfather had no idea how much that night had scared her. Losing him just wasn't an option for her. He was all she had left, and she intended to do everything she could to keep him healthy.

She and Felice had already come up with a new diet plan for him. Fortunately, he didn't mind the changes too much, though he said he was going to really miss the fried foods. But he liked vegetables and fish and chicken, and so far he wasn't complaining about that.

She took the bags inside and laid them on the counter.

"Grandpa?"

No answer.

"Felice?"

Still no answer.

She walked down the hall toward his bedroom, but the door was open. She peeked inside and didn't see them.

But by the time she made her way back into the kitchen, the front door opened and they both came inside.

"Hi, Carmen," Felice said. "We went for a walk."

Felice was a godsend. Carmen didn't know what she would have done without her this past week.

"How was the walk?"

"Hot," her grandfather said. "And I'm slow."

"Which just means you get to see all the beauty in the neighborhood," Felice said with a smile.

"I guess so."

"But you're right about it being hot," Felice said. "I'm very sweaty, so I'm going to rinse off in the shower. I'll be right back."

"Okay, honey." Grandpa took a seat at the kitchen table and stretched out his legs.

Carmen filled up a glass of ice water and brought it to him.

"Thanks." She started to turn away, but her grandfather stopped her.

"Take a seat, Carmen."

"Sure." She sat in the chair next to him.

"You know I feel fine."

"You look good, too. Look at how well you're walking. You didn't even have your cane with you. That'll make you even stronger." She smiled and laid her hand over his.

"What happened with Rafe?"

She pulled her hand away. "Nothing. It just didn't work out."

"Bebita. Tell me."

She shrugged and stood, heading over to the counter. "Oh, you know how these things go. Sometimes a relationship just runs its course and fizzles."

He went quiet for a few minutes, and Carmen began chopping vegetables for the salad she was making for dinner.

"It's been a long time since you've lied to me, Carmen Lewis."

Damn. She turned to face him. "I can only handle so much. My job, taking care of you and the house. Something had to go. So it was Rafe."

Her grandfather looked shocked. "You broke up with him because of what happened to me?"

She looked down at her feet. "Not exactly. Maybe. I don't know. It was all just so complicated, and I don't need complicated right now."

He stood and came over to her, tipping her chin up with his finger. "Look at me."

She raised her head up and met his gaze, saw uncharacteristic anger in her grandfather's eyes.

"I'm old, Carmen. I'm going to have health problems here and there. I'm also in love, and I want a future with Felice, who knows exactly what she's getting into with me. Maybe it's time you face some harsh realities. One, I'm going to die someday."

Her eyes filled with tears, and she shook her head. "Don't say that."

"It's the truth. And when I die, I want to know that you have someone in your life who's going to love you and be your partner in all things, who'll be by your side to love and care for you. I thought that was Rafe."

Her stomach clenched as the pain of missing Rafe became nearly unbearable. She hadn't been able to sleep the past week between worrying about her grandfather and missing Rafe so much she wanted to run over to his house to beg his forgiveness.

Tears fell down her cheeks. "I didn't know what to do, Grandpa.

I panicked that night. I was so afraid of losing you that I thought if I had more time to take care of you, I could handle it."

She heard sounds coming from the garage but then figured it was probably nothing.

"When I had my big stroke, I needed you and I was so glad you were here for me. Just like I was here for you after your divorce from Tod. That's what family does. We're here for each other when we need each other the most. But now I'm better. And you and Felice are doing everything you can to get me on the right track, to make sure I'm the healthiest I can be. I appreciate that. But I have to tell you, Carmen, that it's time for you to take a step back now and find your own life. Because I won't be able to handle you being all alone after I'm gone."

She was about to speak, but he held his palm up to silence her. "Not that I'm intending to go anywhere right away. I'm going to marry Felice, and I'd like some nice long years with her. I like her house because it has a great view of the water, so we're going to move into her place and sell this house."

At her look, he added, "Don't worry. You can stay here as long as you want to."

"That's not the issue. Are you sure Felice can handle everything?"

He laughed. "By everything, you mean me? Yes. She knows all my health concerns. She accepts me for who I am, and the possibilities of what could come up in the future."

She laid her hand over her grandfather's. "That's not at all what I meant. But you've had a live-in nurse, Abuelo."

"And I'll do fine without one. You've got to give up the reins on managing my life and start figuring out how to manage your own, okay?"

He was right. She knew he was right. But letting go was going to be so hard.

She gave a quick nod. "I'll try. Te amo, Abuelo."

"Yo también te quiero, bebita."

His words in Spanish were always a comfort to her. And his conversation had been an eye-opener.

Okay, so she wasn't going to be able to micromanage her grandfather's health forever. He was right about that. And she did have Felice to help her out, and she was always going to be just a phone call away.

And now that she'd burned down her love life, she was going to have to do something about that.

She'd been so incredibly stupid. She'd walked away from Rafe, from the one person she should have been leaning on this whole time. Instead, she'd pushed him away.

Would he even forgive her?

She looked at her grandfather. "What if Rafe doesn't forgive me? I said some awful things to him."

Her grandfather gave her a warm smile. "He loves you, Carmen. Of course he'll forgive you."

The noise in the garage grew louder.

She looked in that direction. "Someone's in the garage."

Her grandfather frowned and followed her to the door.

She inched open the door and saw Rafe out there, moving boxes and some of her furniture pieces around. Her heart did a hard leap. She closed the door and turned to her grandfather.

"It's Rafe. Did you ask him to come over?"

"No."

"What's he doing out there?" She realized she was whispering.

Her grandfather shrugged. "No idea. Looked like he was organizing. Something the garage desperately needed. Maybe you should go talk to him."

The thought of it made her stomach twist.

"I don't know."

"Don't be a coward." He laid his hand on her back. "Go. Talk. Take your time. Felice and I can handle dinner."

Talk about what? About how she'd screwed up the best thing that had ever happened to her?

"What will I say to him?"

No answer. She turned around to realize her grandfather had left.

Okay, Carmen, time to face what you did. She put her hand on the doorknob and opened the door.

He was carrying a box filled with stuff out to the driveway. She walked out there.

God, he looked so good in his shorts and tank top, his skin glistening with sweat.

She'd missed him. She loved him. More importantly, she needed him.

He looked up at her, glaring.

"Don't argue with me about cleaning out your garage, Carmen. I'm just trying to help make more room for you to work on your furniture."

"Uh-huh. And you just thought you'd come over here without asking and do this?"

"Well . . . yeah. Because you've had enough time to think about how much you've missed me. And you have missed me, haven't you?"

"Took you long enough to get over here. God, yes, I've missed you." She threw herself against him and nearly knocked him to the floor. He steadied himself and put his arm around her.

"Whoa," he said. "What's this all about?"

She reached up and swept her hand across his jaw. "I'm so sorry. I've been so stupid. I broke up with you because I was scared that I couldn't give enough time to caring for my grandpa, when all this time I should have been leaning on you to help me. I should have asked you to help me. Because when you love someone, it's a partnership, both the good and the bad."

"I believe you said that same thing to me when I went all silent and uncommunicative with you before."

"You did. And I should have listened to my own advice. I love you, Rafe, and I need you and I want you and I'm begging you to forgive me for the awful things I said."

He pulled her closer. "And I'm sorry it took me so long to come over here. I should have done it the day after you walked out on me, but I stupidly wanted to give you some time to cool off, to think about things and to take care of your grandpa. We can't keep doing this. We have to find a way to communicate better."

She nodded. "You're right. I promise never to push you away again."

"And I promise not to let you walk away from me again. And if you do, I'll follow you to the end of the world."

He kissed her, a soul-searing, powerful kiss that made the hair on the nape of her neck stand up. His hands roamed lower and cupped her butt, and she realized what she would have missed out on had she let this man go. Because when he held her like this, when he kissed her with such deep emotion, she knew exactly where she belonged. She raised up on her toes and aligned her body with his, needing him more than anything. He was her life, her future, and she'd never let him go again.

"Get a room, you two," Kal hollered from across the lawn as he walked outside to his truck.

Carmen pulled back and laughed, laying her head against his chest. "I'm sorry."

He tipped her chin up to look down at her. "Forgiven. No more *I'm sorry*."

"Okay."

"How's your grandpa?"

"Doing well enough to lecture me on being an idiot in letting you go."

His lips curved. "He's a very smart man."

"Thank you for what you're doing in my garage."

"You need a stress reliever, and you need the space to work on the furniture you want to restore."

He always thought of her, and her needs, because he loved her. God, she was so lucky he still wanted to be with her. She would never take that for granted.

"I love you, Rafe."

"I love you, Carmen."

"We were making dinner. Are you hungry?"

"Always."

"Okay. Finish dumping those two boxes first, and then you can eat."

He laughed. "So that's how it's gonna be, huh?"

"That's how it's gonna be."

He planted a quick kiss on her lips and then got back on task. Carmen went inside. Felice was in the kitchen getting the chicken ready for the salad.

"Everything okay?" Felice asked.

"Everything's perfect now. Rafe's cleaning up the garage, then he's going to come in and have dinner with us."

"That's wonderful," Felice said, a happy smile on her face. "I'll set an extra place at the table."

Carmen slid her glance over to her grandfather, who smiled and nodded.

Oh yeah. Everything was going to be absolutely perfect.

Her grandfather was healthy and in love.

Carmen could help take care of Grandpa—when he needed it. But he was right about one thing—it was time to take a step back and let him have his life. Because now it was time for her to have a life of her own. A love of her own.

And had she ever found the love of a lifetime.

It was time for her own happily-ever-after.

EPILOGUE

"HOW LONG DO I HAVE TO KEEP MY EYES CLOSED?" CARmen asked. "I'm getting carsick."

"Just another mile."

"Bleh."

Rafe grinned as he turned down the street and pulled into the driveway. Or at least, it would be a driveway someday soon. Right now it was dirt. But it was dirt and a promise, and he wanted to give it to Carmen.

"Just another minute," he said, turning the engine off. He came over to her side of the truck to open the door.

He saw the disgruntled look on her face and smiled. He took her hand and helped her out of the truck.

"Okay, open your eyes."

She did, and frowned. "What the hell is this?"

"It's a house."

"No, it's not. It's a frame of a house."

He took her hand and led her down the dirt drive. "It's four bedrooms, two and a half bathrooms. It has a huge kitchen and an amazing master bedroom. It has a huge yard for kids and still plenty of space to build a workspace for your furniture restoration—"

She tugged on his hand to stop him midstride. "Wait. What are you talking about?"

"A house. A brand-new, not-yet-built house. For us. To buy."

She blinked and stared at him. "You want us to buy a house. Together."

His lips curved. "Yeah."

He pulled the brochure out of his back pocket and handed it to her.

Carmen stared down at the beautiful color picture of what the house would look like finished. Incredible colors, ample windows to let in light, an amazing island and plenty of space in the kitchen for entertaining, and so many bedrooms. And the lot size was huge.

She lifted her gaze to Rafe. "But how . . . ?"

"I have a friend who builds homes. He's giving me . . . us, a great deal on this one with all the land. I want to marry you, Carmen. Build this house with you. Or if you don't like this one, we'll choose another one. I want you to have your dream—a brand-new house that we can make memories in together. That we can have our forever in together."

Forever. Together. She had thought she'd move into an apartment so her grandfather could sell his house. Not buy a house. She never thought she'd be able to—

Stop overanalyzing everything and just go for it, Carmen. This is the man you love.

"I want forever with you, Rafe. I want this house with you. I love you. Yes."

She laughed, she cried and she threw herself into his arms to kiss him.

And then they walked toward the house that would someday become theirs, where they'd start their forever together.

TURN THE PAGE TO READ A SPECIAL EXCERPT
FROM THE FIRST BOOTS AND BOUQUETS NOVEL
BY JACI BURTON

THE BEST MAN PLAN

COMING SOON FROM JOVE!

ERIN BELLINI SHOUTED OUT FROM HER OFFICE AT RED Moss Vineyards.

"Mom. Have you talked to the caterers?"

Her mother didn't respond right away. It was her most annoying quality. While she waited, Erin jotted down several notes about the bridesmaids. Her two sisters were on site so she had them covered, but she made a note in her planner to text Chrissy, her best friend and maid of honor, to make sure she had received the itinerary Erin had emailed to her.

Erin's mother, Maureen, made an appearance in Erin's office. "You don't need to yell at me, Erin. You could have just sent me a text. And yes, caterers are confirmed. Which I already told you this morning."

"Right. You did. For some reason I hadn't checked it off the list." She typed an X in the spreadsheet on her laptop as well as marking it off on the page in her planner. She looked up at her mother. "And my dress is back from alterations, right?"

"It's in your closet." Her mom made that face, the one where her lips went straight and her eyes narrowed and you knew you were being scrutinized. "You're not getting nervous, are you?"

Erin smiled and took a deep breath to center herself. "I never get nervous. Because I have everything planned. In my planner. In my spreadsheet. In the notes in my phone."

Her mother smiled. "Right. Yes, well, that's you, honey. I'm going out to the vineyards to check on your dad. Call if you need me."

"Okay."

She should call Owen, her fiancé, to make sure he remembered he had to pick up the tuxes. Or maybe she should call Jason, Owen's best friend and the best man. Owen was always scattered and busy and he'd likely forget. Thankfully he had her to organize everything for him.

She picked up her phone and found Jason, then pressed the call button.

"Busy here, Erin."

She shook her head at Jason's gruff brush-off. Since they were neighbors, they'd known each other forever. "I need you to pick up the tuxes."

"What?"

"The tuxes, Jason."

"I'm knee-deep in cow shit right now, Erin. You don't mean now, do you?"

"No. I mean Thursday." She heard mooing. "You delivering babies?"

"Pregnancy checks."

"Oh. Cool." Jason was a large animal vet, so he was always on the run. He had a practice in town, but he also worked the local ranches.

She was scrolling through her emails when she saw one from Owen. Owen never emailed her. He always texted. She frowned and clicked on it.

"I thought Owen was doing the tux thing," Jason said.

"Well, Owen is likely up to his elbows in hops or wheat or whatever it is that brewers do. Or he's likely making sure the brewery and the restaurant won't go up in flames without him when we're on our honeymoon. You know how he is."

"Fine. I'll handle it. Anything else?"

"Yeah." She was trying to concentrate on Owen's email and forgot she was on the phone with Jason.

"Erin. Anything else?"

Her blood went cold. Everything in her went cold, despite the warm May day.

She read the email again. It was a breakup email. Two days before the wedding, and Owen was breaking up with her.

"In a freaking email? He's breaking up with me in an email?"

"Who's breaking up with you?" Jason asked. "Owen is?"

She was getting married in two days. Correction. Apparently she was *not* getting married, because exactly two days before their wedding Owen had broken up with her. Via email.

She felt dizzy and sick to her stomach. She leaned over and put her head between her legs.

"Erin. Are you there?"

"Did you know about this?" she asked, trying not to faint or throw up.

"Hell no, I didn't know. Did he call you?"

Erin straightened, the dizziness making her feel as if she'd just downed a bottle of Bellini's best prosecco in one gulp.

Two days. They were getting married in two days. This had to be a mistake. But as she straightened and looked at the email again, the word "mistake" was written in the same sentence as the words, "us getting married."

"Ahhhhhhhhh!" she screamed, long and loud, then yelled, "That son of a bitch. I will kill him. He broke up with me in an email, Jason."

"He didn't," Jason said. "Are you sure?"

"Oh, he did. And I'm sure. I can read a damn email. I gotta go." She hung up the phone and stared at her lists, tears pricking her eyes as the future she'd envisioned with Owen dissolved right in front of her.

All because of an email. An email! How could he be so cold?

"I will kill him. I. Will. Kill. Him."

She was breathing too fast and she knew it. She was going to hyperventilate if she didn't calm down. She pushed herself out of her chair and forced herself to pace the floor of her office, centering her breathing, forcing the tears back, resisting the urge to crumple on the floor and curl up in a ball and sob like a baby.

How could he do this to her? To them? They'd been perfect together.

Oh, no. She would not cry. Not over him.

"Who are you going to kill?" Honor asked, running in. "You screamed. What's wrong?"

Torn between betrayal, hurt, and utter fury, she couldn't even answer her younger sister. She finally managed to find her voice and pointed at her laptop.

"Owen dumped me. In an email!"

Honor gasped. "He did not." She yelled out the door, "Brenna, get in here now."

Brenna sauntered in. "What's up?"

"Owen dumped Erin. In an email, apparently."

Erin reread the email again, making sure it said what she thought it had said. Maybe she'd misinterpreted it.

But no. She hadn't. There was no misinterpreting the "I'm sorry" and the "We're not right for each other" and "We shouldn't get married." She felt her sisters' hands on her shoulders as they leaned over her to read it.

"That son of a bitch," Brenna said.

"I can't believe he'd do that," Honor said. "That doesn't seem like Owen at all. Did he say anything to you to lead you to believe he wanted to back out?"

Erin finally swiveled around in the office chair to face her sisters. "No, he didn't say anything to me because apparently he was too busy packing for Aruba. For our honeymoon. Where he is right now. Taking *our* honeymoon trip by himself."

Brenna crossed her arms and narrowed her gaze. Erin felt a little vindicated by the fury in her older sister's eyes. "I will personally destroy him."

"You won't get the chance," Erin said. "Because I get the pleasure of doing that."

"Dad might kill him first," Honor said, looking worried. "Or, knowing Mom's temper, you might have to hide the kitchen knives."

Erin stood and started to storm out of the office, but then turned. "Nobody gets to kill him but me."

Their mother walked in right then, a smile on her beautiful face.

"Who are we killing now?"

Their Mom was used to the three sisters always plotting someone's demise. Oh, but she didn't know how bad this was. This was bad. This was murder worthy.

"Owen dumped me, Mom. And he's already left for Aruba without me."

Their mother just stared at her, dumbfounded for a few minutes. "What? He did what?"

She took her mother's hand and led her to the desk, showing her the email Owen had left her. She read it. Then read it again and lifted her head to stare in confusion at Erin.

"This makes no sense, Erin. He loves you."

Erin snorted. "Apparently not. He said he tried to talk to me but I wouldn't listen. I don't even know what he's talking about, because he most certainly never talked to me about ending our engagement. And the rest of it is all blah blah blah whatever where he didn't want to hurt my feelings." She pointed to her laptop, to the life-altering email. "Like *that* wouldn't hurt my feelings? He couldn't even face me, the coward."

"Are you sure he didn't try to talk to you about this?" Honor asked.

"Honor!" Erin said. "Whose side are you on?"

"Yours, of course. I just . . . it's just that we all know Owen. He'd never hurt you like this."

Erin waved her hands at her laptop. "He just did."

Honor sighed and shook her head. "You're right. I'm sorry, of course you're right. He's a terrible person. A coward for not facing you."

"Bastard coward," Brenna added. "So now what do we do? Everything's ordered for the wedding. Flowers, cake, caterer, music. Nothing can be canceled at this late date except the venue here at the vineyard, of course. He couldn't have gotten his cold feet six months ago?"

At Erin's stricken look, Brenna added, "Or, never? I mean, who wouldn't want to marry you? You're beautiful and talented and smart and any guy would be lucky to have you."

"Damn right he would," her mother added.

Erin didn't understand it. As her mother and sisters talked amongst themselves, she turned to face the window, looking out over the vineyards, rows and rows of grapes growing, promising a prosperous future.

She sighed and reviewed the past year in her head. Owen had proposed in his apartment. She hadn't been too surprised because they'd talked about marriage for a year. They'd planned the wedding. Everything had seemed fine. It had been stressful, of course, but all weddings were stressful.

And sure, she'd been preoccupied with her work here at Red Moss Vineyards, plus all the wedding planning, but Owen had been equally engaged with his work. They were both successful in their jobs. Owen had started up a craft brewery and restaurant in Oklahoma City. Erin handled the business aspect of the family winery. Sure, they were super busy. But they made time for each other.

They'd known each other since they were kids. They'd been in love, dammit. She rubbed her stomach, aching inside at the loss of the future they'd planned together.

She couldn't pinpoint one time where warning bells had clanged in her head, where she might have stopped and thought that maybe he was having second thoughts.

And now she had a wedding in two days and no groom. And no refunds at this late date, either.

Fury replaced the hurt, pure anger wrapping an icy wall around her shattered heart.

Well, screw that. And screw him, too. Only she wouldn't be screwing him on her wedding night. Or ever again, for that matter. Which was fine with her.

But she'd have her revenge. And a party to remember.

She pivoted to face her mother and sisters, lifting her chin in defiance. "We're going to have the reception without him."

Her mother shot her head up and stared at Erin. "What?"

"You heard me. Everything has already been paid for. Since we own the winery and the wedding venue, we have the spot reserved. We'll never get our money back for anything else. So let's hold one hell of a party here on my non-wedding day."

Honor came over and put her arm around her. "Oh, honey, don't you think that's the last thing you'll want on that day? To remember it's the day you were supposed to get married?"

"Probably. But it's also going to be a party to end all parties. If he thinks I'm going to cancel, then spend that day crying over him, he's wrong. Dead wrong." Erin shrugged. "So, let's party our butts off on my non-wedding day. We'll call it the Bellini Party of the Summer, instead. What do you think?"

"I'm in," Honor said. "Whatever you want, you get, as far as I'm concerned."

Brenna nodded. "Agreed. It's your day, Erin. So you get to do whatever you want to do. I'm in, too. Mom?"

Their mother sighed. "Wait till your dad hears about this. I'm not convinced he won't fly to Aruba and personally drag Owen back here to marry you."

Erin lifted her chin. "I don't ever want to see him again, let alone marry him."

It took a few beats for her mother to answer. "Okay, then. We'll throw the best party this venue has ever seen."

And Erin would drown her heartbreak in the finest wine the Red Moss Vineyards produced.

It would be one hell of a party.

JASON CALLUM DROVE THE DIRT ROAD LIKE THE FIRES OF hell were on his heels.

He'd tried calling Owen's number three times. Each time, his phone went directly to voice mail. Owen often turned his phone off when he was working back in the brewing area, but he knew for a fact that his best friend was off work for the next two weeks.

Jason glared at his phone. "Because you're supposed to be getting married in two days, asshole."

He tossed his phone on the console of his truck.

He should have never backed off three years ago when Owen said he wanted to ask Erin out.

Then again it wasn't like Jason was going to do it. He and Erin had been friends since they were kids. Just friends.

You like her, dumbass. You've always liked her. You just didn't have the balls to do anything about it.

He gripped the steering wheel, trying to bite back the curse words that wanted to escape from his mouth.

This whole thing was his fault—indirectly, but still his fault.

Three years ago Jason could have told Owen to back off, that he was interested in Erin. Instead, he'd told Owen to go for it, and had swallowed the feelings he'd had for Erin.

He hadn't realized how strong those feelings were until he'd had a front-row seat to watch Owen falling in love with Erin.

And who wouldn't? She was strong willed and smart and capable and beautiful and the way she laughed could instantly make a guy fall crazy in love.

So what the hell was Owen doing?

He turned into the long drive of the Red Moss Vineyards.

He hoped like hell he'd heard Erin wrong, that this was some kind of colossal mistake. Because his best friend wouldn't do this to Erin, wouldn't up and cancel the wedding with only two days to go. That just wasn't Owen, and he knew him probably better than anyone.

He pulled the truck along the side of the main house and got out, brushing off dust and animal hair that clung to his worn jeans. He'd changed out of the boots that he'd been working in and slid into another pair so he wouldn't track cow shit into the Bellini's house. He walked up the wide wood stairs and onto the oversized porch. He knew he didn't have to knock. He'd known this family for as long as he'd been alive. He'd played out back with the Bellini girls since they were all kids.

He walked through the front door and followed the sound of Johnny Bellini's booming voice, some of it in English and some in Italian.

"Dad, you're not going to kill him," Honor said.

"*Bastardo*. He disgraced my daughter. That is just not done."

Erin rolled her eyes. "First, I am hardly disgraced. Pissed? Yes. Disgraced, no. And second? By the time I'm done talking to everyone about what he did to me, it'll be his reputation that's ruined. That'll be enough."

"Hey," Jason said, stepping into the room. "I was on the phone with Erin and I heard. I came right over to make sure she was okay."

His gaze shot to Erin, who looked as upset as he'd ever seen her. Erin was never flustered, never upset, never out of sorts. She was the one sister who always had her shit together.

Today she didn't have it together. Her dark raven hair was piled high in a crown on top of her head. Erin never let a hair fall out of place, but right now the crown sat a little lopsided and tendrils had escaped, framing her flushed face. The pencil she'd stuck into the bun on her head threatened to topple the entire shebang. And her normally sharp green eyes were clouded, as if she was on the verge of tears.

Jason wasn't sure he'd ever seen Erin Bellini cry. Not even when he'd pushed her off the slide when they were eight years old. She'd just gotten up, brushed herself off, then come over and punched him right in the jaw.

He figured that's when he'd first fallen in love with her.

Now she just looked sad. But damn, she still looked beautiful, and he had no right to think that.

"I'm not okay, Jason." She walked over and leaned against him.

He put his arm around her and held her close. "I'm sorry, Erin."

He'd do anything he could to take this pain away from her, including kicking the shit out of his best friend.

"Have you heard from him?" she asked.

"No. I tried calling him on my way over and his phone went right to voice mail each time."

"Damn. Has he said anything to you?"

"About calling off the wedding? No. You know I'd have talked him out of it. What was he thinking?"

She tried to smooth her hair into place, then walked back into the living room. "I don't know. I wish I could talk to him."

"No. You will not ever speak to him again," Johnny said. "I, however, have a lot to say to him."

"Johnny," Maureen said, "you know you're not going to say anything to him."

"What about his parents?" Honor asked. "Has anyone called them? Aren't they supposed to drive in tomorrow from Dallas?"

"They are," Erin said. "I hadn't even thought about calling them."

Jason pulled out his phone. "Let me do that."

Every set of Bellini eyes rested on him as he was about to call Owen's dad. "I'll just step outside."

The phone call with Owen's dad was short, but just about as much of a punch to the gut as hearing Erin scream. When he hung up, he saw Erin standing just outside the front door.

"They know?"

He nodded. "But not for long. They just got off the phone with him about an hour ago. They're in shock, Erin. They didn't know anything before now."

She walked forward and took a seat on the front step, cradling her arms around her knees. She lifted her gaze to his. "Did he tell them anything?"

He took a seat next to her. "Just that he changed his mind, and he knew what he was doing was wrong and would make a lot of people unhappy, especially you, and that he flew to Aruba because he needed some distance."

She sighed, and he felt the weight of her sigh as if he carried her pain himself. "I don't understand any of this. Why didn't he just talk to me?"

"I don't know. Why didn't he talk to *me*? I'm his best friend. If he had second thoughts, you'd think he'd want to sound them out with someone. It seems to me like he didn't talk to anyone. Not you, not me, not his parents. So I don't get it, either."

"See, none of this makes sense to me, Jason. Owen and I always talked everything out. I mean, maybe we hadn't done a lot of talking lately, but with the wedding planning, my job, his job, we've both been busy." She swept a stray hair away from her face. "I thought everything had been fine. He'd told me he was fine.

"Clearly it had not been fine. Couldn't he have said something to me? Like, 'Hey, Erin, I don't want to get married'? That would have been a great start."

Jason read the anguish on her face and he wanted to pull her close, to comfort her. But he also read the tension in her body and knew now wasn't the time.

Damn. How could his best friend do this to . . . his other best friend?

Erin straightened. "Well, anyway, screw him. I've decided we're still going ahead with the reception."

"What?"

"You heard me. Everything is paid for and arranged and it's not like at this late date we can cancel anything. So we're going to have one hell of a party."

"You don't have to do that, Erin. Everyone will understand if you want to cancel."

"But see, that's the thing. I don't want to cancel. I might not be getting married, but I'll have the best damn non-wedding reception this town has ever seen. And I'll expect everyone to be there. Well, not Owen's family, of course. But everyone else should come. You'll come, won't you?"

If there was one thing he knew about Erin Bellini, it was her determination. And he could tell from the look on her face that she was determined not to spend this weekend acting like the jilted bride. But there was no way to know how that non-wedding party of hers was going to play out. So he planned to be by her side. He wasn't going to be the guy who let her down.

"Hell yeah, I'm coming. And I'll wear the damn tux, too."

He got up and held his hand out for her.

She grinned and slipped her hand in his. "Good, because you and I, Jason? We are gonna dance Saturday night."

He was counting on it. Owen may have screwed her over, but Jason was going to show her that life went on.

It might not be her wedding on Saturday, but Jason was going to make sure that Erin had the best night of her life.